T0354492

THE LION'S DEN

NORMA COOK

THE LION'S DEN

iUniverse books may be ordered through booksellers or by contacting:

iUniverse
1663 Liberty Drive
Bloomington, IN 47403
www.iuniverse.com
1-800-Authors (1-800-288-4677)

Because of the dynamic nature of the Internet, any web addresses or
links contained in this book may have changed since publication and
may no longer be valid. The views expressed in this work are solely those
of the author and do not necessarily reflect the views of the publisher,
and the publisher hereby disclaims any responsibility for them.

Any people depicted in stock imagery provided by Thinkstock are
models, and such images are being used for illustrative purposes only.
Certain stock imagery © Thinkstock.

ISBN: 978-1-5320-0243-4 (sc)
ISBN: 978-1-5320-0242-7 (e)

Library of Congress Control Number: 2016916798

Print information available on the last page.

iUniverse rev. date: 11/03/2016

CHAPTER 1

The early-morning air was cool on Della's face as she crawled out of the one-man tent. She quietly zipped the front flaps, buttoned her light jacket, and started across the moonlit meadow toward the overgrown path leading to the river. Skirting around the sleepy log cabin, which, she imagined, protected her from roaming predators and wild animals just by its stalwart presence, she could hear the rush of the water. As she stepped out of the scrub, the dark river lay before her, gurgling and lapping at its banks. Dusky barrens stretched beyond to where the shadowy foothills of the Appalachian Mountains rose in the distance. The stars were still shining, although the dawn was starting to lighten the edges of the inky sky, and she knew that, soon, a pinkish glow would dance on the rippling current.

With the ghostly mist rising from the water, conditions would be perfect for getting her shot. Della had been waiting for days for the rain to stop drizzling down. It was nothing new. As a photojournalist, she was used to crouching for hours in adverse conditions, waiting for news to happen in front of her camera. Quite often, it was not just raindrops she dodged but gunfire or worse. She sighed as she opened the flap on the camouflaged blind that housed her camera and tripod setup and checked the light meter to see if she would soon be able to get a decent exposure. Her subjects had yet to arrive, and they were shyer than their human counterparts about having their photos taken.

Della sighed as she settled in to wait. As always, her thoughts turned to Aaron, her partner whom she had left behind in Pakistan. They had been sent on assignment to Afghanistan by the news magazine Today to cover the hunt for bin Laden. They had been roaming all over Afghanistan for months, staying in seedy hostels, camping in the hills, hiding out in caves—waiting, watching, and listening with nothing to show for their efforts. Disgruntled, they had returned to the city of Kuwait. Aaron had gone back to his usual haunt, to hang out with the locals at the shisha cafe. Blending into the background, pretending to be stoned and harmless, he'd overheard a man he recognized as a "person of interest," a courier from Pakistan, tell another man that he had a package to deliver to the Lion Sheik in Abbottabad. Recognizing what it would mean to the American government to have proof that Pakistan was harboring the head of al-Qaeda and America's most wanted international war criminal, Osama bin Laden, Aaron had unobtrusively left the café and called his contacts with the magazine and the CIA. And he and Della had pulled up stakes and moved their headquarters to the small town of Abbottabad, Pakistan. There was a $25 million bounty on bin Laden's head, and this could put Della and him first in line to collect it.

A gentle sound outside the blind brought Della's mind back to the present. Flexing her cramped muscles, she pressed a button on the camera, lighting the viewfinder display. On the screen, a group of shadowy figures appeared out of the lavender mists, their gray forms silhouetted against the breaking dawn sky, which painted the digital landscape with muted shades of pink, purple, and gold. Two majestic caribou, a buck and a doe, stepped into the foreground and dipped their heads to the water to drink. The composition was incredible, the diffused lighting was perfect, the color saturation amazing. Della paused to check the light meter one last time and then gently pressed down on the shutter release, just as all hell broke loose. Brilliant lights stabbed through the woods behind her as the roar of a monster machine shattered the quiet stillness. Dust billowed, and the light blinded her as Della crouched in the blind, paralyzed with terror. Her heart was beating out of her chest, and she couldn't draw breath into her lungs. Her mind was back in the Middle East, even though her body was here in the Canadian wilderness. She stumbled out of the blind and dropped to her knees in the dead grass, clasping her hands behind her head. With the last gasp in her quaking body, she shouted, "Don't shoot. I'm an American citizen!"

The door on the huge vehicle opened. A rack of lights on the roof, shining toward her, stole almost all of her vision. All she could see was the silhouette of a beast of a man striding toward her through the dusty air. She kept her eyes downturned as he stopped in front of her.

"What the hell, woman?" the masculine voice asked incredulously.

Della looked up. She thought it odd that the soldier wasn't carrying a weapon. Hope dawned in her foggy brain that the man standing in front of her might be on their side. He cautiously approached her and reached out a hand. She flinched away, expecting a blow to the head.

"I'm not going to hurt you," he said calmly. "Can you tell me who you are?" He once again cautiously reached out to her. "Here—let me help you up."

With the beep of a remote control device, the overhead lights on the vehicle went off, and Della could see the man's face. He was definitely not Saudi. Brown, wavy hair fell over his forehead, framing darkly lashed blue eyes. His brow was furrowed, not with anger but with concern. His cheeks were clean shaven, and his strong jaw and full mouth were more Gentlemen's Quarterly than World at War Magazine. He was wearing camouflage, but it was the kind hunters wear, not military issue.

Trembling, Della gripped his forearms to steady herself as she rose to her feet. "I'm Della Rawlins," she said shakily. "I've been sent here by Today ... I mean, National Environmental Magazine," she said, just catching herself in time, "to shoot the caribou."

"Could have fooled me," the man said. "Looks more like you've been caught in a war zone."

Della realized she wasn't in any imminent danger, and she felt foolish and embarrassed and shell-shocked all at the same time. She was furious, and the hackles rose on the back of her neck.

"Yeah, well, if you hadn't barged in here like a weekend warrior, I wouldn't have been terrified. Who do you think you are, crashing through the woods in a military-issue Hummer, of all things, dressed like a soldier of fortune? Hasn't anyone told you that the war here in Canada is over?"

"Well, now that you mention it, I guess the gear is a little over the top," the guy said ruefully, scratching his head. "But, hey, I have an image to uphold. I'm Brad Jamieson, owner of Jamieson's Outdoor Outfitters," he said, extending his hand. "Your tent is parked practically on my front doorstep. This is my family's property. I was just wondering who was out here squatting on my land."

Ignoring the proffered hand, Della bit out, "Well, the caribou owned it long before you did. And the Algonquian and Mohawks were happy to live here without having to put fences around everything. What is it about white men that make them feel they have to lay claim to the land and its natural resources? Whatever happened to 'live and let live'? Anyway, for your information, I was invited to use this location by a member of the Jamieson family, who just happens to be your brother."

"Well, that's news to me. I guess Ryan didn't deem it necessary to inform me. By the way, some of us white men have more of an interest in protecting the land rather than exploiting resources or the native people. But that's a discussion for another time. Can I offer you a cup of tea and a bite of breakfast—and maybe an apology for ruining your morning?"

Della huffed, out a breath, still fuming, and retrieved her Nikon from its tripod inside the blind. "Now that you've scared off the caribou and stunk up the blind with your man smell, it's just as well I call it a day and move my gear somewhere else," she said peevishly. "This was a perfect location, though."

"Want a ride up to the cabin?"

"No thanks. I need the exercise."

Noticing—and not for the first time—the trim, athletic, and definitely female body in the slick North Face jacket and Sportskin leggings standing before him, he tended to disagree, but he thought it wise to hold his tongue. Shrugging his shoulders, Brad said, "Suit yourself," and strode back over to the camouflage-painted Hummer, which Della now noted was blazoned down the side with the company logo of Jamieson's Outdoor Outfitters. He swung up into the driver's seat and expertly backed the rig up the path to where he could turn in toward the cabin.

Still peeved, Della trudged up the path, debating whether she should pack up her gear and spend the afternoon scouting other locations or take the mighty, great white hunter up on his offer of a cup of tea and see if he had any ideas on where the herd might have migrated, having vacated "his" property.

CHAPTER 2

Della approached the cabin warily. Brad—whom she had secretly dubbed "G.I. Joe"—had the door open and was busily unpacking the Hummer. The back of the vehicle was packed with boxes and bags and all sorts of gear.

"Planning on staying awhile?" she asked cautiously, not wanting to appear nosy.

"Couple of weeks," Brad replied, hefting a huge duffel bag over his brawny shoulder. "I always come up to the cabin to field-test new products we're considering listing in our catalog. Nothing goes in the new line until it's checked out."

"Hmmm, that's very conscientious of you," she said.

"We have a reputation to uphold." He grunted, grabbing another weighty bag to balance his load. "Our company has been around for over fifty years. People expect us not to sell junk."

"Of course," she replied.

"Wanna grab a box of groceries?" he asked, noticing her discomfort in the way she was twisting the camera strap and fiddling with the dials.

"Sure," she said, grabbing a cooler. "I can help you unpack.

* * *

You're definitely planning to eat well," Della said, grinning as she hefted the heavy cooler onto the countertop in the rustic kitchen, opened the cover, and pulled out a couple of T-bone steaks.

"Sure thing," he replied, lighting the pilot in the compact, propane fridge. "I have to maintain my manly physique," he said, grinning back. "I'm not a wieners and beans kind of guy."

"Righto," Della said, thinking about the packages of dehydrated trail meals she'd been living on for the past four days. That and a jar of peanut butter and crackers was all she'd had room for when she'd packed her stuff to backpack in to camp. At least, she figured, she wouldn't be attracting bears.

"So how do you know my brother?" Brad inquired, his eyes narrowing.

"Oh, we met in Bolivia," she said, smiling as she remembered. "He was following the Inca Trail and climbing the Machu Picchu, communing with condors in the Colca Canyon."

"Oh yeah, I remember that trip," Brad said, lighting the propane range and setting the kettle on to boil. "He was writing for our adventure tourism magazine, Out There. The pictures of the condors were spectacular."

"He's a very talented photographer," said Della.

"Yeah, and a bit of a wing-nut," Brad said ruefully, reflecting on the antics of his younger brother, who loved chasing every outdoor adventure he could find and hated being confined to a desk "bean counting" as he put it.

"So what were you doing in Bolivia?" Brad asked, removing the boiling kettle from the range and filling a ball-shaped infuser with loose tea.

"My partner and I were covering President Morales's takeover of the energy industry. Bolivia has the second largest reserves of natural gas in South America, but the country is one of its poorest. Morales wanted to put the industry under state control to stop the exploitation."

"I guess that's not the least of his worries, with the country being one of the world's largest producers of coca. Talk about exploitation. I was involved a few years ago when it came out that the Bolivian military was abusing dogs in military training. They would tie the animals down on wooden platforms, stab them to death, and remove the organs, smearing the blood on the faces of the soldiers. It was horrific. You could hear the dogs screaming in agony. Such needless cruelty," he said, shaking his head.

"Yeah, the world can be a cruel place," Della reflected, her heart aching for Aaron, whose fate was yet to be determined.

"Cream or sugar?" Brad asked, waving a carton of milk.

"Ah, such luxury," Della replied. "I'm trying to get used to powdered skim milk."

"So what are you doing photographing caribou in the great Canadian wilderness when you could be off somewhere helping to topple governments?"

"Well, that's a long story," Della said. "Suffice it to say that I ran into a little trouble in Pakistan and was 'encouraged' to take a little hiatus from the political arena." The truth was that she had been forcibly recalled by her editor at Today after Aaron had been taken prisoner and she had evaded capture in Abbottabad. She'd taken this assignment from National Environmental to photograph the caribou in order to pay her rent. She needed to regroup, build her resources, and make some connections to get back. Noting the shadow that crossed her face and the lost look in her eyes, Brad asked gently, "You want to talk about it?"

"Not particularly," she said, shaking herself out of the melancholy. "What I need to know is where those caribou have gone. I need to find another location to get some pictures."

"Well, I dunno. But if you like, once I get sorted out here, we can climb up on Pointe Peak and have a look-see. From that elevation, you can see for miles around. It would save a lot of time and legwork."

"Brilliant idea," Della said, knowing she had only two weeks to get the shots and get back to the city.

"I have some rifle scopes and binoculars to test, so it'll be a good opportunity for me as well. By the way, what sizes do you wear in clothing and footwear? Wouldn't be a medium and a size seven shoe, would it?"

"Close enough," she replied. "Why do you want to know?" Her eyes narrowed as his appraising gaze ran down her body.

"The suppliers always send me samples in average sizes in both men's and women's apparel. I can fit you out with some first-class hiking and rock climbing gear."

"Hey, I prefer my hikers already broken in." Della grinned, indicating her battered, well-worn boots. "We've been together a long time, and they haven't let me down yet."

"That's fine, but these rock climbing shoes can save your life on steep slopes like Pointe Peak. Shove them in your backpack and give 'em a test-drive."

* * *

After putting the groceries away, Della and Brad spent the rest of the afternoon taking all of the product samples out and examining everything. He insisted she take all of the ladies' wear, which included a very expensive, formfitting windproof suit for climbing.

"Lightweight, breathable, water-repellant, and abrasion resistant," she read. "Should be made from spiderweb for all the science that went into making that." She laughed, noting the spider motif on the packaging.

"That's not so far out," Brad said. "Did you know that spider web is the strongest natural fiber on earth?"

"Fascinating," she replied as she threw the three hundred-dollar outfit on her pile. "Hey, I could really use this," she said, pulling out a portable shower outfit, which consisted of a black poly bag you filled up with water and a shower head connected by a hose. "I haven't had a shower in four days."

"If you're gonna use that, you had better take this, too," Brad said, tossing a plastic bag containing a portable shower enclosure toward her.

By the time they had sorted through all of the bags and boxes, it was late afternoon, and Della felt it was time she went back to her tent to get ready for supper.

"Why don't you stay here in the cabin?" Brad suggested when she said it was time for her to make tracks. "There are two bedrooms, a chemical toilet, running water, and no wild animals. It's practically the Hilton. I'll even put a chocolate on your pillow," he joked, biting off a piece from a Hershey bar.

"It's very tempting, believe me, but I snore like a lumberjack, and I wouldn't want to intrude. I've already overstepped my boundaries by 'parking my tent' on your land. I'll be fine where I am."

"Aw, don't be silly. We're family friends now, aren't we?" He smiled, but sensed she didn't want to surrender her independence so didn't press further.

"At least take the bigger dome tent. It has a nice waterproof fly and lots of room for the extra gear."

"No, really. I'll be fine."

"Okay," he said, not for the first time that day. "Suit yourself."

Della left the cabin and walked back to her tent. She unzipped the door and pushed the huge box of outdoor gear inside. With her bedroll, pack, and bear-proof food bag already in there, she hardly had room to take off her boots.

Later, as she got out her small camp stove and heated water to mix with her dehydrated "hunter stew," her nostrils were assailed by the smell of grilling burgers, and the strains of country music drifting on the evening air.

I'm not the first woman to be sabotaged while trying to stake a claim for independence, she thought, as her traitorous stomach growled hollowly.

CHAPTER 3

The morning sun was just topping the hills when Brad awoke. He was so comfortable snuggled in his high-tech sleeping bag, nestled in his feather bed. He rolled over and looked at his wristwatch—6:00 a.m. It didn't matter where he was or whether or not he set an alarm, his inner alarm clock woke him up at six on the dot every day.

He rubbed his eyes, unzipped the bag, and swung his legs over the edge of the bed. Padding over to the bedroom window, he looked out over the sunlit meadow to where the little beige bump was nestled among the late-blooming wildflowers. Another structure had sprung up not far from the tent, and Brad groaned, "What the hell, woman," as he beheld Della inside the light gray nylon shower enclosure, happily lathering her hair. The September sun slanted low across the horizon, shining right through the material of the shower walls and throwing her naked body into clear silhouette. "How the hell did the mountain men stay celibate for months?" he asked himself, out loud, forcing himself to turn away from the window as he headed toward the bathroom, trying to figure out how he was going to pee. That's a clear fail on the "material guaranteed to ensure privacy" feature, he thought to himself.

* * *

Having washed, shaved, and dressed, Brad checked to be sure the shower was vacant before heading across the meadow, carrying a bag and two mugs of steaming coffee.

"Anybody home?" he called.

"Yeah, I'm up," Della answered, unzipping the tent and stepping into her hikers. She was dressed in the leg-hugging rock climbing pants and a white, sleeveless tank top that was "scientifically designed to wick away moisture and keep you dry and comfortable on the trail."

"You're an early riser," Brad said, handing her a mug of coffee, which he'd treated to a dollop of milk.

"Ahhh," Della breathed as she inhaled the fragrant steam. "Nectar of the Gods. I'm still running on Pakistani time."

"Right," said Brad. "The jet lag must be wicked. I wasn't sure if you wanted breakfast, so I brought a couple of muffins," he said, handing over a paper sack. "I don't like a heavy stomach when I climb, but I have lots of trail food for energy on the way up."

"Sounds good to me," Della said.

Brad approached her with a strange-looking pack. "This is a PortaOasis drinking pack," he explained. "You fill it with water, and you wear it under your climbing pack. The plastic hose comes over your shoulder under your jacket, and you can drink when you get thirsty without having to stop and unscrew a water bottle."

"Neat," Della said. "Show me how to put it on."

Brad moved to her back. Pushing aside her thick, dark ponytail, he admired the fine contours of her well-developed shoulders and tried to ignore the soft rise of her breasts as he fastened the water pack securely to her slender frame.

"Won't the water get warm?" she asked.

"It's not supposed to," Brad replied. "But I guess we'll find out."

Reaching inside the tent for her daypack and the jacket from yesterday, Della once again checked over her camera, which she had fitted with an adjustable telephoto lens.

"Hope we get a bead on those caribou," she said as they headed over to the cabin to pick up Brad's pack.

***

They had been hiking for an hour through the woods, following a barely visible trail that snaked through the conifers and deciduous trees. The ground had been steadily rising, and Della could already feel a burn in her calf muscles. "Great workout," she commented as she paused to take a swig of water from the mouthpiece.

"We're getting close to the boulders," Brad said. "We'll soon have to stop and gear up. I dunno how much rock climbing experience you've had, but there's a hard way and an easy way to climb this peak."

"Little bitty mountains like this one don't scare me much," Della said. "I grew up in Michigan and spent most of my summer holidays in the Porcupine Mountains, hiking and camping. I went to rock climbing school in Grand Rapids, did lots of free climbing and trad climbing on the Upper Peninsula, up around Silver Mountain, but I'm nowhere near as accomplished as your brother. I saw him climb the Pinnacle in Marquette and ice climb on Glacier Mountain out in British Columbia. He's as nimble as a mountain goat."

"Yeah, he's fearless, all right," Brad said, laughing. "He's gonna crack open that damn fool, stubborn head of his one day."

"Tell me about it," Della agreed. "My boyfriend is just like him, a daredevil. It's no wonder they get along so well."

Brad's heart did a little swan dive at the word boyfriend, but he plodded on anyway. "What does your boyfriend do?"

Her brow furrowed, and that shadow came over her face again as she said, "He was my partner at Today magazine, a writer. He liked high-profile conflict stories. I took the pictures."

"Oh, so you liked chasing the excitement, too, hey?" Brad teased her, hoping to make her smile again.

"Not so much anymore," Della said. "Aaron was captured in Pakistan. He's still there as far as I know. He's being held as a prisoner of war. I don't know if he's dead or alive."

"Wow, I know the Middle East is a crazy place, but isn't he protected under the third Geneva Convention?"

"Not if he's considered an 'unlawful combatant.' The laws governing deprivation of liberty for security reasons in international armed conflicts can be a bit hazy, especially when the other side wants to incite further hostilities by holding hostages."

"Crappy situation," Brad said somberly. "Hope our government is doing everything it can to see him get home safely."

"Well, my dad's the United States senator from Michigan, and he's been keeping the pressure on the Department of Defense and our representatives at the United Nations. But Pakistan's counterterrorism laws allow enforced disappearances to continue to happen. Even though the UN describes it as a 'violation of international human rights law,' all they can do is call on the Pakistani government to carry out a full review of its security-related legislation to be sure they are conforming to their international law obligations. In other words, 'Brother, be thine own keeper.'"

"A lot of good that'll do." Brad snorted. "Maybe the International Press Corps or Associated Press can help."

"All they can do is get the word out. No one has the balls to go in and extract him after what happened with the capture of bin Laden. It's too much of a risk." Della shook her head. "It's so hard to just sit back and watch the wheels of government turn so slowly. He's running out of time. I feel so helpless." Her eyes filled as she buried her face in her hands.

"Look, Della, you made it out alive," Brad said, taking her by the shoulders. "Your guy knew the risks. He played his cards, and this time, he lost. You never know what twists there are going to be in the road. Don't lose hope—not while there's a chance he may get out alive. Keep the pressure on the government. Things are volatile now, but you never know when people can be used as bargaining chips. I know you have your eye on things. And your old man is a wily, old bird. He'll be a great guy to have in your corner when the time is right."

"Yeah, you're right," Della said, wiping her nose. "What's that old saying? God helps those who help themselves?"

"Yeah, something like that," Brad said, a worried look in his eyes as he gave her a one-armed hug. "Come on. Let's go. All we can do today is find those caribou."

They resumed their trek up the trail. Della's pack seemed lighter to her after having unloaded her emotional baggage onto Brad's wide shoulders. It felt so good to get everything out in the open and hear someone else's take on the circumstances of Aaron's captivity. Brad was certainly a rock of a guy–smart; worldly; insightful just like Aaron, but cautious; prepared for everything; and tuned into her physical and emotional needs. She had to admit, he was also sexy as hell, but different from the type of guy she was used to.

CHAPTER 4

By midmorning, Della and Brad finally broke out of the woods at the base of Pointe Peak. The September sun was warm on their backs, but the wind remained cool at this elevation. The mountain rose like a giant, arthritic hand, its swollen wrist and fingertips veering northwest instead of north. Its base was strewn with large boulders, from which the grizzled fingers rose, sheer cliffs with vertical fractures. The topmost portion was much smoother and veered outward, looking to be a pretty technical climb.

Brad was sitting down, pulling climbing shoes, harnesses, ropes, and helmets out of his pack. "How does it look to you?" he asked Della.

"Not bad at the beginning, but the top part looks a bit difficult," she replied, shading her eyes as she scanned the smooth face for visible hand and footholds.

"It's not as bad as it looks," Brad replied. "Ryan free climbed it when he was practically an infant, and he drilled bolts in to make it safer for the rest of us. When we get up there, the ropes are already in place. You can clip in, and I'll belay you. It's a lot faster coming down, obviously, because we can rappel."

Della was sitting, putting on the smooth leather climbing shoes with the soft rubber soles. They'd come packed with extra foam, and even though they weren't broken in yet, she'd gotten them to fit quite well by padding them here and there to conform to the contours of her feet. They felt really good.

"Nearly ready," she said, buckling the climbing harness around her waist and legs and adjusting the helmet comfortably. Some fancy gloves completed the outfit.

Similarly attired, Brad collected the rest of their gear and piled their heavier packs along with their boots near the base of a tree. "We'll leave this stuff here for the trip back. Just take your camera, and I'll take the scopes and binocs. These light packs are way easier to climb with," he said, handing her a light nylon backpack.

They started toward the boulders, and the going was pretty easy, with lots of hand and footholds on the way up. It was great to be independent of the safety lines, although Brad had been sure to place a thick safety pad on the ground in case one of them accidentally fell. They made great time, climbing to about five hundred feet in about fifteen minutes.

The view even from this elevation was excellent, much like the view from a gondola ride up a mountain. They were far above the treetops, and you could see the river in the distance, but they weren't yet far enough up to be able to see the barrens or down into the forest where the caribou might be grazing. Della took out her camera and got some nice shots. The telephoto lens allowed her to bring the distant landscape into sharp focus—but still no caribou.

The next part of the climb was far more difficult. But even so, Della felt she could climb traditionally, putting her own fall protection devices into fissures in the rock and clipping into them with carabineers as she moved up the rock face.

"I really think I'll be fine," she said insistently.

"I don't want to take any unnecessary risks," Brad said, expertly tying a figure eight knot in the working end of the belay rope and threading it through Della's crotch loop and up through her waist loop. He did a figure eight retrace and ended off with a double overhand safety knot at the end. He checked to see that all her buckles were correctly fastened and the knots were tight and secure before looping the second rope's belay end through his belay plate. He clipped the looped rope and guard onto the loop on his harness with a locking carabineer. With this setup, Brad could feed the safety rope to Della as she climbed and could stop her fall should she lose her grip or footing on the rock.

"What's the first rule of belaying?" Della asked, testing his knowledge.

"Never let go of the dead end." Brad demonstrated how, by holding fast to the bottom part of the belay rope, below the plate, he would cause the rope to lock and the climber's fall would be arrested.

"Okay, I'm good to go," Della said, shouldering her light pack.

Brad was impressed with her technique as she carefully found and tested handholds and footholds, making excellent progress up the craggy rock face.

"Hey, can you give me some slack?" she called.

He'd become momentarily distracted by the flexing of her shapely calf muscles and her perfectly round ass as she nimbly scaled the rock wall. "Whoops, sorry," he said and dutifully gave his full attention to the job at hand.

Soon Della had made it to the ledge that separated the fractured rock section from the smooth rock at the top of the peak.

Brad climbed up after her, and when he pulled himself up over the edge, his face and shoulders were shiny with sweat.

Della sat with her knees bent and her back to the wall, having had time to recover from the exertion. "Piece of cake," she grinned, taking a swig of the still-cold water from her PortaOasis.

"Not bad," Brad agreed still breathing hard, and taking time out to rehydrate as well. "Some view, hey?"

The landscape was fantastic. They could see all the way out to where the coastal plains ended at the edge of the distant Atlantic Ocean. The view of the Appalachians' permanent ice caps shining on the majestic peaks was spectacular. The river looked more like a ribbon from up here, but they could see down through the trees to some small forms moving on the barrens.

"Look!" Della cried, pointing excitedly, "Caribou!"

"Hey, you're right," Brad said, pulling some equipment from his pack. He put a rifle scope to his eye and said, "It would be quite a shot to make from here. I think it would require more rifle than your standard 308."

"Hah. But not more lens than a 300 mm," Della replied, putting the Nikon with the long telephoto lens to her eye. "I think I need to use the tripod to hold it steady, though," she said, attaching the camera to the tripod with the mounting screw.

"Hey, I can take pictures too, with these," Brad said, pulling out a huge pair of binoculars. "Check 'em out."

Della adjusted the glasses to her eyes, "Wow, not a bad resolution," she said, impressed. "Your hunters can get the bears and moose to smile before they shoot their lights out." She smirked. "Hey, moose, say cheese!" she said, adjusting the binoculars down to take his picture.

"Smart-ass!" Brad grinned. "Some hunters appreciate being able to have a picture of their moose and eat it too, you know."

They sat in companionable silence for a while, just taking in the view, enjoying the rest, and sharing a snack of some trail mix and beef jerky.

"Look at that bald eagle," Brad said, pointing to the left,

where a huge bird hung almost motionless in the crisp air. "She's hunting. Probably sees a mouse or rabbit down in the woods."

With that, the bird swiftly dove, and then rose up through the trees, a small animal gripped in its talons.

"How do you know it's a female?" Della asked.

"Well, bald eagles don't have gender distinct plumage, but the females are usually about a third larger than the males. Now, I guess you could get scientific and do an internal investigation. But this guy, Mark Stalmaster, found that, by measuring the bird's beak depth and toe claw measurement and doing some fancy computations, you can find out whether the eagle's female or male."

"How do you know so much about animals?" Della asked.

"I have a bachelor's degree in biology and ecology, a master's in conservation and natural resources management, and a PhD in environmental science policy and management."

"Wow. How do you fit all of that into your head?" she joked. "Your parents must be proud."

"Not really. They wanted me to get a degree in business management and marketing so I could run the family business."

"If a child is raised to think with his own brain, he will probably be destined to thwart his parents' plans in pursuing his own educational path," Della said sagely.

"Sounds like someone was a bit of a rebellious kid herself," Brad guessed, smiling.

"Oh yeah," she said. "No White House internship for me. I went to Boston University, mastered in photojournalism, minored in poli-sci, subminored in partying. That's where I met Aaron."

"Aaron?"

"My boyfriend. You know, the one who's being held

hostage in Pakistan," Della reminded him, her eyes once again clouding over.

"Oh, that's right. Sorry," he said, mentally kicking himself for bringing it up again.

"My brother, Ryan, went to Rochester Institute in New York for photojournalism," Brad shared, hoping to steer the conversation out of dangerous waters.

"Yeah, and the way he talks, he hated every minute of it except for escaping to the big city to party every chance he got." Della laughed, lightening the mood.

"Do you want to climb higher? Or go back down?" Brad asked, getting to his feet.

"I'm no quitter," she said. "And I have this thing about completion. Can't stop till I conquer the damn thing."

"Great, I like a woman who knows what she wants and goes for it!" Brad grinned at her.

"You betcha," she replied, thinking to herself, Whoa baby, put the brakes on that thought!

***

Later, as they rappelled down from the summit, Della reflected on what a great time she'd had with Brad. There was none of the competitiveness she had with Aaron or Ryan. He was so concerned for her safety and comfort. It was such a different way of relating to a guy. She and Brad were more like a team, a unit. It felt kind of nice knowing that someone had your back. It was different.

CHAPTER 5

By the time Della and Brad reached the base of Pointe Peak, got out of their climbing gear, and repacked their packs, it was four o'clock. They still had an hour's hike to get back to camp, and the air was getting chilly.

Della put on her jacket and said, "Thanks, Brad. That was an amazing climb."

"My pleasure," Brad said, winding up the rope and shouldering the heavier pack. "We accomplished our mission, found the caribou, tested some new products, and got some great shots. I'm looking forward to a preview later on. Can I persuade you to come over for a steak barbeque for supper?"

Remembering the mouthwatering aroma drifting over to her camp from last night's grill, Della delightedly took him up on the offer.

"Do you think the caribou will come back to the river to drink?" Della asked. "They never really went too far away."

"Hard to say," Brad replied. "They start to migrate from the coastal plains, where they have their calves in the spring, to the forest, where they spend the winter. They usually follow the same route every year, but they haven't really started the move yet. I'd say they'll be around for maybe another week or two. The herd used to be huge, maybe over a hundred thousand head, but the clear-cutting of the forest has encouraged a bigger population of moose to grow, and more moose attract more wolves. The wolves and coyotes have had a detrimental effect on the herd. Then there are parasites like the brain worm. Many years ago, the government here introduced about three hundred reindeer from Norway to increase the food supply because the caribou herds had been reduced by overhunting. The reindeer were herded to different parts of the east, and they carried the parasite."

"So did the caribou catch it directly from those animals?" Della asked.

"No. Snails and slugs crawl over the reindeer droppings, and the larvae penetrate their bodies. Then a caribou comes along and eats a leaf the slug is on, so the parasite gets into its stomach, and then into the spinal cord, and eventually into the brain. It causes all kinds of strange behaviors and most often results in death."

"That's awful," Della said. "Doesn't the government check animals out before introducing them into new areas?"

"Not always," Brad replied. "And they often create a bigger problem than the one they were trying to fix in the first place."

"What about the moose? Are they infected?"

"They aren't finding it so much in the moose population as with the caribou, but moose don't herd together the same way. There have been isolated cases, but nothing like with the caribou. The eastern herds are the only ones affected right now."

"Wow, it's a good thing it hasn't affected the domestic food supply," Della commented. "I would really be disappointed if it meant we couldn't have our steak barbecue tonight! But when I make the salad, I'm going to be sure to wash the lettuce really well!" She shuddered, thinking about the parasites.

"Good plan," teased Brad. "But if the bugs don't get you, the pesticides and herbicides will." He laughed.

"'Killed by food.' That would be a horrible thing to have to have written on your headstone," Della said.

CHAPTER 6

Brad and Della got back to the cabin at around six o'clock. The afternoon was waning, and the sun was dipping toward the horizon, coloring the sky with hues of yellow, pink, and orange. The riverbank was aglow with the slanting rays, and Brad, remembering with amusement her tirade from the day before said, "I think I'm going to take a dip in the river to wash off my 'man smell.'"

"Yeah, about that," Della said sheepishly. "I'm sorry I was so mean."

"No need to apologize," he said. "I am truly sorry I messed up your shoot. I'm going to make it up to you, though. A buddy of mine is a helicopter pilot, and we have an agreement that, when the caribou start to herd, he's going to fly in and take me on a run to watch the migration. If you're still here, you can come up, too. You can take some photos to round out your story."

Della lit up like a Christmas tree. "Are you serious? That would be fabulous!" She threw her arms around his neck and said, without thinking, "I could just kiss you!"

Catching her around the waist, his gaze dropping to her smiling mouth, Brad said seriously, "Don't let me stop you."

Embarrassed and suddenly shy, Della said, "Hey, aren't

you going for a dip?" She hoped that the heat in her cheeks was hidden by the glow of the sun on her face.

"Yeah, are you joining me?" he asked, teasingly.

"Are you kidding? That water is freezing!" She shivered just thinking about it. "I'll just wash up a bit and change my clothes, and I'll meet you back at the cabin."

"Chicken," he challenged, hoping to change her mind.

She laughed it off as he turned toward the cabin steps and instantly felt guilty. How could she be so attracted to this man when the guy she was supposed to be in love with was rotting in a prison somewhere in Pakistan? What kind of a person was she?

I have to stop thinking that way about him, she told herself firmly. I have a job to do, and I'm going to keep my mind on that. She marched across the meadow, firming her resolve to be a better person.

**

Brad watched her through the bedroom window as he stripped off his hiking clothes and grabbed his swim trunks and a towel. That's temptation looking for a place to happen, he thought. She's such a great girl, with so much on her plate right now. I have no business messing with her. Just have to keep things light between us. We'll just be friends.

But his body felt differently. Her lips were so very kissable. He had been tempted to pull her close, pressing those soft breasts against his chest and fitting himself into that tempting space where her toned legs met in those tight leggings.

Ah, fuck, he thought—and not for the first time that day—I hope that water is damn cold.

**

Della was rocking in the weathered, wooden rocking chair on Brad's veranda. She had packed away all of her gear and had freshened up and changed into her old, comfy jeans, which were so soft and faded that they fit her body like a second skin. She had thrown on a fresh tank top and a cozy, fleece-lined football hoodie and had headed on over to wait for Brad to return from the river. The thought of a sizzling hunk of charring beef on the coals was making her empty stomach growl in anticipation. She had brought a couple of ration packs of lemon cake with her for dessert but was thinking that her humble offering would certainly be eclipsed by the main course.

Brad appeared, trudging up the river trail with a striped towel slung around his neck, hair dripping like he'd just finished running a marathon.

"How was it?" Della asked, noticing the goose bumps covering his arms and chest.

"Very refreshing," he replied, rubbing his hair dry with the towel. "But now I think I would like to get into something dry and warm. I see you're supporting the Patriots. Strange for a girl from Michigan?"

"Yeah, I just wear it to bug my dad. He's a big Detroit Lions fan."

"Always the rebel," he laughed as he opened the cabin door and said, "Come on in or stay there and relax. I'll only be a minute. Why don't you grab yourself a beer from the fridge," he called over his shoulder.

Remembering the little white pill she would have to take later on to allow her to combat the sleep disorder she'd suffered from, ever since returning from Afghanistan, she called back, "No thanks, I'll just have a soda."

It was getting dark, so Della grabbed a box of matches and lit the kerosene lanterns that graced the corner sconces on the kitchen walls. She took one outside, too, and hung it from a hook in the veranda roof over the charcoal grill.

Soon Brad reappeared, took two luscious T-bones out of the fridge, and grabbed himself a beer. He expertly rubbed the meat with some barbecue spice and left it on some waxed paper to rest while he grabbed a bag of charcoal and some starter and headed out to the grill.

"Nothing like a real barbecue over charcoal," he said, dumping a pile of briquettes into the grill pan and dousing it with starter.

"Smells like downtown New York," Della said and wrinkled her nose as Brad lit a match and set the coals on fire, sending black smoke billowing toward her.

"We'll just give that some time to burn off, and then we'll get this show on the road," Brad said, setting the wire grill over the now lightly flaming coals to heat up.

He left once more, heading toward the kitchen, where he took out the vegetables to make the sides.

"You seem very comfortable with cooking," Della said admiringly.

"Yeah, well, when you've been living on your own in the city, eating out all the time gets to be a drag," Brad said. "You get tired of overly seasoned food and huge portions. You're better off learning to cook for yourself."

"No Mrs. Jamieson to greet you at the door, slippers in hand?" Della teased.

"What country did you say you were from?" Brad laughed. "I haven't heard of women doing that since Beaver Cleaver was a kid. And to answer your question, no, I'm not married."

"Well, that's good," Della replied. "You won't have to explain what you're doing out here in the wilderness with a strange woman."

"No worries," Brad said, poking the graying coals with a stick. "Just having dinner with a friend."

***

Soon the smell of charring beef scented the air, and the potatoes roasted in their foil jackets on the edge of the coals. The freshly washed lettuce leaves were chopped and tossed with some sliced garden vegetables to make a mouthwatering salad. Della shook some oil, vinegar, mustard, and honey, seasoned with a dash of salt and pepper, in a mason jar and placed it on the kitchen table.

"Steaks will be ready in two minutes," Brad called, reading the temperature on the meat thermometer.

"Yup, everything's ready!" Della called back, sliding some sautéed mushrooms and onions into a serving bowl.

"Et voilà," Brad said, placing the steak platter on the table with a flourish of his dishtowel. "Dinner is served."

They filled their plates with the delicious-looking food, and the first bite of steak made Della close her eyes in rapture. "This is the very best thing that has crossed my lips in a very long time," she confided, chewing contentedly.

"Even a vegetarian couldn't complain," Brad said, helping himself to a forkful of salad. "Mmmm, that dressing is divine. I must get your recipe!"

***

After the meal was finished and Brad and Della had boiled the water and shared the dishwashing duties, they wandered back out to the veranda with steaming cups of coffee. Sitting down on the front steps, Della gazed up into the inky sky. The stars were out by the thousands, and the moon was on the rise, almost full.

"There's no way to capture the night sky with a camera and do it justice," Della said, raising her ever-present camera to her eye and pointing the lens toward the heavens. "Once, when we were in Chile, Aaron and I took a trip out to the Atacama Desert near Paranal. The sky there is so black and crystal clear, and weather conditions are perfect about three hundred and twenty nights out of the year. There's an observatory there, and I got to talk to some astrophotographers about their work. When you see the terrestrial landscape in the foreground with the universe beyond, it shows you the connection between earth and sky. It can make you feel very insignificant or very much a part of nature, depending on your viewpoint. It's beautiful."

The starlight shining in Della's dark eyes, Brad thought, was pretty beautiful, too. And he wondered, as he saw that melancholy cross her face like a cloud across the moon, if she was thinking about the man who was being held in a far-off prison.

"Let's see the pictures you took from up on the peak today," Brad said, hoping to pull her out of that dark place.

Della turned on the display on the back of the camera, and pictures of the caribou appeared on the small screen. There were close-ups of some of the animals grazing and wider shots of groups of caribou, standing or lying down with their young. The calves were adorable, following close to their mothers and bending their little necks to eat the grasses and plants, which were abundant on the plains.

"What do they eat in the winter?" Della asked.

"See those large, flat hooves?" Brad asked. "They use them to dig through the snow for lichen. Some people call it reindeer moss."

Moving backward through the pictures that Della had taken, Brad saw there were some really great shots. One showcased several of the antlered animals splashing through the water in the river. The shot was backlit, with the light reflecting off the water, and the animal in the foreground seemed to be traced with silver. It was breathtaking.

"I think that's the last one," Della said, arrowing back one last time, just to be sure.

"Nope, you saved the best till last," Brad said in wonder as he gazed at the glorious frame. The background colors—the pinks, purples, and golds—took his breath away. The mist rising from the river cast a ghostly lavender glow over the animals, which, poised for flight, seemed ready to spring right off the screen. "That's your money shot."

"Oh my gosh," Della said unbelievingly. "I must have pressed the shutter release just as you came crashing in, down at the river that first morning. It's so natural! A different feeling than I had planned to capture but so much better. Absolutely amazing."

"The best things are always unexpected or unplanned," Brad said, "It's almost like fate steps in and takes a hand."

***

It was getting late, and Della stifled a yawn as she rose to bring their coffee cups in to the kitchen sink. "I think I'd better call it a night," she said, turning toward Brad, who had come in behind her. "Thanks so much for a wonderful day. I really had fun."

"Me, too," Brad said, wishing she didn't have to leave to go sleep in that little tent all by herself. "Hey, I was gonna try my hand at fishing tomorrow morning. Wanna join me?" he asked. "But you have to get up early to catch the trout when they're hungry."

"That's not a problem for me, remember?" Della smiled. "I hope you don't want me to put worms on the hooks, though. That grosses me out. I always feel like I'm hurting the poor things and they try to squirm away. Ugggh!" she said, shuddering.

"No worms will be harmed in the catching of these fish," Brad assured her. "I have a whole box full of new lures to try out."

"Okay, you're on," she said, picking up her camera and heading down the cabin steps. "See you tomorrow."

CHAPTER 7

Della was up at daylight and poked her head out of the tent to get a read on the weather conditions. It was a little overcast and cool, so she put on the windproof and water-repellent jacket and pants and her rubber boots and jammed a toque on her head. With weather conditions not conducive to showering, she would just have to deal with not feeling completely clean.

She trotted on over to the cabin to see if Brad was ready. Two spin cast rods and reels lay on the veranda with a tackle box and dip net. A silver thermos and compact cooler accompanied the fishing gear, and a pair of rubber hip waders sat near a bench, waiting for an occupant.

"Anybody home?" Della called.

"Yo," Brad called back, stepping out of the cabin dressed in a fleece-lined jacket, fishing vest, and cargo pants. He jammed a canvas hat on his head and thrust his stocking feet into the hip waders. "Ready," he announced.

They picked up the fishing gear and headed down the path toward the river.

"What kind of fish are we after?" Della asked, not knowing much about sports fishing, even though she was from Michigan, home of the Great Lakes and some of the best freshwater fishing anywhere. Her dad would have been mortified at the extent of her ignorance when it came to the sport.

"I'm hoping to net a couple of trout to panfry for our breakfast," Brad said, sorting out the rods and tackle and preparing the lines to attach the lures. Reaching into the tackle box, he took out a shiny, spoon-shaped gizmo with hooks, some lead weights, and a hook on a filament line. He attached a swivel to the line and began to tie in the weights, the shiny bit with the hooks, and lastly the filament line with the hook at the end.

"The fish aren't stupid enough to just swallow the bare hook, are they?" Della asked.

"I'm gonna put some corn on the lower hook to get their attention. That hangs down below the lure, which looks like a baitfish moving through the water. The fish sees the shiny 'fish' and tries to gobble it up, and bam, you've got him hooked. We're gonna give them a fighting chance, though," Brad said, taking out a Leatherman tool and cutting the barbs off the hooks. "That'll make it easier to remove the hook if the trout is too small to keep."

Della was impressed with the humane way in which Brad prepared to fish. "Do you have to have a special license to fish in this river?" Della asked.

"Well, it's a salmon river, so you do have to have a license. But you're not allowed to fish when the salmon are running in the spring. There are only certain times of the year when salmon fishing is allowed, and you can only keep the mature ones, not ones in the early stages of development. Signs are posted along the rivers on how to identify them and what's allowed at different times of the year."

"What about the trout?" Della asked. "Are they protected?"

"Not as much as the salmon, which is a more commercial species," Brad answered. "But in some rivers, anglers can only use lures with one hook. It gives the trout a better chance to get away."

"Well, that evens up the odds," Della said.

"True," said Brad, "although some of the anglers on the river don't respect the government's authority. That's why we have to have wardens and wildlife officers patrolling the rivers. They have the power to confiscate your fishing gear and your ATV, and even your car—if you're found to be breaking the rules."

"Wow," said Della. "They sure take it seriously."

"They have to if we want these species to be there for future generations."

"For sure," Della agreed. "Speaking of sustenance, do you mind if I pour myself a coffee?"

"Go ahead," Brad said. "There're donuts in the bag, too. Help yourself."

Della watched as Brad scanned the river, looking for the sweet spot in which to cast his line. Facing upstream, he threw his line out in that direction.

"Why'd you throw the line there?" Della asked, sipping on her coffee and munching a donut. "Won't it just move downstream anyway?"

"Wow, you're full of questions today," Brad commented, using a quiet voice. "No wonder you're a good reporter. Just look at the currents in the river. The fish hang out facing upstream so they can see food coming toward them. You find a spot where the water runs from shallow to deep, and there will usually be trout there. You throw your line out ahead of the spot, and your bait looks like it's just naturally drifting downstream."

"Brilliant," said Della. "Ummm, why are you talking so quietly? Can the fish hear you?"

"They can sense sound vibrations on the surface of the

water, and they are very spookable. They can see you, too. That's why you should cast upstream—that way, their tails are toward you."

"Okay, I'm shutting up now," Della said, watching Brad reel in and cast out again.

Suddenly the tip of his pole jerked down, and he instantly pulled upward and started to reel in. "Della, grab the net!" He motioned to her excitedly. "I have one on the hook."

Brad kept a steady pressure on the line as Della placed the net in the water. He covered her hand with his as they scooped the flapping fish into it, laughing as they admired the two-pound beauty.

Brad caught five more fish but let three go, as they were too small to keep.

"Your turn," he called to Della, baiting the hook with corn and motioning for her to join him on the riverbank.

"You're doing fine on your own," Della protested. "And I'm having fun just watching."

"Now you know you're not getting away with that, Miss 'I Gotta Conquer It.' Come here, and I'll show you how to do it."

Reluctantly, Della made her way over to where Brad stood—knee-deep in the water. She tentatively entered the river, trying not to lose her balance on the slippery rocks. Brad caught her arm and gently led her to stand in front of him.

"See that pool just in front of that little riffle? That's where we're going to throw our line." Putting the rod in her hands, he once again covered her hands with his, and together they drew the rod back and cast the line upstream. With a gentle plop, the lure sank into the water, and the line started moving downstream. Suddenly, Della could feel the pressure of the head of the rod bending over, and the line drew taut.

"I think we've got one!" she exclaimed excitedly.

"Keep the pressure on the line now. Easy, though ... We don't want to lose him," Brad said, helping her to reel in the line. He grabbed the net, and leaning down, he scooped the flashing, silver trout into the net.

"Success!" he cried triumphantly as Della exclaimed, "I think it's the biggest one of all!"

It was midmorning when the mighty anglers decided they had caught their limit, and they trudged up toward the cabin with their catch in their net, wrapped in some moss.

Noticing movement out of the corner of her eye, Della turned her head and stopped dead in her tracks, whispering, "Oh look, Brad! Bear cubs."

Sure enough, two small black bears were wrestling and playing with each other in the meadow in front of the tent. They were close to the Hummer at this point, which was parked just in front of the cabin.

"Careful now, Della," Brad whispered, scanning the woods. "Where there are cubs, there's usually a mother bear."

With that, a loud grunting sound came from behind the Hummer. Momma bear had scented intruders who were threatening her babies, and she wasn't happy.

The seven hundred-pound animal reared up on its hind legs, making a guttural bawl, looking ready to charge.

Brad dropped the net with the fishing gear, grabbed Della, and shoved her under the truck.

"Roll over to the middle!" he yelled. Della needed no persuasion. He wrapped her in his arms and lay on top of her. The animal was pacing around the perimeter of the vehicle, her huge nose snorting and snuffling and grunting. Suddenly, a large paw swiped in under the left running board, and Della turned her face into Brad's neck and started to whimper. He pulled her closer, and not knowing what else to do to distract her, he started to kiss her. Her lips parted, and his tongue tangled with hers, the kiss going deep and wild. Her body went molten with sensation, and she squirmed closer, fitting her body to his hard contours. She felt so good in his arms. Her passion matched his as he nuzzled her neck, blazing a trail down to where the jacket strained across her breasts. She caught his earlobe in her teeth, her warm breath playing havoc with his senses. The bear had lost interest in them by now, had discovered their netted lunch, and was happily feasting on the fresh trout. Oblivious to the danger having passed, the couple strained toward each other. His hands had found her soft breasts, and her long fingers stroked his massive erection through the soft material of his pants.

Brad came suddenly to his senses and regretfully pulled his lips from Della's. He peered out from under the Hummer and watched the mother bear lumber over to where the cubs were licking peanut butter off their paws. The tent was pretty much a write-off, all of its contents strewn across the meadow.

Della's hand rested against the pocket of Brad's pants. She felt something hard digging into her palm. "Car keys?" she whispered.

"Oh yeah," Brad said, pulling them out. He pressed a button on the remote control, and the car alarm blared, startling the mother bear. She took one last look at the truck, herded her family in front of her, and lumbered off into the woods. Della closed her eyes and slumped in relief. Brad tried to rearrange her clothing, softly apologizing for messing her up. He was mortified that she would think he had taken the first opportunity to take advantage of her—and when her defenses were down. But the truth was, he hadn't been able to stop himself.

Della was just glad to be alive, and she thought that Brad could have taken her right there on the ground with the mother bear chewing on her head, and she wouldn't even have noticed.

***

Slowly, they untangled themselves from each other and crawled out from beneath the Hummer. "Thank God you decided to bring that tank," Della said, pointing at the Hummer.

"Yeah, it certainly proved its worth today," Brad said, grateful there was no damage to either the vehicle or them. "Looks like your tent is a bust, though."

Sadly, Della surveyed the wreckage that had been her home away from home. "Looks like I'm gonna have to bunk with you after all."

Della had brought her camera with her to the river and had snapped some great candids of Brad catching fish. Thinking about their catch, Della looked around for the net. When she located it, she sifted through the wreckage and found that two trout were left untouched! "Hey, breakfast is not a write-off after all!" She grinned, holding up the two moss-covered trout. "If you don't mind eating after a bear."

***

After they had feasted on their morning's salvaged catch, Della and Brad spent the rest of the afternoon cleaning up Della's campsite. The tent itself was ruined, but much of the outdoor gear and the pack containing her clothing were fine. The little rascals had feasted on the peanut butter, but judging by the torn packages of dehydrated foods, they'd found that trail food was not up to their standards. Most of the rations she'd had to last her the rest of the week had to go in the garbage. So much for "bear-proof" packaging!

"Good thing you taught me how to fish," Della commented, throwing a mangled package of "Swiss meatballs and gravy" into the black, plastic garbage bag.

"Yeah, and lucky for you, I have a shotgun or two with me because tomorrow we're going duck hunting."

"Wha-a-t-t-t?" she stammered. "You mean like aim the stick at the bird. And honk, honk, bang, you're dead?"

"Like, yeah," Brad said, doing his best impression of a blonde. "Thought you just came back from a war zone."

"Yeah, but the only shooting I did there was with a camera. Sure, I've seen other people shoot guns—even at people—but I have never shot anyone or anything in my life."

"Well, you're all into survival mode now, babe. I can't believe a girl from Michigan has never fired a gun. You put the folks in Detroit to shame."

"Please tell me you're not gonna make me shoot bunnies, too." Della fretted, worrying her bottom lip with her teeth.

"Of course not," Brad said, noticing her biting her lip and remembering what it had felt like against his mouth. "We catch bunnies in snares."

The look of shock and horror that spread across her face was too much for him. He could no longer keep a straight face and cracked up at her expense, causing her to swat at him in disgust.

* * *

It was bedtime, and Della, who had managed to find her sleeping bag and both the top and bottom parts of her pajamas intact in the tent wreckage, was sitting up in the middle of the feather bed in Brad's spare bedroom, wondering why she had been so adamant about staying in the tent alone. With luxuries like hot and cold running water and an actual bathroom in Brad's cabin, she was sitting in the lap of luxury.

"Ready for me to turn out the lights?" Brad asked from the doorway, noting the guarded look in her eyes. "You know that bears can't get in the cabin, right? There's a big iron bar across the inside of the door, and anyway, bears aren't nocturnal."

But it wasn't the bears that had Della's nerves on edge; it was the thought of sleeping so close to this man who could turn her world upside down with just a mind-blowing kiss. She hadn't brought up the morning's incident, thinking it better to sweep the whole episode under the carpet and let sleeping dogs lie. How could she have acted so brazenly? And with a man she had just met? She felt so guilty and disloyal to Aaron but chalked the whole incident up to loneliness and stress.

"Yeah, I know." Della faked a yawn. "I'm really tired, but can I have a drink of water before I go to bed, please?"

"Sure," Brad said, taking a tumbler out of the kitchen cupboard and filling it using the pump at the kitchen sink. He brought it into the bedroom and handed it to Della, who looked so adorable sitting there in her pink pajamas, her long, dark hair, freed of its confining ponytail, curling softly around her shoulders. His fingers brushed hers as he passed her the glass, and she remembered his touch as he had stroked her cheeks and held her jaw gently as his mouth had plundered hers under the protection of the Hummer.

"G'night, soldier, see you at oh-eight hundred," he said as he saluted her and left the room, blowing out the kerosene lantern with a soft huff.

"G'night, Brad," she answered softly.

CHAPTER 8

Maybe it was because of the day, which had been fraught with tension, or maybe it was because she'd lost her bottle of little, white pills, but sometime during the night, Della's mind traveled back to the Middle East. It was May 1, 2011, just before midnight. Della and Aaron had been informed by their contact in the CIA that something big was going to happen. They had already identified the custom-built compound in Abbottabad to which the courier had delivered his package as the place where Osama bin Laden was in hiding. The CIA contact had told them that, in exchange for their tip—which had been decisive in the American president deciding to go ahead with the mission—the task force would turn a blind eye to the presence of the news team of Giles and Rawlins at the execution of the order.

Aaron and Della knew there was going to be a helicopter raid on the compound, but they didn't know from which direction the special ops team would be approaching. They had decided to split up, each of them taking a camera, in order to be sure that they had all the bases covered.

***

Della's heart pounded as she crouched on the rooftop

of the concrete building located across the narrow dirt road from bin Laden's compound. Through her telephoto lens, everything looked quiet and tranquil. The lights had gone out one by one on the various levels, until only the security gates were left illuminated. She glanced at her watch, shielding it from view as she pressed a button on the green light screen; it was ten to one. The night was so dark that she could barely make out her hand in front of her, and there was no moon.

Suddenly, she could hear the muted chop of the aircraft. The two modified Black Hawk helicopters had traveled in over the hilly terrain to evade radar detection and were now coming in low over the compound. She could barely make out its shape as the first helicopter hovered over the courtyard. Her camera clicked and whined as she took frame after frame in the low-light conditions. She gasped as the tail grazed the wall of the compound, no doubt due to the downwash from the rotor not being able to fully diffuse in the heated courtyard. The pilot quickly buried the nose into the ground, and nobody on board was hurt in the soft crash landing, which ended with the copter coming to rest at a forty-five-degree angle to the wall. The second helicopter landed outside the compound, and the Navy SEALs scaled the walls to get inside.

Della's camera clicked away as she focused on the drama taking place before her. She could hear the explosions as the soldiers breached walls and doors to gain entrance to the lion's den. Then a familiar face appeared over the third-floor ledge. Quickly focusing her camera, Della couldn't believe her eyes. She was staring into the face of evil—that of "the Sheik" himself, Osama bin Laden. She zoomed in on him and shot frame after frame until he disappeared from view as a SEAL fired at him.

In the street, a crowd had begun to advance on the compound, yelling angry words in Arabic and threatening the invaders with every weapon at their disposal. Some even threw rocks in their furor to protect their own. By the gate of the compound, Della saw a familiar figure, dressed in the regional garb of loose-fitting tunic and pants, throwing rocks at the advancing mob and gesticulating wildly. "Osama bin Laden. Osama bin Laden!" he shouted. It was Aaron.

Della remained rooted to the spot as the crowd converged on her partner, beating him with sticks. An authority figure in a turbaned headdress dealt a final blow that rendered Aaron unconscious. She held her hand over her mouth and bit her palm to stop herself from screaming as blood bloomed on the side of Aaron's skull and ran in rivulets down his face and neck. They hauled him away, dragging his feet in the dust as the SEALs left the compound and boarded the aircraft, carrying a body bag between them, which Della knew contained the body of Osama bin Laden.

Della knew she had to get out of the area fast. She crouched and ran to the rear of the roof. Throwing her leg over the ledge, she gained a foothold in a close-growing tree. She shimmied toward the trunk and carefully climbed down toward the street. She ran around the building, keeping to the shadows, winding a dark burka around her head to cover her American features and her camera. She swiftly made her way back to the street, back to their apartment, but suddenly she was grabbed from behind and spun around. A swarthy, dark-faced man with breath that reeked of garlic and curry leered at her, his eyes blazing with the fire of jihad.

She screamed with all her might, twisting to break free of the terror of capture.

*   *   *

"Della, Della! Wake up!" Brad called, gently patting her

face. "It's okay. You're just having a nightmare." He gripped her shoulders and forced her to look at him.

Slowly, the terror drained from her face. Her body went slack, and she started to sob. Brad held her, stroking her back and pushing the hair out of her face, pressing her face into his strong shoulder.

"It's okay, sweetheart. Everything's okay now," he crooned, rocking her as she sobbed against his chest.

"Oh my God. Oh my God. They have Aaron. I think he's dead." Della wept inconsolably. "What am I going to do?"

"Shhhh. It's going to be okay, sweetheart." Brad lay down beside her and wrapped her in his strong arms. "I'm here. Nobody's going to hurt you."

Della cuddled instinctively into Brad's chest, seeking refuge from the torturous memories. She wrapped her arms around his solid body, drawing comfort from his nearness.

After a while, her sobbing stopped, and she drew a shaky breath as the tension left her body. The soothing strokes of Brad's warm hands on her back and the clean male smell of his skin against her cheek had lulled her into a haven of comfort and protection. She opened her eyes and placed her lips against the strong column of his throat. She could feel the steady beat of his heart and heard his swift intake of breath.

"Della?" he asked.

"Shhhhh. Just hold me," she murmured, kissing his jaw and nuzzling him in the hollow behind his ear.

"I can't do this. I want you so badly," Brad whispered, pressing his hard length against her stomach, his cock pulsing with heat, straining to gain entrance to her body.

"I want you inside me," Della spoke against his lips. "I need to feel alive. I want you here with me. Take me away from the memories. I want you so much," she said, her body moving restlessly against his, driving him wild.

"Della ... we can't. I don't have any condoms." He groaned.

"It's okay," she said showing him the implant in her inner upper arm. "I'm on birth control, and I'm STD free."

"Well, that makes two of us," Brad said and grinned.

Grabbing the hem of her pajama top, he stripped it off over her head. His hands found her ample breasts, and her nipples instantly rose in hard peaks. His mouth took possession of them, his tongue teasing the sensitive tips, sending spears of pure desire deep into her core. Her fingers sought his hardness, and she took him in her slender hand, her long fingers sheathing him, moving up and down in a rhythm of ecstasy, making him ache to be inside her. He quickly rid her of her pajama bottoms, and he cupped her tender mound. The Brazilian wax she had treated herself to before leaving New York made her smooth against his palm, and his growl of approval against her throat made her feel sexy as hell. His fingers found their way between her slick folds, and she gasped as his thumb grazed her sensitive clit. He slipped a finger into her hot pussy as she undulated against his hand, increasing the friction between their bodies. Suddenly, he shifted position, and her hand fell away from his cock. A disapproving groan came from her throat.

"It's okay, baby. I don't wanna come yet," he whispered, his tongue on her clit, sucking her juices into his mouth and making her shiver with pleasure. He kept teasing her until he felt her clamp down on his plunging fingers as a fierce orgasm rocked her body. He continued to wring waves and waves of sensation out of her as the tip of his thumb teased her clit, bringing her to the edge of oblivion. And when she thought she had finished, he poised the tip of his cock at her entrance and gently pushed his way, inch by inch, into her hot, sweet wetness.

"I had no idea you would feel this good. You're so tight," he murmured as he sought her lips in a blazing kiss. "Come with me this time, baby," he panted as he started to move slowly inside her.

Della had never experienced sex like this. He made her feel like she was the most desirable woman on the planet. Her tongue was in his mouth, entwined with his. Then his lips were on her nipples, sucking and licking. She thought she would explode from the heat of their joining. Her body quickened again, and Brad followed her over the edge, his seed spurting into her core as they came together in rapturous harmony. It was like the desert coming to life after a rain. Beautiful, radiant, life-giving, exquisite joy.

***

They slept peacefully in each other's arms until the sun was well over the treetops. Della was the first to open her eyes. She smiled when she saw the dark fan of Brad's lashes pressed against his cheeks. "Those lashes belong on a girl," she whispered. "So pretty."

His eyelids fluttered open just then, and he said lazily, "Good morning, beautiful." His arms tightened around her and he kissed her warmly on the neck. "And by the way, men are not pretty; they're handsome."

"Beauty is in the eye of the beholder. So is pretty." Della smiled at him, resting her head on her hand and leaning down to kiss him gently on the lips.

"Did you sleep well?" he asked, his hand running up over her ribcage to tease the tip of her breast.

"Oh yes. I slept like a log." She grinned, cuddling closer.

"You don't snore like a lumberjack," Brad assured her, "Unless I slept so soundly I didn't hear it."

"How about you?" she asked teasingly, reaching for his hardening cock. "I think you might have a little problem with wood."

"I wouldn't call that a problem we can't fix, would you?" he asked, rolling her onto her back.

She grinned, kissing his lips and wrapping her legs around his waist.

***

It was much later, when Della and Brad had finally gotten out of bed, that Della caught a glimpse of her glowing face and "sex hair" in the bathroom mirror. The guilt returned, but the voice of reason in her head told her that, from what she had seen on that hellish night in Abbottabad, Aaron was dead. In order to recover from the horror of that night, she would have to move on and lay his memory to rest. She touched her lips, still swollen from her long night with Brad, and the heavy feeling she had been carrying in her chest eased.

***

Brad was at the stove cooking breakfast when she made her way to the kitchen. He expertly flipped eggs in a frying pan, and the air was fragrant with the smell of bacon frying and coffee brewing. He smiled as he saw Della in the doorway and caught her around the waist, laying his lips on hers.

"Hungry?" he asked, his mouth moving to kiss her in the soft hollow below her ear.

"Starved," she replied, wrapping her arms around his neck and returning his kisses.

His attention turned back to the stove as the acrid smell of burning toast assailed their nostrils. "Whoops," he said, grabbing some tongs and lifting the blackened bread from the wire rack on the burner and throwing it into the trash. "You know how toast goes—not done, not done, not done, burnt."

"It's okay." Della laughed. "Too many carbs anyway."

They attacked their breakfast like they hadn't seen food in months. Everything tasted so good.

Outside the kitchen window, the sun was shining, the trees were just starting to show their fall colors, and the birds were gathering together in flocks, soon to be vacating the northern territories in their southern migration. It was a perfect fall day.

Looking across the meadow to a gap in the trees where the barrens beyond were visible, Della could see movement.

"Look, Brad!" she said, excitedly. "There's a whole bunch of caribou!"

"Yeah, you're right," he said, grabbing the binoculars and walking out onto the veranda. "Looks like several hundred head."

"I'm gonna grab my camera and go down by the river to see if I can get a wider shot," Della said.

"Looks like the migration has started," Brad said. "I need to give Ted a call to see if he can get the chopper out here."

CHAPTER 9

Several hours went by from the time Brad contacted his buddy, Ted. And in that time, many more caribou had joined the herd, moving northward and inland from the coastal plain. Della was amazed by the sheer number of animals and the force of the instinct that drove them to travel the long journey, which would bring them into the cover of the forest to wait out the long winter months. Watching the little calves running to keep up with their elders, she wondered how many of them would survive the ravages of the wolves; the sparse food; and the harsh, bitterly cold weather.

"How far do they have to travel?" Della asked Brad, who was mulling over some maps and charts.

"Depends on where they live," Brad answered. "This herd will travel over 1,200 miles annually. Some individual animals have been known to travel as much as 3,700 miles in a single year. These guys are part of the George River herd, which spreads across the northern part of eastern Canada from Quebec to Labrador."

"How many animals are there altogether in the George River herd?"

"There used to be around 384,000 at the turn of the millennium, but the numbers have shrunk to a little over 27,000 in recent years."

"Wow, that's a huge decrease," Della said. "Besides the habitat destruction, the overhunting, and the increase in predation and disease, is there anything else that caused the decline?" she asked.

"Well, as a matter of fact, yes. Did you hear in the news a few years ago about a huge number of caribou that drowned while crossing a river in northern Quebec?"

"Yeah, I think I remember something about that. Tons of dead animals were found floating down the river," Della said. "Why would that happen? I thought caribou could swim."

"They can," said Brad, "but only about six miles at a stretch. The herd will generally lose a few of the weaker or older animals on its annual migration, but what happened in Quebec was a man-made tragedy."

"How so?" Della scented the rotten stench of politics lurking behind the story.

"What happened was that Hydro Quebec built a reservoir on the headwaters of the Caniapiscau River. The caribou followed a migration route that had them cross the Caniapiscau about seventy miles upstream, just above the Limestone Falls. The caribou had gotten used to the low water flow in the Caniapiscau while the reservoir was being filled. The waters of the upper Caniapiscau River, which flow north, were diverted into the La Grande River of the James Bay watershed to the west. That September, there were exceptionally heavy rains, and the reservoir had filled up completely. A decision was made to partially release the headwaters back into the Caniapiscau because the power stations on the La Grande River couldn't yet turbine the full water flow. According to the power company, any major addition of water to the La Grande River would have been diverted around the power stations for months—even years— and would have seriously damaged the floodgates, which were designed only for temporary use during exceptional climatic events."

"So the caribou didn't realize that the Caniapiscau was too wide and too strong for them to get across," Della concluded sadly.

"Exactly. That was the conclusion of the biologists and wildlife officers, along with local residents familiar with the river and the migration route of the animals, who had opposed the development for years."

"Yet another example of white man's arrogance, thinking they can just interfere willy-nilly with the natural environment for their own selfish gain, making changes that have tragically detrimental repercussions."

"I have to agree," said Brad. "The government, the power company, and even the wildlife authorities were jointly responsible for the death of over ten thousand animals."

"So what's being done today to assure that it doesn't happen again?" Della asked.

"Well, in this area, the Quebec Indian and Inuit Secretariat recommended that the reservoir's water levels be lowered by about two feet for several months of the year to avoid the use of the floodgates during extreme rainfalls when the caribou are migrating in late summer and early fall. No water has been diverted back into the lower Caniapiscau since 1985. Also, a fence was installed to divert the herd from the danger zone near the Limestone Falls."

"Yeah, but what's being done to make sure this doesn't happen anywhere else?" Della persisted.

"What happened here taught wildlife and conservation specialists a valuable lesson. No wildlife expert had foreseen anything more than the usual mortality along the rivers of this region. They had no idea that the caribou would follow their instincts regardless of the fact that conditions were too dangerous for survival," he explained. "So now, before any major development is undertaken—like a hydro development or the construction of a pipeline or even the construction of a highway—wildlife experts and conservation groups are consulted to see what impact the project will have on the environment and wildlife of the area. Native groups are invited to share their views and propose solutions so that the least amount of harm can be done to the natural ecosystem."

"What kinds of things have these interest groups been able to achieve?" Della asked.

"You'll see on some of the Canadian highways that fences have been constructed to keep the animals from being killed by traffic and to save the lives of people using the highways. Governments have built wildlife corridors over the highways so that the animals have a safe way to move from one side of the highway to the other. Some provinces have even installed live cameras so that you can go online and actually watch bear and moose and caribou using the overpasses. It helps get the word out that we need to protect wildlife and make accommodations for the animals when our needs interfere with theirs."

"What about the really greedy companies who ignore the advice and try to break the rules?"

"That's where I come in," Brad said. "The organization I head watchdogs basically any kind of project that can impact wildlife through habitat destruction—proposed hydro developments, nuclear power plants, airport construction, highway development, things like that. We monitor the planning from the very beginning and advise the government on potential problems. Heavy fines and penalties can be levied if companies don't comply."

"Which organization are you part of?" she asked.

"The World Wildlife Organization," he answered.

"Oh my God!" Della exclaimed. "I've met dozens of your agents all over the world. We ran into them in Namibia and Sumatra, where they were involved in protecting the rhinos. And we even did a story on TRAFFIC, and their efforts to stop the illegal trade of elephant tusks."

"Yeah, there's a lot of work to be done," Brad said.

Suddenly, a familiar vibration could be felt in the air, and the chop of a helicopter's rotors disrupted the peaceful quiet.

"That'll be Ted," Brad speculated, hurrying outside and shading his eyes as he looked up over the trees. A large, green helicopter with the WWO emblem on the side hovered over the meadow and then descended to touch down lightly on the grass. The wash from the rotor stirred up debris, and Della put her hands over her face to protect her eyes from the flying dust and pebbles.

Brad waited until the rotor stopped and, ducking his head, ran over to open the cockpit door.

"Hey, boss," a tall man with sandy hair and a lanky build said, pulling off his headset and climbing out of the aircraft and extending his hand. "Good to see you alive and well."

"No worries, Ted," Brad replied, shaking his hand and thumping him on the back. "How's the world been treating you?" Together, they walked over to the cabin.

"Not bad," Ted replied, spotting Della standing on the veranda. Taking off his aviator sunglasses, he said, "Hello! And who, may I ask, is this lovely lady?"

"This is Della Rawlins, a good friend of mine," Brad said. "Della's a photojournalist. She's on assignment to photograph the caribou for National Environmental. Della, this is Ted Hunt. He works with me at the WWO."

"Nice to meet you." Della smiled and shook his hand. "Brad has been filling me in on the caribou, and I'm so excited to be here for the migration."

"Yeah, there's a fine crowd of them on the move already from what I could see flying in," Ted said. "Should be a regular wagon train moving northwest."

"Brad promised to ask you if I could tag along to see it from the air and get some shots," Della said hopefully.

"Sure thing." Ted grinned, winking at Brad. "There's always room for one more, especially when she's a fine-looking chick with an eye for an outstanding buck."

"Funny guy," Della said to Brad, nodding her head at Ted.

"Want a drink or something before we take off?" Brad asked Ted.

"Naw, maybe on the way back," he replied. "You guys ready?"

"Sure," Della answered for both of them, grabbing her camera and heading toward the chopper.

"You got yourself a lively one," Ted ribbed Brad, out of Della's earshot. "Nice outdoorsy type, too. Where'd you find her?"

"Down by the river, actually," Brad replied.

***

Ted started up the engine, and the rotor whined and started to spin overhead. Della was seated next to him in the front bubble of the aircraft, a headset covering her ears, while Brad was seated behind them with a collection of maps spread out on the seat next to him. The aircraft rose from the clearing; a small dust storm swirled from the whir of the blades. It reminded Della of the many times she had been in and around helicopters during her time in the Middle East, especially that fateful night in Abbottabad. This time had a much different feel to it, though - With the sun shining on the water and reflecting off the colorful trees lining the riverbanks, her tension eased, and she started to enjoy the ride.

Ted turned eastward, heading toward the coast and the edge of the coastal plains. A long line of Caribou was forming, mostly males as far as she could see. It was hard to tell, as both the males and females had antlers. But she noticed that these animals looked more solid, and there were no calves among them. Flying along the coast, Ted turned back, hovering a little lower over the column of animals. Spooked by the noise, they picked up their pace, returning to a slower walk as the strange bird flew over. They were like a line of soldiers marching to war, their gray hides camouflaged against the grasses and low plant life that covered the coastal plains. The sight of the mass of moving animals amazed Della, who was busy clicking away with her camera. A couple of times, Ted dipped lower so that she could get a more intimate shot of the female caribou who were traveling at the front of the herd with their calves.

Brad moved toward Ted and spoke into a mike that was built into his headset. "We need to fly up around Musquash Falls when you're ready. They've almost finished construction on the dam at the hydro development, and I want to see how they're progressing."

"Roger that," Ted replied, veering in a more westerly direction to follow a wide river that snaked across the landscape below.

Soon they flew over what looked like a large scar on the landscape. Mammoth earth-moving equipment could be seen at work, reshaping the land. A large concrete barrier, over one hundred feet high, stretched from one bank of the river to the other, forcing the level of the water behind it to build to ominous heights. On one side, the water spilled out through a series of pillars, behind which the rushing water would turn turbines, generating the clean electricity the power hungry cities on the lower mainland craved. To Della's eyes, the swollen river behind the dam looked so deep and so wide that no caribou would have any hope of trying to swim across it.

"Is this development lying in the path of the migration?" Della asked worriedly.

"No, the route crosses the river far downstream. What we're worried about here is the flooding of the upper plains should the water rise," Brad said, pointing at the forested area on either side of the river. The company has guaranteed that it will be no more than twenty-five square miles."

"What would the effect be if the flooding were more extensive than that?" she questioned.

"For one thing, there would be an increase in phosphorous in the water due to the rotting vegetation, Brad explained. "And that would affect the algae that the fish eat. There would also be problems with ice buildup when the winter comes."

"What about the environment with regard to the caribou?"

"See that reservoir there?" Ted pointed. "The substrate of this river is mostly sand. When the water is backed up behind a barrier like that, the sediment drops to the bottom and only clear water spills over. Because there's no sediment to replace the substrate that the extra water washes away, the downstream gets dug out, making the water deeper."

"Yeah, and the riverbanks get eroded, too; because there's no sediment to replace the material that naturally washes away, the river gets wider," Brad added.

"So potentially, if this was the place where the caribou crossed the river, the same thing could happen here that happened in Quebec?" Della concluded.

"Smart one, isn't she?" Ted commented to Brad.

"Yeah," Brad said, fondly touching Della's shoulder. "Luckily for the George River herd, they cross the river quite a bit away from here, so they shouldn't be affected. Also, the company has strict directives about the level of water to be maintained in the reservoir."

"Winter brings another set of problems," said Ted, "because if the water is flowing too fast, frazil ice can form. It's kind of slushy and backs up against the stable ice cove behind the reservoir. Then the water spills over the dam, and flooding occurs. They have to slow the water by keeping the level low so stable ice can form."

"How does the hydro company manage all of this? It seems like a lot to deal with," Della said.

"The company has to come up with a plan to address all of the concerns—whether it's the amount of mercury the fish would be exposed to, the salinity of the water, or the temperature of the water," Brad said. "They have to come up with a program that describes in detail how they plan to sample and measure and track the effects the development is having on the ecosystem, and that program has to be approved before the project can even be approved to start."

"So that's why you guys are up here today—to make sure that the hydro company is building the development according to spec," she said.

"Yeah. You didn't think we were just up here on a joyride, did ya?" Ted kidded, taking the helicopter down low so that he and Brad could get a closer look at the hydro project from the upstream side.

After a while, Ted set the helicopter down in a cleared area not far from the heavy equipment. The men disembarked, put on hard hats, and went to meet with the foremen and engineers who were set up in some temporary buildings on the site. Della took the time to jot down some notes and take a few shots of the dam and the surrounding area to use as reference material for the story.

After not too long, Ted and Brad came back to the helicopter, and they prepared for takeoff.

"Seems that everything is on track," Brad said in response to Della's unasked question. "There's a briefing this week with the Department of Energy and the Department of Wildlife and Conservation. I'll bring up those points we talked about and see that they're addressed." Brad said to Ted, making notes. "Altogether, they're complying with all of our recommendations, and everything is progressing on time."

"I like the ones that play by the rules," Ted said, grinning at Della. "You don't want to see Brad get mad."

"True that," admitted Brad, biting the end of his pen.

***

The afternoon had been an eye-opening experience for Della. She hadn't fully realized the scope of the impact that something like a hydroelectric development could have on the wildlife and habitat in the surrounding environment. The politicians claimed the project was going to produce twenty-eight hundred megawatts of clean power. But at what cost? And to what extent was the true impetus behind this kind of development? Was it undertaken to line the pockets of the power companies and fill the coffers of the government? Like so much of humankind's interference with natural resources, this project may too, be driven by a lust for power and wealth. It was sad to see the animals and natural environment have to suffer to appease man's greed. Della was so proud of people like Brad and Ted who put so much effort into doing something positive and bringing those who would abuse to justice. She would be proud to help them by telling this story.

CHAPTER 10

The ride back to the cabin was uneventful, and when the helicopter put down in the meadow, Brad once again invited Ted in for a drink and a snack before he left on the long flight back to New York.

Just as Brad opened the cabin door, the strident ringing of his satellite phone drew their attention.

"Wonder who that is," Brad thought out loud. "Nobody calls me here unless it's an emergency."

"Brad Jamieson," he said, picking up the receiver. "Hello ... Ryan?" he said, putting his hand over his other ear. "Yeah, I can hardly hear you ... You're where? ... Yeah she's here ...

"Oh my God ... Yeah, I'll tell her ... Yeah, Ted's here ... She can hitch a ride back with him ... Yeah, thanks, bro. See you soon." He hung up and then paused and said, "Wow."

He exhaled, placed his hands on Della's shoulders, and gently steered her over to the settee. "Ryan's at Clark Air Base in the Philippines. Just flew out of Pakistan. The American and Pakistani government have just negotiated the exchange of three American prisoners of war in exchange for an Algerian arms dealer and a couple of others who were being detained at Guantanamo Bay. One of the POWs is Aaron," he told her.

"Oh my God!" Della cried, putting her hand over her

mouth, the shock spreading in a pale wash across her face. "He's alive?" She started to cry.

His face tense, Brad turned to Ted and asked, "Can you fly her into New York? The POWs are being flown from Clark into Travis Air Force Base in California, and from there, the government will arrange transport to their home towns." In a quiet voice out of Della's earshot, he added, "Some of them are in rough shape and may not survive the flight home."

"Sure," Ted readily agreed. "Are you coming, too?"

"No, I don't want to slow you down with the extra weight, and I also have to close up the cabin before I can leave. As soon as Ryan lands in California, he's coming to New York to pick Della up and take her back with him to California."

"Okay, I'll go get the chopper ready to leave," Ted said.

Brad turned back to where Della was still sitting on the settee, looking dazed. He sat down next to her and took her hands.

"I can't believe that all of this time while I've been here with you, Aaron's been over there, probably being treated like an animal. I really thought he was dead," she said.

The guilt was eating her alive; Brad could see it in her eyes. She was visibly shaking, twisting her hands into knots. He was worried about her flying into New York on her own. He told Ted not to leave her until Ryan got there to pick her up. He knew he could trust his brother to look after her until he could get back.

"Della," he said, taking her chin in hand and turning her face to look her in the eyes, "You have to be strong now. There's nothing you could have done over there. He's coming home, and that's the important thing. You have to be strong for him now. Can you do that?"

Della nodded her head, crying softly. And he stood up, pulling her to her feet. "Don't worry about your stuff. Just take your camera with you, and I'll send the rest to your editor at the magazine. What's his name?"

Della gave him the details, and Brad gently led her out to where the chopper was prepped and ready for takeoff. Ducking their heads, Brad put Della aboard the helicopter, and Ted helped buckle her in and put on her headset. Her face registered shock and disbelief as the chopper lifted off the ground, and Brad shaded his eyes as the machine turned and headed in the opposite direction, away from him. Before long, the green bird disappeared from view, and he was left there, alone.

CHAPTER 11

On that fateful night in Abbottabad, after Aaron had been taken prisoner, members of al-Qaeda had been summoned to take him, unconscious but still living, away for interrogation ...

***

Aaron awoke in a world of pain. The parts of his body that weren't covered in bruises, welts, and open sores were so numb from pain that he no longer felt them. He was suspended from the ceiling by the wrists, bare to the waist, and a mixture of blood and sweat ran down his face and over his chest. A small shard of light seeped through the seams of the padlocked shutters that kept the old warehouse locked down and inescapable. But for the most part, the space was unlit, dank, and musty. Armed guards stood outside the only door. He could hear them talking in Arabic and knew that it would only be a matter of time before another round of interrogation began.

He thought of Della and prayed that she had made it out without being captured. It was bad enough what these animals would do to him, but the indignities they would make a woman suffer were unthinkable. He would never tell them about her. There was no way that these terrorists could connect him with his partner. He and Della had had an evacuation plan in place, and he knew that she had had time to get back to their apartment and grab her go bag. With her passport and identification papers, all she had to do was dial the preprogrammed number on the disposable cell phone. He didn't even care anymore if she got the story out, as long as she got out alive.

Suddenly, the door was wrenched open, a bare bulb flickered to life overhead, and five men dressed in the ragtag garb of Taliban fighters entered the musty space. Four of them pointed their automatic rifles at him, while the fifth came to stand in front of him, his arrogant features a mask of control as he assessed the prisoner's condition.

"You have made quite a nuisance of yourself tonight, prisoner Giles," he said in heavily accented English. "You and your American brothers have the audacity to think you can just walk into this country and interfere with what we do and who we do business with. Who are you working for? And who do you report to?" he asked, nodding to one of the guards, who shoved the butt of his rifle into Aaron's ribs, making him groan as a blood-encrusted gash reopened.

"I am a reporter, sent here to participate in a cultural exchange. I am not an agent of the government."

A staggering blow across his face snapped Aaron's head back, and a spray of blood spurted from his nose and splattered on the ground.

"You lie!" the officer roared, his balled fist raised to deal Aaron another blow. He drew his face up close to Aaron's cheek and said, "You were seen around Abbottabad with an American woman and a known CIA operative. What is your purpose here?"

"I know no woman," Aaron ground out between his teeth.

"My assignment is of a cultural nature. I am here alone. I had nothing to do with the attack on the compound."

"You are very unwise to anger me further," the officer snarled, lighting a cigarette and grinding the glowing end into Aaron's cheek.

His body shook, and he bit off a scream as the smell of his own burning flesh filled his nostrils.

"You will tell me the name of the other Americans and where they are hiding. Now!" he roared, kicking the bone that projected through the open flesh of Aaron's left leg.

Fighting the haze of pain that blurred his vision and threatened to shut down his consciousness, Aaron denied over and over. "I am a reporter, not CIA. I am no threat to you."

"You attacked the people of this town. You tried to stop the authorities from protecting our people from the infidels," he spat. "You insult us with your lies."

He gestured to the armed guards, and two hurried forward to unlock him from his restraints. Together, they dragged him to a grated hole in the floor. They forced his broken body into the tiny space until his bones felt as if they would break under the pressure of the confinement. He wept bitter tears as the officer said, "You will learn to obey and tell me what I need to learn, or we will be feeding your American entrails to the dogs."

Then they left him in the dark, filthy water dripping down onto his broken body as he cried bitter tears and prayed for his own death.

CHAPTER 12

Della had almost made it back to the apartment. People were running through the streets, shouting and brandishing anything they could use for weapons. Della kept to the shadows, stepping into doorways and melting into shrubbery as she made her way to the alley where she knew she could catch a minute of sanctuary. Suddenly, a rough hand grasped her arm and spun her around. A swarthy face leered at her, shiny with sweat and grime, his teeth yellowed and broken, and his breath reeking. He pushed her back into the doorway of the rooming house, his hands like metal bands. Della squirmed in the voluminous burka, trying to break his grip, biting and scratching like a wildcat as he swore in Arabic and pushed her down to her knees. He had drawn back his hand as if to slap her across the face, when suddenly his body was jerked away from her, and he was thrown to the ground. A short struggle ensued between him and a soldier dressed in dark fatigues. The soldier dealt him a blow to the head with his automatic rifle, and the attacker slumped to the ground. Her savior dragged the limp form behind a stone wall and grabbed Della by the arm.

A familiar voice spoke to her. "Della, it's me. Come on." He threw his shoulder against a flimsy wooden door, breaking it open and pushed her inside and up a narrow flight of stairs.

"Quick, grab your stuff. I have a chopper waiting, but there's not much time. Let's go!"

Quickly, Della located the small duffel containing her and Aaron's passports and identification papers, a change of clothes, and a handgun. Her hands shook as she quickly stashed her camera in the bag and turned to leave.

"Is there anyone else living in this building?" the soldier asked.

"No, nobody's been here for the past month," Della replied.

Throwing a bunch of books and papers on the floor, the soldier lit a match and tossed it into the pile. The fire crackled to life, its tongues greedily licking the leaves of the books. He threw a nearby oil lamp on it for good measure and, grabbing Della by the hand, rushed her down the stairs and out into the dark night.

They ran like the hounds of hell were on their heels, out past the last of the houses and into the desert. Topping a rise, they could see the dark form of a Chinook helicopter ahead of them. The soldier spoke into a radio mike in his helmet, and the rotors started turning overhead. They ran toward the open door—armed guards quickly loaded them aboard, and the aircraft rose into the inky night sky.

Suddenly, an explosion rocked the airwaves, and a plume of fire and smoke rose from the direction of the compound. The radio crackled, and a voice came over the cockpit radio. "Captain, the vulture has been terminated. Operation Neptune Spear is complete. All units secure and cleared to return to base."

"Roger that, and the falcon's in the nest," the pilot replied.

And a cheer rang out from the soldiers as the helicopter flew out across the desert toward the safety of their air base in Bagram.

Della slumped against her rescuer in relief. She had made it out by the skin of her teeth. But Aaron was still down there. She prayed for his sake that he was dead.

She turned toward the soldier, who offered her a bottle of water. "Did they blow up the compound?"

"No, just the downed Black Hawk," he replied. "Did you see what happened to Aaron?" he asked. "We couldn't locate him. Lucky you made it back to the muster point in time."

"I saw them beat him unconscious and take him prisoner," Della replied sadly. "There was no way that you could have gotten to him."

"That's too bad. He was a good man. At least we got you out."

She looked into his exhausted, grimy face, and said, "Thank you, Ryan. I owe you my life."

***

Finally, the helicopter slowed, and Della could see the lights of the air base below her. They descended to the tarmac, where the aircraft landed. And the strong, capable hands of the airmen helped her out of the helicopter. She was left in the care of a medic as Ryan said to her, "I have to leave for a bit, but these folks will take care of you. Get you something to eat and make some phone calls home to let everybody know you are all right. I'll be back later tonight, and tomorrow we'll be able to fly you back to New York."

Della put her hand on Ryan's arm. "Ryan, what about Aaron?" she asked.

"There's no way we can go in and extract him right now," Ryan explained. "Abbottabad is locked down tighter than a drum. They won't even release a body back to the States.

We'll just have to wait until the heat is off—it's going to take some time."

"Can we even find out if he's alive or dead?"

"Right now, we can't trust a word they say. They want us to think that we haven't been very effective in hurting their cause, so we're not going to get good intel."

"So, what you're saying," Della said, "is that we just have to wait."

"Yeah, sit tight," Ryan said, patting her knee. "Patience."

With that, Ryan left, striding off in the direction of a larger helicopter emblazoned with the three-pronged insignia of the Navy SEALs special warfare unit, which represented their operational capacity on land, sea, or air.

CHAPTER 13

Della's patience was wearing thin. She had been back in New York for two weeks, and not one iota of news was coming out of Pakistan. It had been released to the public that the Navy SEALs special ops had, under the direction of the CIA, captured and killed bin Laden. He had been harbored by the Pakistani government, which was trying to do its best to claim that he had been acting without the knowledge and consent of the authorities and that the government was not in any contravention of international law. She had pored over the reference material and law books with a team of lawyers from her father's office and the Department of the Secretary of State, but they couldn't find any grounds that would force the Pakistanis to release their detainees. The US government was holding just as many—if not more—Middle Eastern nationals as prisoners, and neither side was willing to negotiate for their release. Della could picture the president's face on the TV screen saying, "We will not negotiate with terrorists."

"We're not making any headway here," Della's father said, taking her by the hand and sitting her down on the edge of a settee. "It's just as well you let our people carry on with the work here, and you try to take your mind off of it by going back to the magazine. You're just getting in the way."

And it was true. Everyone understood Della's impatience

and need to find the solution that would lead to Aaron's release. But getting even the slightest shred of information could take years. These types of negotiations took a methodical approach. No hotheaded, heavy-handed method was going to work.

Recognizing the truth in what her father had to say, Della reluctantly packed her bag and moved back to her apartment. She called her editor and asked if he had any assignments on his desk that she could take on temporarily, to keep her from losing her mind while she waited for news from Pakistan.

"I don't have anything political that's not assigned right now, but I'll call around to some contacts and see what's on the go," her editor, Phil Brennan, promised.

The phone rang a couple of hours later, and Phil asked Della whether she would be interested in a wildlife shoot in Canada. National Environmental was planning a feature on the woodland caribou and needed someone to fly into the Canadian wilderness to cover the northern migration, as the photographer the magazine had booked had broken his leg in a car accident.

Della needed something to do and a means to pay her rent, so she packed her backpack with a couple of changes of clothes, some food, and little else, save for her camera equipment, and started searching the directory listings for an outfitter who would fly her into eastern Canada, where the migration would start. Just as her finger was poised on her telephone's touch pad, the phone vibrated in her hand.

"Della Rawlins," she identified herself.

"Hi, Della. It's Ryan. How are you?"

"Going crazy with inactivity. I'm trying to get hold of someone to take me into the Canadian wilderness. I have an assignment to shoot some caribou for National Environmental Magazine."

"What part are you heading to?"

"Somewhere east of the Great Lakes, between the Appalachian mountains and the coast. Somewhere I can backpack into."

"I may have just the spot for you," Ryan said. "My family has a log cabin on a salmon river in eastern Canada. A bunch of caribou spend the summer there, have their young, and then migrate northward for the winter. The timing would be just about right for them to be on the move. If you like, I'm going to be in the area and can drop you off within a couple miles of the place. You'll have to hike in unless you have an off-road vehicle, but it's not hard to find. I don't have the keys to the cabin, but you can always pitch a tent for a couple of days."

"Sounds perfect," Della agreed. "I'm used to roughing it."

"I'll be back to pick you up in a couple of weeks. If you need me before then, you can just hike out to the general store and call me. It's only about three miles away."

"Yeah, I can take my cell phone if there's service there. It can work off regular batteries for short calls, anyway."

"Yeah, you might catch a signal once in a while. At least you won't be completely cut off from civilization."

***

That was then. Now here she was, flying back to the "war zone" and away from the man who had brought her comfort and given her a haven from the world of madmen and their conflicts and fighting. She was on her way back to the man she supposedly loved, but what her heart felt for him was no longer clear. Was it genuine concern for him or a sense of responsibility that drove her to return to his side? A week ago, the world had been turning too slowly, but now everything was happening too quickly. What the future would hold was uncertain.

***

The helicopter touched down at Mitchel Field Air Force Base just outside Long Island. Ted shut down the engine, and the rotor spun to a gradual stop overhead. He took off his headgear and, turning to Della, said, "Here we are, all safe and sound. Let's go over to the commissary and get something to eat, and I'll give Ryan a call and see where he is."

Della didn't want to hear talk of food. Her stomach was so queasy, but she followed Ted over to the old-style military building and stepped inside.

"Something to eat?" he asked her.

"No thanks. Just a coffee," Della replied.

He seated her at a table and went over to a coffee urn, returning with two steaming cups and some sugar and cream. He took out his cell phone and punched in a number.

"Yo, Ryan," he said loudly, covering his ear. "Yeah, we're here at Mitchel. What's your ETA?" Several minutes of silence went by on Ted's end. "Okay, we'll sit tight. See ya soon," he said, signing off.

"They're bringing the POWs directly here," he told Della, his expression unreadable.

"They're about twenty minutes out."

***

It wasn't long before three army helicopters could be seen approaching the air terminal. The huge hangar doors rolled open, and two choppers landed inside. Della and Ted approached the craft that had put down outside on the tarmac. The door swung open, and Ryan stepped out. Taking off his uniform hat, he turned to Della and took her hands in his.

"Della, I'm so sorry, but Aaron died in flight. He was just too far gone for the doctors to save him. They transfused him and shocked him three times on the way here, and they did everything they could at the hospital at Edward's. But his body was riddled with infection, and he was barely conscious."

Inside the hangar, three flag-draped caskets were on a conveyer, being transferred to three waiting hearses.

A familiar figure walked toward her, and she left Ryan's side and flew into his waiting arms. "Daddy," she cried.

"I'm sorry, baby. We were too late," the gray-haired man said, holding her tightly in a bear hug and rubbing her back.

"You tried your best," she muffled into the front of his overcoat. "I thought he was gone the night they took him prisoner in front of the compound. I just couldn't let him go until I knew for sure."

"It's over now, baby," the senator said. "Let's go home."

CHAPTER 14

The next few days were a blur. Aaron's parents had to be notified of his death, and arrangements had to be made to send Aaron's body home for cremation in Boston and then his ashes sent back to New York for inurnment. Funeral arrangements had to be made, and notifications sent to Aaron's friends and colleagues. Because of the government involvement in the recovery and repatriation, special notices had to be printed and sent to officials and heads of departments with letters of thanks from the family. There were flowers to order, a caterer to hire, speakers to arrange—and the list went on and on. The senator loaned Della one of his staffers to help her keep it all straight and on track.

The day of the funeral arrived, chilly and overcast. Della dressed in a somber gray dress and a dark wool coat. Slipping a pair of leather gloves into her handbag, she took a final look in the mirror before she went to her father to tell him she was ready. She had lost weight, and there were dark shadows under her eyes and hollows under her cheekbones. She tied a crimson scarf around her neck in an effort to reflect some color onto her face, and she pinned a gold and enamel emblem of the Navy SEALs, which Ryan had given her, onto her lapel.

Thinking of Ryan made her smile. He had been her rock

through the days since Aaron's return home. He had been so considerate—taking her to lunch and sharing stories of how he and Aaron had gone to great lengths to keep his identity as their CIA contact in Afghanistan a secret. He made sure she got some rest and had spoken to her editor at the magazine to arrange some bereavement leave. When it came to asking someone to do a tribute to Aaron at the funeral service, Ryan was the natural choice.

In contrast, she had had practically no contact from Brad. He had sent her a very formal text just after it had been made public that Aaron had passed away, telling her how sorry he was with the turn of events. Still, there had been no telephone call or personal contact. Flowers had arrived from Jamieson's Outfitters and the World Wildlife Organization, but nothing had come from Brad himself. It was as if they were strangers or, at best, business acquaintances. It was almost like what had passed between them in eastern Canada had never happened. If she had felt alone before meeting him, she sure as hell felt alone, abandoned, and rejected now. She pulled a couple of Kleenex from the box strategically placed on the hall table and blotted at the moisture that threatened to ruin her mascara. Straightening her shoulders, she walked down the wood-paneled hallway of the opulent hotel suite to the room her father was using as his study.

***

The long, black limousine bearing the state insignia pulled slowly up to the curb in front of the old, stone cathedral. It had been Aaron's wish to be cremated in his home state, but he wanted his ashes returned to New York and a memorial service held there to allow his friends and peers in the press corps to pay their respects. Della and he had each written their private requests in duplicate and had sealed them in envelopes kept with their go bags—just in case anything should happen to them in the field. Tears had streamed down Della's face as she had unfolded the lined piece of notepaper, bearing Aaron's distinctive scrawl. He had ended the note with these sentiments:

I leave this world, saddened by the inability of humankind to reconcile differences, accept each other's cultures and beliefs, and above all to live in peace. I am thankful for the love I have found in my life and for the friendship and respect shown to me by people from many corners of the globe. I lived my life holding up a mirror to the world, hoping to bring about change and make it a better place. If I have failed, I'm sorry. But if I have made even a small difference, it was worth it. Della, I love you now and will in the next life and in all that come after. Don't hide from love if I am gone. Know that I reside in a corner of your heart as you do in mine, forever.

At the funeral home in Boston, after Aaron's body had been prepared for viewing and before the cremation took place, she had slipped the note into the inner pocket of his suit jacket and laid a kiss on his still lips, thankful that his ordeal was over, and he could finally be laid to rest.

CHAPTER 15

The organist played a requiem on the ancient pipe organ as the mourners and dignitaries filled the pews of the old cathedral. Brad hung up his wool overcoat in the vestibule, entered the sanctuary, and took a seat in the back. The bell tolled as six pallbearers carried the flag-draped casket table upon which the simple urn containing Aaron's ashes rested up the long, red-carpeted center aisle of the church. The mourners were escorted in, led by Aaron's mother and father, followed by his two brothers and their wives and children, and then Della, flanked by Ryan and her father. Brad's eyes bore into the back of Della's head so intensely that it was a wonder she didn't physically feel the pressure. The clergy called the gathering to worship, and the service commemorating the life of Aaron Kenneth Giles commenced.

About three quarters of an hour into the service, the bishop called upon Ryan Jamieson, a close friend of the deceased, to give a tribute to his fallen friend. Ryan stepped up to the podium, adjusted the mike for his tall frame and began. "Senator, ministers, friends, family, and colleagues of Aaron Giles, thank you for coming today to join with us in celebrating the life of an extraordinary individual. Not only was Ryan a loving son and brother to his own family and a true friend and esteemed colleague to many gathered here today, but he was also a true patriot.

"Aaron spent his short life reporting on conflict around the world. He had a keen sense of justice and injustice. He had been brought up to know right from wrong, and he felt that, when the greed of men with a thirst for power overrode the needs of a country and deprived people of their basic human rights, the world ought to know. He called on the global community to challenge the dictators, depose the despots, and oppose the oppressors to allow even the weak and the hungry to have a voice. He did that because he knew it was the right thing to do.

"Aaron believed in justice. He, along with the rest of us, had seen the face of a militant Islamist, the son of a Saudi oil millionaire, tell his followers that the United States was evil and that they should declare jihad, Holy War, against its people. This man hoped to destroy our country by attacking the very fiber that makes it strong, doing it through terror, and using his own people as weapons of mass destruction.

"Aaron hated a bully—especially one who would strike out and then hide in a hole so that no one could hold him accountable for his actions. We put a $25 million price on his head, but Aaron would have delivered him for nothing. All he wanted was to see that justice was served.

"Aaron died a hero. He suffered for his beliefs, but he never betrayed a trust. He endured physical pain and atrocities of both body and mind, but he would not submit to the forces of the enemy. He would take the sins of a whole country to bear on his shoulders. We can only marvel at his courage and passion, and thank God that he lived among us.

"It is my honor and privilege, on behalf of the US military, to award posthumously the Medal of Honor to our fallen comrade, Aaron K. Giles."

Ryan left the podium and laid the polished case containing the US military's highest award for bravery next to Aaron's urn, going to sit next to Della, whose head lay on her father's shoulder as she softly sobbed into a Kleenex.

Brad watched as Ryan's arm went around Della's shoulders, and he nodded and smiled at something she said. He wished that he could be the one sitting next to her to lend his strength and support, but he wanted to give her the space and time she needed to mourn. He didn't need to complicate matters by making her feel as though she had, in any way, betrayed or abandoned Aaron in his hour of need. God knows he had spent a fortune sending a team of mercenaries over to try and locate Aaron's whereabouts in Pakistan after he and Della had become close. But the outcome would most likely have been the same if they had found him before the negotiations for his release came through, judging by the poor state of Aaron's health when he returned home. There probably would have been a few more dead terrorists, though.

The service soon ended, and the congregation rose as the flag-draped table was wheeled down the aisle by the pallbearers, followed by the family. Della walked down the aisle holding her father's arm, her eyes downcast, while Ryan followed close behind her. Standing outside in the churchyard, accepting the condolences of strangers, Della thought she saw a familiar figure in a dark overcoat walking away from her toward the parked cars. She looked for him again when they gathered at the cemetery, but he wasn't there. A feeling of emptiness consumed her as she felt Aaron's loss and her own loss as his mortal remains were laid to rest in the columbarium.

***

Afterward, a reception was held back at the hotel, and

Della went through the motions of shaking hands, sipping tea, and accepting messages of sympathy. She was most touched by a letter that had been sent from a grade five class in a school in New Jersey who expressed their gratitude to Mr. Giles for helping to find Osama bin Laden. The children said that they had lost so many people—moms, dads, uncles, and aunts—in the 9/11 World Trade Center attack, and they would feel safer knowing that he was no longer a threat to the people of the United States of America. Even though killing Osama bin Laden wouldn't bring their families back, at least he wouldn't be able to take other children's families away.

Books of condolence had been prepared by firehouses and police precincts around New York state, calling what Aaron had done heroic and paying tribute to their fallen comrades who had also died in service to their fellow man.

When everyone had said their good-byes, leaving Della and her father to themselves, her father asked her what she was going to do now.

Della had given it some thought. "Well, I have the piece on the caribou to write for National Environmental. And who knows after that? I'll have to wait and see. I found writing about conservation engrossing. I know there are a lot of stories out there that need to be told. I'd like to start a fund, too, for the families of reporters and news people who have been taken prisoner in foreign countries. They need to know that there are people who understand the workings of foreign governments and can work with the embassies and the Department of the Secretary of State to see that these people have every chance of making it out alive."

"That's a great idea, honey," her father said approvingly. "The wheels of government turn slowly. Sometimes, with the resources and discretion of outside forces, much can be accomplished in a shorter period of time."

Della stared into the flames of the hearth, reflecting on the life of danger and intrigue that Aaron had seemed to thrive on. She knew that it was important to him to get the story and that it was just as important that the story be told. She had ridden along on Aaron's coattails for so long, but now she was looking for something more permanent, more steadfast in her life. She wouldn't become a martyr or a pawn to be used in the world of foreign politics. Lots of wars on her own home turf needed to be fought. There were plenty enough daredevils out there who were prepared to take on the world.

CHAPTER 16

Della answered the doorbell to a courier bearing a package wrapped in brown paper. It bore the insignia of the National Environmental Society. Quickly, she signed for the delivery, and before she had the door closed, she was excitedly ripping off the wrapper. Inside was an advance copy of the November issue of National Environmental Magazine. She ran her hands over the familiar, glossy, gold jacket, which beautifully framed her prize-winning shot of the startled caribou. The printers had hardly had to retouch the frame at all. Every technical component of the shot was perfect. The rich colors of the breaking dawn were breathtaking, deep azure and violet hues bleeding into pink and gold, the colors dancing in myriad sparkles on the rippling black surface of the water. The barrens and distant peaks of the mountains were laid down in tones of charcoal and black, while the caribou showed up as ghostly gray figures, the two in the foreground highlighted in white. The lavender mist rising up from the water softened the edges and gave it a surreal feeling, almost dreamlike, as though the animals were about to disappear. The caption served to anchor the theme of the story, "The Vanishing Woodland Caribou: Where have they gone?"

Della pulled out the accompanying letter from her editor and quickly scanned the text:

Dear Ms. Rawlins,

We are pleased to forward to you an advance copy of the November issue of our signature publication National Environmental Magazine, featuring your excellent story and photography. We are happy to inform you that your cover shot entitled "Gone before Dawn" has been recognized by our board of governors as some of the finest wildlife photography that has ever graced the cover of our esteemed magazine. It has been awarded the National Environmental's Gold Seal Award in recognition of your superb skill, and we expect that more accolades will be forthcoming once the issue hits the newsstands. Please accept the accompanying check in the amount of ten thousand dollars, which is in addition to the freelance fee we have forwarded to your agent, in appreciation of the valuable contribution you have made. We look forward to seeing future submissions from you as we add your name to our distinguished list of contributing writers.

Please have your agent contact my office at his earliest convenience so that I can provide him with a list of upcoming projects that we feel would be a good fit with your writing style, and we can see where we can book you in. I have included a copy of our standard contract so that we can negotiate an expense arrangement for your next assignment.

I will be looking forward to hearing from you soon.

Yours truly,
Bill Mahon

"Aaaaaahhhhh!!!!" Della screamed, jumping around like a madwoman, causing her father to poke his head out of his office with his glasses pushed all the way down his nose.

"What in blue blazes is going on?" the senator demanded, expecting maybe to see aliens landing out on the front lawn.

Della waved the gold-embossed letter under his nose and said, "Dad, you're not going to believe it! Not only did my story and photographs about the caribou make it into National Environmental; it made the cover! And it was awarded the National Environmental's Gold Seal Award for excellence in wildlife photography! Won't that be excellent to add to my résumé?"

"I'd say the conservationists are going to be beating down your door!" he said. "Do you know how many lobbyists are after us each month with presentations on every creature that ever broke a toe? To get National Environmental's endorsement is gold. Congratulations, sweetheart."

"They awarded me ten thousand dollars. I'm going to add it to the contributions people made to the Bring the Journalists Home fund I started after Aaron's story came out last month. There are some cases that have come to my attention already, and I want to get some networking started to see how we should proceed. It's really important to me, Dad. If I can help some other people who are being persecuted for just doing their jobs, then Aaron won't have died for nothing."

"He died doing this country a great service, Della. Don't ever think his death meant nothing. He is an inspiration to millions of people worldwide."

"What about the dissenters though? Are they right, Dad? Should the United States just stay out of other countries' business? Do we have a right to use taxpayers' money and power to bend these countries to our will. And do we have the right to pay for it with lives?"

"These are the difficult questions that fall on the shoulders of the president and elected leaders of this country. There are so many facets to every conflict, be it economic, cultural, territorial, or historic. So much has to be balanced. But we can't stand idly by while people are abused and deprived of their human rights by self-serving government leaders who live like kings while the common people beg in the streets for scraps. We don't just try to bend them to our will—we try to hold them to a higher ideal."

"It's pretty disheartening when our own people can treat animals with the same kind of disrespect."

"That's true. And that's why we need people like you to tell their stories. There are just as many issues in play, but these animals quietly disappear unless someone shines a spotlight on the issues. There are laws in place to uphold our ideals in our own country. At least we can see that they're enforced here and also have a say in what happens to countries that are not doing enough to protect endangered species worldwide."

Della's thoughts turned to the WWO and the man who had put so much of himself into the conservation effort. She wondered what he was doing now. She'd had no contact from him now in almost a month. Maybe it was time to send him a wake-up call.

CHAPTER 17

Brad shuffled some papers around on his desk and shifted restlessly, almost knocking over the cup of coffee that his secretary had thoughtfully left at his elbow. At least ten things vied for his immediate attention, and his concentration today was shit.

The morning had started as usual with his stop at the newsstand across the street from the office building housing the headquarters of Jamieson Enterprises. While picking up a copy of the local newspaper and a copy of the Wall Street Journal and Financial Times, his attention was drawn to a familiar image, framed in a familiar, gold jacket. He picked up a copy, turning to the editorial page where Bill Mahon sang the praises of National Environmental's newest contributing photojournalist, Della Rawlins. He read about the Gold Seal award and thought to himself, Good for her! I knew that shot was going to get some attention. I hope she sees how her efforts in writing about conservation can get things done. It's a lot more gratifying than trying to help institute changes in foreign governments. He didn't like the Idea of Della putting herself in the line of fire as she had with Aaron, even though he knew he had no right or say in how she lived her life. The thought of her coming to the same end as Aaron killed him.

Brad glanced again at the gold-framed magazine lying

near the edge of his desk. The picture of the caribou reminded him of the dreams that had been haunting his subconscious ever since that night before he, Ted, and Della had taken that helicopter ride to follow the migration. Images of her body wrapped around him, moving with him, her tongue mating with his, her breasts slick with sweat from their joining, the tips hard and aching for the suction of his mouth—all this swirled through his brain. Damn! He was hard again. He had been plagued with this for the past number of weeks. His libido had seriously been knocked out of neutral. It was so annoying. He was seriously considering dosing himself with saltpeter, or at least buying some tight-fitting underwear.

He jumped as the intercom chimed on his desk phone.

"Mr. Jamieson, a package just arrived for you," his secretary reported.

"Yeah, okay, Stacey. I'll pick it up on my way to lunch," he said grumpily, not wanting to further sabotage his scattered morning's work by adding yet another iron to the fire.

"But sir, it's so big. I don't know where to put it."

Biting off a terse retort, Brad got up from his desk, muttering about distractions, and opened the door to the reception area. A huge, rectangular package leaned against the wall, taking up almost one whole side of the office. Brad looked it over for identifying address information, racking his brain as to whether promotional material was expected for any upcoming sales campaigns. Usually he received an e-mail when anything was being sent in, but nothing was up on his daily calendar. The package was just addressed to Brad Jamieson, care of Jamieson Enterprises, with their corporate address, no return address. Strange.

"Should I call security?" the young blond girl asked, noting Brad's puzzlement about the strange delivery. She picked up her handset, preparing to punch in the speed dial code.

"No, I don't think so, Stacey. It's too big for a letter bomb. Feels like something in a frame. I'll take my chances. Ryan said he was sending me a souvenir from the Algiers. Maybe it's that."

Stacey followed him into the office as Brad hefted the awkward bundle. He unwrapped the outside paper and unwound sheets of cardboard and bubble wrap from around the framed print. When it was finally unveiled, it was a huge blowup of Della's "Gone before Dawn," beautifully printed on canvas and signed by the artist herself. He quickly removed the suddenly tacky-looking, yet hideously expensive watercolor of flying waterfowl on the wall to the side of his desk and replaced it with the newly acquired art. Under the track lighting in the ceiling, the picture was even more powerful.

"Wow, that's very impressive. From anyone I know?" Stacey asked, noting the artist's signature in the lower right-hand corner.

"I don't think you've met her, but we're going to be hearing a lot about her work in the near future."

"Right, boss," Stacey said. "Maybe I could call the maintenance guy and get him to mount it on the wall on the other side of the office so you can see it all day long."

"No, that's quite okay," Brad said, dismissing her as he reached for the white envelope that had fallen out on his desk when he had unwrapped the print.

Stacey raised her manicured eyebrows as he said cryptically, "I need to get some work done sometime today."

Brad slit open the letter, which was just addressed "To Brad" and pulled out the single, folded sheet.

Dear Brad,

I hope that you are well. I haven't heard from you since I left you in Canada, and I wondered if I had said or done anything on that last day to hurt or insult you. Please know that no malice was intended. I hardly remember anything about that day when I learned of Aaron's death, only the sadness of knowing that he was gone and the relief of knowing that his ordeal was over.

It was a surreal feeling to go through everything, from the claiming of the body to placing his urn at the cemetery, I feel like I've lived this time in someone else's body.

I wanted you to have a copy of the print. We pretty much made it together. It is my finest work to date, and I wanted you to share in the joy of having created it. The subject matter mirrors what happened to me when I got the news of Aaron's imminent homecoming. I can identify with the caribou's need for flight, even though they were reluctant to leave that haven of comfort and safety. But the fear of the unknown sometimes makes us all bolt.

I'm hoping that you understand, and please know that I do not regret anything we did. I want to thank you for the courtesy and respect you showed me during the short time we spent together and for everything you taught me about the caribou and about conservation. I have been the biggest pain in my father's butt since you opened my eyes to the issues surrounding the destruction of wildlife habitat and the carelessness we've exercised in wildlife management. I intend to be a strong voice in the future to see that some of these wrongs are righted and that we become better trustees of the natural environment. Time better spent than the futility of toppling governments, hey? I'll leave that to the daredevils, like your brother.

I wish you well in your work with the WWO. I hope that I can contact you or your office in the days going forward in order to source accurate information for future projects. It is heartening to know that there are still a few people in the world who would stand against the greed of men and not try to exploit the innocent and destroy what we were entrusted to protect. Thank you for your generosity of mind and spirit.

I have one last thing to thank you for. Ryan told me that you had organized an extraction attempt for Aaron by hiring mercenaries to go into Pakistan after the capture of bin Laden. I can't believe the insane amount of money you must have had to pay out to mobilize a team of mercenaries in the most hostile territory on the planet. As you probably know, I've started a fund for bringing home journalists who have been detained in foreign countries. I'm hoping that you will let me reimburse you in whole or in part, as I have committed funds to this organization that I have earned myself, and it would give me closure to be able to settle that debt with you on Aaron's behalf. I thank you for trying when everyone else was sitting on their hands. It means a lot.

Your friend,
Della

Brad reread the letter and thoughtfully slipped it into his inner jacket pocket. He had wanted to give Della lots of space to deal with her emotions and with Aaron's loss. He was sorry for her to have misinterpreted his distance as disinterest or anger. Nothing was further from the truth. He hadn't been part of that world. Ryan had been a major player and was better able to know how to help Della heal from those wounds.

It had been his intention to go and see Della after enough time had gone by to offer her a position as a staff writer for the WWO. Putting together briefs and environmental assessment reports might not be the kind of writing she was used to, but someone with her eye for detail could be invaluable in that position. And besides, they would be working together every day and sometimes late into the night. He was pretty sure that the chemistry they had felt between them wasn't just a result of being scared of bears or the isolation of a couple of healthy, red-blooded individuals being left alone in the woods. He admired her mind and her adventurous spirit. She fit so easily into his head and into his arms, and she had made major inroads into his heart as well.

He wasn't fool enough to think it would just be a matter of baiting the hook and reeling her in. He hadn't quite figured that part out yet, but he was pretty sure it might involve the use of cute baby animals. Yeah, that always worked in advertising. Who could resist cute baby animals?

CHAPTER 18

Ryan rolled his head and tried to stretch his legs in the cramped seat of the Boeing 747. How he hated flying coach! If he had been going to Algiers on Jamieson Outfitters business, he would be in a first-class seat, probably enjoying a bourbon now with his feet reclined and extra pillows for his neck. But today, he and two other agents of the US government were flying on the taxpayers' tab, and the taxpayers wouldn't think much of sending home a trio of Algerian prisoners who had just been released from Guantanamo Bay prison, first-class.

President Obama had been pleased with the offer from the Pakistanis for a prisoner exchange, as the UN had been very critical of his government for holding prisoners on the US base in Cuba, where methods of interrogation were, by most standards, pretty barbaric. Their censure was very embarrassing to the president, and he had vowed to close Guantanamo Bay during his first year as president. Unfortunately, in the aftermath of 9/11, it had become crucial for the government to have the capability of extracting information from prisoners without being bound by its own human rights legislation. Obama was under pressure from Congress to keep Guantanamo Bay open, as the latter was vehemently opposed to incarcerating suspected terrorists on US soil. The number of Guantanamo detainees was now down to twenty-four, and the offer of the prisoner exchange presented an opportunity to get rid of three more of them without any hassle from Congress.

From the CIA's perspective, however, it was not advisable to allow former terrorists back into their own countries. Their findings confirmed that one in seven previously released prisoners returned to terrorist activities.

When the net had tightened in Pakistan and Afghanistan after the 9/11 attacks, many of the al-Qaeda ranks had fled to Algeria. As head of covert operations in Africa, Ryan had been responsible for monitoring terrorist activity. So when it had been confirmed that the US government was going to release these three Algerian prisoners in exchange for three American POWs, extra surveillance had to be set up.

From what they had learned of these men during their stay at Guantanamo, two of those now in his custody were only minor bad boys—low-level Taliban fighters with not much information to offer. The last member, however, was a different story. Ibrahim Shafir Sen had been arrested in Afghanistan on suspicion of supporting terrorism. He had been sent by the American authorities to Guantanamo for interrogation but had proven to be a hard nut to crack. Despite all of the methods brought to bear on him to give up information—which wasn't much, with the new directives imposed on the CIA interrogators by Obama—Sen had remained silent.

The other prisoners had not been so resilient and had identified the man as Ibrahin bin Sharikh, who was not only a supporter of terrorism but also a known arms dealer and a leader of an al-Qaeda cell in Kashmir. He had recruited and trained members and had provided them with illegal weapons. He was an integral member of al-Qaeda, which was keen to exploit the two nuclear powers of India and Pakistan, both of whom claimed full rights to a divided Kashmir. It was apparent now why the Pakistani government was interested in his release. It had been an executive decision on the part of Ryan's superiors, with Washington's approval, that Sharikh be released as Sen and be allowed to resume his former activities, thinking he was unexposed. Using Sharikh to monitor al-Qaeda's activities would not only provide valuable intel on the group's attempts to acquire nuclear weapons, but it would also provide unmistakable proof about the importance of prisoner interrogation in extracting information.

Ryan reflected on the necessity of using "enhanced interrogation techniques" and "alternative sets of procedures" to extract information from prisoners. The US president wanted to uphold the fundamental American principle that the military does not control the streets of America. But when terrorist threats came from within, what choice did the government have but to mandate military custody for dangerous terrorism suspects? It would be irresponsible to put legislation in place that would challenge the president's ability to collect intelligence. The countrys' law enforcement agencies had to incapacitate these terrorists to protect the American people. but when American citizens could be arrested and essentially put away without trial, how did that uphold constitutional rights? Ryan was glad that these moral and ethical issues were not for him to decide. One thing he did know was that these people were intent upon bringing down his nation, and if it was his job to stop them, he couldn't do it with his hands tied behind his back with red tape.

The intercom crackled as the captain's voice announced that they were starting their descent into Houari Boumediene Airport. Ryan signaled to his two accompanying agents to prepare for landing and to disembark.

The plane touched down about fifteen minutes later, and the captain came on again, telling the travelers to stay seated while the prisoners deplaned. It had been a condition of their release that they were to be flown in on a commercial jet. The Algerians were taking no chances on letting an armed foreign military force into their airspace. The men were led off the plane with their hands shackled in front and their ankles shackled. Each had a belt around his legs, over the knees, to which the handcuffs were attached. The men had been given an injection before takeoff to guarantee their cooperation, and they crossed the tarmac at a stumbling gait under an armed Algerian guard to a waiting bus.

Ryan and his accompanying agents, along with the prisoners, were taken to a military facility, where the prisoners underwent a medical exam and Ryan signed them over into the custody of the Algerian government. Ryan and his agents were then escorted back to the airport, where a US military envoy waited to take them to the embassy. They would stay there until their return flight back to the US, which wasn't scheduled until the following day.

No foreign country had been permitted by the Algerian government to build bases in the country. Access had been gained, however, when the US-based Halliburton and the Bechtel Corporation, who had made oil-rich western Africa the fifth largest source of US imported oil, had set its eye on the northern Sahara, notably Algeria. The oil field giant decided a military presence was needed, and what was billed as a NASA base was established alongside the main airport of Algeria's southern garrison, doubling as a US military and CIA listening post.

Ryan and his two accompanying agents were taken by underground tunnel from inside the American embassy to the underground entrance of the NASA facility and were met by armed American guards, who inspected their identification and allowed them admittance to the base. They were escorted to a briefing room, where they were met by a uniformed officer.

"Good afternoon, gentlemen," he said, extending his hand to Ryan and then to the other two men. "I'm Major Thomlinson, CO of this US military base. As you know, the Algerians are not favorable to the US government operating a base in their country, so our presence here is top secret. As our guests, we expect you will take every precaution to ensure that it stays that way. You will be operating under the same confidentiality guidelines as you would in any other covert operation. Our facility is at your disposal. You'll be leaving the base soon to make contact with some of your team. They are set up in a house close to that of Ibrahin bin Sharikh's family. He is expected to return there when he is finished being processed by the Algerian government. Your team will brief you and bring you up to date on their activities." He picked up a phone on his desk and called for their escort.

"Col. Jamieson, I'd like a word with you," the major said, having dismissed the two accompanying agents into the care of a junior officer.

When the door was closed behind the others, the major sat on the edge of his desk and relaxed his military demeanor. "I hear the CEO is getting soft on the interrogation of prisoners at Guantanamo Bay."

"Yes, sir," Ryan said, not knowing what was coming next.

"Damn fool," the major remarked. "These people are so intent on bringing down the West that they would stop at nothing to undermine his authority. The only chance we have of stopping them is to gather information, and the diplomatic approach is not going to get us anywhere."

"No, sir," agreed Ryan.

"Son, I know you have a job to do here, and you can't do it with your hands tied behind your back. Just know that we've been operating in this country for a long time now, and we have a finger on the pulse of what goes on here. If you need information or support, we have your back. The release of this Sharikh is going to cause some major ripples in the pond. There are others who have been elevated within the organization to take over in his absence, and escalations in hostilities from within will happen with his release. If you identify a weak link in the organization and need to use extraordinary force to gain information, just know that we will support you, whatever it takes. This place is a time bomb, just ready to go off at any time. When the time is right, you can't be waiting on some pussy bureaucrat in Washington who's waiting for a bill to pass before taking action. Keep me apprised of the situation as it unfolds, and I will do whatever I can to support you."

"I appreciate your offer, sir. I hope it won't reach critical mass on our watch, but you just don't know. We will keep our eyes and ears open, and we will certainly rely on your intel to identify where we need to concentrate our efforts."

"Good to know we're on the same page, son."

Ryan shook his hand and turned to the door to rejoin his unit, and they were taken to a nearby dormitory where they changed into street clothes and prepared to enter the city.

The three Americans were taken into the city separately. The two agents accompanying Ryan were of Algerian descent and were dropped off near a bus stop close to the city, where they easily blended in with the locals. Ryan, with his complexion darkened and his head shrouded in a traditional headdress, was dropped off at the local market, not far from the watch point. He wandered around the stalls, covertly taking in the lay of the land and taking note of individual vendors who were known to be trading in contraband of all kinds. He stopped to buy some fruit and noted a stall across the way displaying used housewares and assorted goods.

On a rickety shelf near the tented roof of the stall, a brightly colored bit of material caught his eye. Munching on a juicy pear, he casually moved closer to get a better look. The vendor, busily engaged in bartering with several women over pots, ignored him, allowing him uninterrupted time to confirm what he suspected.

Sitting on the shelf that contained assorted camcorders, radios, and other assorted electronic equipment, probably stolen from unsuspecting passersby, was a familiar camera strap, embroidered with the stars and stripes of the American flag. It was attached to a battered, single-lens reflex camera, which looked like it had seen better days.

The vendor, having unsuccessfully finished his business with the two women, noticed Ryan looking at the camera and immediately engaged him in his sales pitch. Ryan asked to see a couple of the other models on display, examining the features and looking through the viewfinders, leading the seller to finally hawk the piece he was interested in. He looked it over, telling the guy he was asking too much for a camera in such bad condition. Turning it over, he noted the initials scratched into the paint, and he opened the compartment that held the digital storage card, noting that it was missing. The seller, desperate for a sale, offered him a ridiculously low price for the battered Nikon, which Ryan countered with an even lower offer. Smiling an almost toothless smile, the vendor shook his hand and took the bills Ryan held out.

Concealing the camera under his robe, Ryan strolled on through the crowded market, making his way toward the residential area.

CHAPTER 19

Reaching the alley where the watch point was located, Ryan checked to be sure no one was observing before slipping inside the door. Inside, he was met by a locked door, and he knew a security camera was watching his every move. He pulled out a plastic ID card and gave the password, and then the door opened to an armed guard who checked the card through an electronic scanner and stepped back, letting Ryan inside.

Climbing a staircase to the second floor, Ryan was greeted by a man dressed in the local garb, smiling widely, his teeth a flash of white in his dark face.

"Hi, Samson," Ryan greeted the man, stepping forward and clapping him in a friendly hug.

"Hey, man," the man replied. "It's been a long time."

"Yeah, but with the amount of time we've spent together electronically in the last few months, you'd think we were going steady." Ryan grinned. "The package has been delivered, and now we wait."

"Yeah, there's a lot of activity at scene one." Sam indicated the array of electronic equipment with lights flashing and monitors displaying and recording interior views of the subject's residence. Several agents were in place, headphones on, watching and typing notes onto computer screens. "Looks like they're planning a welcome home party."

"Great." Ryan grinned. "Hope they keep the beer flowing. Keep your ears on; it's going to be a long night."

"Sure, boss." Sam grinned. "Let the games begin."

The sun sank and rose again over the horizon before the group hunched in front of the computer screens and monitors stirred from their posts. Almost all of the guests had either gone home or were passed out drunk.

Stretching and reaching for his fifth cup of strong, black coffee, Ryan said, "Looks like things are winding down for now. Looks like some of the team can take a rest break. I have transcripts from the overnight. I'll take a copy with me back to the base and get it encrypted to send a full report back to Washington. I want to get started on the analysis right away.

"Oh," Ryan said, turning to Sam, "and I have a small mission that I would like for you to handle personally for me."

"Oh yeah?" Sam asked, eyebrows raised.

Pulling out the camera from his discarded street clothes, Ryan showed it to his trusted friend. "This belonged to a really good friend of mine. It was in Abbottabad the night bin Laden was killed, in the possession of an American photojournalist who was captured and held as a prisoner of war. It's interesting how it turned up here in Algeria. I can't take it with me back to the States, so I need you to arrange for it to be sent back. It's very important that it not be tampered with in any way. I don't want you to let it out of your sight until it's on its way back to its rightful owner."

"Yes, sir," Samson replied, knowing better than to ask why his boss wouldn't entrust the transport of the camera to the people at the base. "I'll be sure to take good care of it. Should I send it to your home office?"

"No, it's too sensitive for that. Send it to my brother at

Jamieson Outfitters," he said, digging a business card out of his wallet. "Registered mail, address it to Brad Jamieson."

The three agents reconnoitered back at a meeting point outside of town at midday. A car picked them up and took them to a drop-off point, where they were able to get back to the base through a Halliburton office to prepare for the return trip home.

Before they left for the embassy, Major Thomlinson met again with Ryan for a debriefing as to the night's activities. He once again pledged his support to the mission "with any means needed"—meaning equipment, personnel, and expertise. Nodding his acknowledgement, Ryan thanked the major and left to join the men.

Before he left, he turned back to the major and, handing him a portable drive, said, "Oh, by the way, would you mind having this encrypted and sending it back to Washington? I'd rather not take the risk of it falling into the wrong hands going through airport security."

"Of course, son," he replied, taking the device from him. "I'll look forward to hearing from you soon."

Saluting sharply, Ryan left for the embassy and home.

CHAPTER 20

Della sat at her desk at home. The office looked as if a bomb had gone off. There were papers everywhere. Photos, newspaper clippings, notes, and folders all competed for space. The faces of eighteen men and women stared back from the bulletin board in front of her, a biography pinned neatly beneath each one. Corresponding manila file folders jammed the cabinets below, containing case histories, background information, and reports from investigators in the field, along with transcripts from senate sessions, court proceedings, news reports, and e-mails—basically every scrap of information that could be gathered on each missing journalist. Della had hired a team of two full-time investigators, a lawyer who specialized in international human rights law, and an administrative assistant who was responsible for entering all of the incoming information into the steadily growing database.

Over in a corner stood a smaller filing cabinet, upon which sat a potted Star of Bethlehem with small, white flowers alongside a small silver-framed photo. Inside, there were only five folders—two green and three black. This was the closed file. Della ran her fingers over the index tabs, smiling as she opened the second green folder and added a news clipping. The story was about the return home of freelance writer Amanda Lindhurst. Amanda had been captured, along with her boyfriend, Australian photojournalist Nigel Brennigan, while on a story in Somalia. They had spent fifteen months held hostage—starved; beaten; and, in Amanda's case, sexually abused—while their governments had tried unsuccessfully to secure their release. Both governments had to maintain a hard line about not supporting terrorism by giving in to ransom demands and were between a rock and a hard place as to how far they could go in offering support.

Both governments had offered the terrorists $250,000 each, the sum of which had been rejected.

Amanda's family had gotten in touch with Della's organization, and with her help and that of other donors, plus the Canadian and Australian governments, they were able to raise the $1.2 million it took to secure their release. About $600,000 of that had gone to pay the ransom, and the rest had covered expenses, including the $2,000-a-day fee paid to a private hostage negotiator.

With a sense of pride, Della closed the door of the filing cabinet, knowing that it was only through the support of the private sector that these people were alive. Governments were under a lot of scrutiny about supporting terrorist activities, but that was cold comfort to families standing helplessly by while their loved ones wasted away in foreign prisons. Della lovingly touched the silver-framed photo of Aaron and then touched the velvety petals of the small, white flower on the plant, representing hope. It felt good to know that her efforts were making a difference.

Her cell phone suddenly rang, jangling her nerves and jolting her out of her reverie. The call display read "unknown caller," and she answered the call with trepidation, wondering who was calling unannounced.

"Hello?" She said, hoping to project an air of confidence and authority.

"Hello, Della," the warm male voice answered. "It's been a long time. How are you?"

"Oh ... Brad," Della replied, glad she was sitting down because, even though she had expected him to call, hearing his voice made her heart flutter and her mouth go dry.

"Yeah," he replied. "Sorry I wasn't in touch sooner. I thought you might need some time to deal with the whole situation, and I didn't want to complicate things. I want you to know that I've been very concerned about you and have kept in touch with Ryan to see how you're doing."

"Oh yeah, your brother, ever the spy," she replied wryly. "Where has he disappeared to anyway? He told me he was going out of town, but I haven't heard a word from him."

"He hasn't taken any assignments from the magazine for a while," Brad said, "but I'm not sure exactly where he is right now. He'll turn up eventually. Della, I wanted to call you, first of all, to thank you so much for the print. I knew it was a winner the first time I saw it on your camera, but blown up on canvas, it's breathtaking."

"It's definitely a great shot," Della said modestly. "A happy accident, really. I felt that you definitely had a part in creating it."

"I can't claim anything, but I'm delighted my blundering in on your shoot worked out so well for you. Uh ... the other reason I'm calling is a little more self-serving, I'm afraid."

"Oh really? What is it, Brad?" Della asked, intrigued.

"Well, there's this awesome wildlife shelter called Hope for Life operating in eastern Canada," he said. "The founder and operator is an old friend of mine from college, Hope Switzner. She's been running it since the nineties, taking in orphaned and injured animals; rehabilitating them; and, where possible, releasing them back into the wild. They also provide excellent educational programs, not only with in-class presentations and tours but also distance education, taking classes right into the sanctuary with live, on-camera interactive TV, allowing students who wouldn't ordinarily be able to visit the sanctuary to see and ask questions in real time. They're doing some excellent work."

"Wow, sounds great," Della said. "Are they looking for a donation? I'd be glad to contribute," she added, taking out her personal checkbook.

"Well, I'm sure they wouldn't refuse your generosity, but that's not why I called you," Brad said, getting down to the point of his call. "You know how I'm down a photojournalist with my little brother out of town?"

"Righhhtt?" Della drew out the word.

"Well, I really wanted to do a feature story on Hope for Life for our magazine, especially now as they are entered in a community funding competition, sponsored by a national insurance company. I thought the timing would be good to raise some awareness. They could stand to possibly gain up to a hundred thousand dollars in enhancement funding for their facility."

"So you want me to write the story, huh?"

"I always knew you were a bright girl. We need pictures, too."

"So what are you proposing?" Della asked as she brought her personal calendar up on her computer.

"Well, what are you doing next weekend?" Brad asked, hoping she wouldn't hear the nervousness in his voice. He felt like a sixteen-year-old schoolboy asking a girl out on a first date.

"You mean besides meeting with Senator Adams, consulting with our lawyer, and writing briefing notes for him—Oh, and meeting with our field investigator, who'll just be getting back from Iraq, not to mention paperwork ... not much."

"Awesome! Want to fly out with me early Saturday morning? We'll have all day Saturday to visit the center, and I'll have you back home on Sunday morning in time to get your homework done." Brad wheedled shamelessly, "You should see the baby foxes. Hold on, I'll send you a picture," he said, pulling up the photo app on his cell phone.

"Oh my God. How cute is that!" Della exclaimed, once she'd responded to the ding of the e-mail arriving on her phone and opened the video file. "Okay, you got me," she said, smiling at the video of the tiny foxes tumbling over each other as they played in their enclosure.

"Thanks, Della," Brad said, mentally wiping the sweat off of his brow. "I know how busy you are. Congratulations on the Lindhurst case, by the way. I could see your stamp all over it."

"Yeah, we played a part," Della said, pleased that he could see past the anonymity her organization tried to maintain.

"You do great work," he said warmly.

"So do you," Della acknowledged. "I'm glad to be able to return the favor."

They arranged their rendezvous time and place while Della furiously sent e-mails, shifting her schedule and delegating what tasks she could to her assistant. Her father agreed to meet with Senator Adams over a game of golf, and so she was able to make the time to do the trip.

She couldn't wait to see Brad again.

CHAPTER 21

Della pulled her long, dark hair into a thick ponytail. Her terrier, Jack, jumped up on her jean-clad legs excitedly, hoping that her putting on her "walkies" jacket meant an outing to the park was imminent.

"Not today, buddy," Della said, crouching down to scratch the little dog behind the ears. "Madeline is coming over later," she told him, making a mental note to leave a couple of twenties on the counter with a note to thank her long-suffering assistant for looking after Jack at such short notice. "Maybe she'll take you for a walk."

Della picked up her keys and the satchel that held her "essentials"—which included her camera and notebook—and headed out, leaving a disappointed Jack behind.

She arrived at the New York offices and headquarters of Jamieson's Outfitters and Out There magazine with fifteen minutes to spare. A security guard opened the door for her and directed her to take the elevator to the tenth floor. She stepped out onto a rustic plank boardwalk and looked around appreciatively at a decor that brought together a collection of real potted trees, river stone, and natural-looking plants. She passed a couple of meeting places where rustic chairs and low tables were arranged in comfortable groupings. You would swear that you were outdoors. A carved sign directed the way to the reception area, and Della hurried along, anxious to be on time.

The office space was decorated like the inside of a Highcroft hunting barn. Rough planks covered two walls, while the outside wall was lined with rustic-looking, double hung windows, which appeared to be looking out onto a wooded yard. The secretary's desk was vacant, and the door to the inner office stood open. Della could hear Brad's voice and headed in that direction. Standing in the doorway, she saw him sitting behind a desk, the top of which was a slab of wood that looked like a cross section cut from the trunk of a giant tree. The pedestal it sat on was the actual tree trunk, hollowed out on the inner side to accommodate the CEO's knees. The whole thing had been coated in acrylic, and it gleamed in the natural sunlight. She noticed that the circular wall behind him was also window-lined, with an outdoor view. She glanced across at the newly installed print and knew that it could not have found a better home.

"Very impressive offices, Mr. Chairman." Della smiled when Brad finished his call and stood to greet her.

"Why, thank you." He grinned back, slipping a worn leather jacket over his casual, chamois shirt. "It's the only way I feel like I can breathe, having to work in the city," he said.

"How did your architect create a forest outside your window?" Della couldn't help but ask.

"They built a twelve-foot, walled balcony right around the tenth floor. It's covered in ivy so you can't notice it behind the evergreens, and it's open to the sky. There's a stream and a waterfall out there in the back."

"Wow, you have your very own Central Park. How cool!" She thought of Jack and his instinctive need to be in the outdoors. How he would love it here!

"Maybe you could come over some weekend, and we'll go camping," he teased. "I promise there are no bears."

"Deal. I'll bring the s'mores."

"Well, let's get out of here, shall we?" Brad smiled and ushered her toward his private elevator. Stepping into the glassed-in elevator capsule, Brad pushed some buttons, and the car rose up the side of the building. Surprised, Della raised her eyebrows questioningly, but Brad only said, "You'll see."

When the car stopped, he placed his hand on Della's lower back, and they stepped out onto the roof of the building. It was quite windy, and Brad took her hand, leading her over to where a familiar green helicopter perched on a helipad like a giant dragonfly. A guy dressed in coveralls was checking over the aircraft.

"Where's Ted?" Della asked, looking around for the lanky, sandy-haired figure of the pilot.

"He's not coming today," Brad replied. "We'll just have to make do without him." He grinned and opened the cockpit door, reaching for a pair of aviator sunglasses.

"Wow, I didn't know you could fly," Della said, taking his hand as he helped her climb into the passenger seat.

"Yup, another fun fact you didn't know about me," he teased her. "I have an amazing repertoire."

"Not to mention a lot of toys," she added as they put on headsets and Brad started a preflight check.

Soon Brad got the all clear from the nearby air traffic control tower. The rotors overhead geared up, and the helicopter lifted off the helipad. Manipulating the control stick, Brad turned the bird to face the East River, and they headed out, leaving the giant skyscrapers behind as they flew over miles of city suburbs.

Della couldn't help but flash back to her last trip in the same helicopter—when she had been accompanying

Aaron's remains back from Boston to be inurned in New York, his adopted home. The pain must have shown on her face because Brad's voice crackled over her headset, "You all right?"

"Yeah, I'm fine." She nodded. "How far to the reserve?"

"A little under six hundred miles. Should take us about an hour and forty minutes."

"Cool." Della grinned. "Just a walk in the park!"

CHAPTER 22

The landscape started to change as the couple flew toward the east coast of Canada.

"We have to make a pit stop in Halifax to fill up and go through Canadian customs. Oh shit, I forgot to mention to you to bring your passport."

"No worries," Della replied, digging through her satchel and pulling out the small folder. "I'm a journalist—I don't leave home without it."

Relieved, Brad spoke into the headset and made contact with the Halifax authorities. He got clearance to land at the Halifax Airport, and as promised, they were met by a border guard, who checked their credentials and approved their entry into Canada. Soon after refueling, they were on their way again. And Della felt her excitement rising as Brad filled her in with some background information about the Hope for Life Wildlife Sanctuary, and its founder, Hope Switzner.

Pretty soon, Brad lowered his altitude, and Della got a close-up view of the lay of the land.

They were flying over natural woodland, and a narrow dirt road wound below them, sometimes hidden from view by the dense forest.

"There it is up ahead." Brad pointed to where an area had been cleared out of the virgin forest and some buildings nestled, surrounded by neat pastures and outdoor enclosures. A long, tall building stood to one side. And below them now, there was a large parking area, where several school buses and a number of cars waited.

There was a nearby meadow, out of the way of the public space, and Brad gently put the helicopter down with minimum disturbance. He shut down the aircraft, and pulling off his headset, he turned to Della. "Ready?" he asked.

"You bet," she said, excited as a schoolkid as she hopped down out of the helicopter and ducked her head under the blades of the rotors.

As they strolled toward the main building, Brad pointed out the different buildings that housed various species of animals. There were pastures where deer grazed, the young fawns resting, camouflaged in the shade, or following their moms around, bleating for a lunch. A large bull moose with a huge rack of antlers gazed balefully out at them from behind another sturdy fence. His leg was splinted, and a large bandage covered one whole shoulder.

A group of schoolkids was following a guide along a neat walkway toward a pasture housing a small herd of caribou. Della took out her camera and found an interesting angle for a shot of the group, the members of which were animatedly asking questions of their friendly and knowledgeable guide.

"He has a great rapport with that group," Della commented to Brad. "You can tell he's good with animals. He even has the two-legged ones eating out of his hand."

"Well, that's a great compliment," said a voice behind them. A tall, willowy woman with an unruly mop of light brown, curly hair grabbed Brad by the shoulders and gave him a smacking kiss on the cheek. "Hi, handsome," she said.

"Hi, yourself," Brad replied, a huge smile lighting up his admittedly gorgeous countenance. "You're looking great,

Hope, you old flirt. One of these days, I'm gonna call your bluff and chase you out behind the barn."

"Promises, promises," Hope teased back, pinching his cheek. "Now stop fooling with me and introduce me to your pretty friend," she said, turning to Della and holding out a farm-roughened hand.

"Hope, this is Della Rawlins. She's the photojournalist I was telling you about. She's going to write a story about the sanctuary for Out There. We're gonna see if we can drum up some support so you can build that new waterfowl enclosure you were telling me about."

Sparkling blue eyes crinkled at the corners as a huge grin split her face in two. "Well, hot diggity dogs," Hope said, doing her best impression of Elly May Clampett. "Right this way, folks! Come and I'll show you my critters." And linking arms with her guests, she said, "You folks get the VIP tour!"

Della spent the afternoon fascinated as Hope led her and Brad from enclosures to the barn to different outbuildings housing all kinds of "critters"—from raccoons and rabbits to coyotes, bobcats, and lynx. There were even some wolves, although they were housed well away from the public areas.

"Where do all of the animals come from?" Della asked, taking notes.

"All of our animals, with a few exceptions, have been rescued from the wild. They were either injured or orphaned or abandoned by their parents, and people either call us to retrieve them, or they bring them to us. We have them seen by a veterinarian, and we decide on a plan of action to try and rehabilitate them with the hope of ultimately returning them to the wild."

"What if their injuries would prevent them from being able to fend for themselves in the wild?" Della asked, chewing on the end of her pen.

"Well, if the animal's temperament is suitable, we try to find them placements in zoos. Some we keep ourselves for our educational programs. They accompany us when we go out to do live demonstrations."

"And if their temperament isn't suitable?"

"Sometimes animals have been so abused by humans that they can't be trusted to not injure their keepers, and sometimes they've been badly injured and are in chronic pain. Then it's not only a danger to us but also a cruelty to the animal itself to let it continue to suffer."

"So you believe in euthanasia?"

"Yes. It's the kindest solution when there is no way the animal can do for itself and can't be integrated to live with humans."

"What's your opinion, then, on no-kill shelters?" Della asked, knowing this was a contentious issue with the ASPCA.

"We believe that there is every hope to rehabilitate injured and orphaned wild animals to be released back into the wild. That's our focus. With domesticated animals, we would hope that shelters do their best to find their animals a 'forever' home. We abhor cruelty to animals and support all kinds of rescue programs that try to remove animals that have been mistreated or abandoned and place them in new homes. We do not believe in using animals for experimentation or product testing. We encourage all of our visitors to have their pets spayed or neutered to control the pet population. If everyone did his or her part, there would be no need for healthy, adoptable animals to be euthanized. Laws have to be enforced and fines levied by governments at all levels to protect animals from abuse at the hands of humans."

"Here, here," Brad said, putting his arm around Hope's shoulders and trying to lighten the mood a little. "Professor Burke in Animal Rights 101 would be proud of you."

"He would be more than proud of you, too, with the work you're doing in animal welfare," Hope responded, her eyes glowing with respect and admiration. "You are an inspiration to us all, right, Della?"

"No doubt about it; the man is a saint," she laughingly agreed.

"Don't give me too much credit." Brad chuckled as he opened the door to the fox house.

CHAPTER 23

Inside the generously proportioned shed, kennels lined one wall. Little, pointed faces peeked out at them as they entered. And in one corner, an adult female wagged her gloriously fluffy tail and started a keening sort of whine as she lay curled up in a blanket inside her enclosure. The animal looked and acted so much like Jack did when she came home from work that Della's heart melted at the sight. Hope opened a nearby kennel, and three tiny, red foxes tried to elude capture. She managed to grab one guy by the scruff and took him out. Della was charmed by the miniature face with the black-tipped ears and white-tipped little tail. He made several playful attempts to chew on her fingers.

"Ordinarily, we avoid handling young animals as much as possible if they're to be released to the wild. The more they imprint on humans, the less likely they are to successfully transition to independent living. We avoid talking to or around them. We insert bottles of formula into real fox furs to act as their surrogate mother until they can be weaned. But these guys were born in someone's basement. Their mom had found a way inside through a broken window, and luckily the people living there were keeping an eye on the den. When the mom didn't return after several days, probably having been shot or run down by a car, the family intervened and tried looking after the pups themselves. When they realized they didn't know enough to rear the little guys, they brought them to the center. Unfortunately, by that time, they had lost their fear of humans. And the family had been feeding them puppy chow, so they didn't know how to forage for food. They had even tried to litter train them."

"So what are you going to do with them now?" Della asked worriedly.

"Oh, I know a lady who works with foxes to allow them to be adopted as pets. She breeds silver foxes herself and actually keeps five as her own pets," Hope said. "They're pretty smart animals, but you have to understand their nature. They're definitely not like dogs."

"Oh really? How so?" Della asked.

"Well, they don't cuddle with their keepers like dogs would with their owners. Sometimes they'll look for attention, but a scratch on the ear tip or a small pat is enough. They have tremendous energy and need a lot of time each day outdoors in a safe enclosure. They love to hide, so all of their kennels, inside and out, should have boxes or places for them to be able to hide out. You'll see on the outside of the shed in the outdoor area, we have a tower where the foxes can climb up and survey their domain from an elevated platform. They love being up high like that. We usually keep our kennel doors draped with blankets—at least partway—to help them feel safe. Some owners have a separate room in their houses, with doggie door access to the outside enclosure. Usually, chain-link fencing is used for outside enclosures, but it has to be buried so that the fox can't dig underneath and escape. Chicken wire is also used as a further barrier to be sure they can't squeeze their heads through the holes in the fence, and the roofs have to be closed in as well. Some people will make pitched roofs with fiberglass panels, lined with chicken wire. They have to have lots of space to run and play."

"Do they catch live prey?" Della asked.

"If we're raising them with the intention of releasing them to the wild, we feed them wild prey that has been killed and frozen. Once they're old enough, live prey is introduced to the outdoor enclosure so that they can develop and hone their hunting skills. We watch them carefully to see which animals catch on, and we supplement them until they're able to fend for themselves. If you're trying to adapt a fox to be a house pet, it's important to remember that they will follow their instincts. You have to keep other small house pets—like rabbits and guinea pigs and hamsters—in cages or rooms that aren't accessible to the fox."

"Do they sleep in their kennels?" Della asked.

"Some do," Hope said, "but some owners will let them sleep in their beds with them."

"They're pretty smelly," Della said, wrinkling her nose.

"It's their urine," Hope said, taking the little fox from Della and returning it to its cage. "It actually smells a lot like skunk."

"Maybe by neutering the males there would be less marking," Brad suggested.

"It usually makes them less aggressive and not as active, but it doesn't take the odor out of the urine," Hope said.

"Can they be litter trained?" Della asked.

"Some can," Hope said. "Dixie over there is around 90 percent reliable. We use her in demonstrations and for in-class visits. She's very calm and tame and is a real help in settling in new arrivals." Dixie was the adult female who had reminded Della so much of Jack when they'd entered the fox house. She had seemed so happy to see Hope, even wagging her tail. You could tell that she had a deep trust in her keepers.

"Do you have any males?" Della asked.

"Not in this shed, but we have one outside if you want to meet him. His owners gave him up when they had to move, so he's been partially domesticated. He'll be leaving soon to go to a zoo in Wyoming."

"Sure," Della said enthusiastically, following Hope through to the outdoor enclosure.

"Wow, this is great!" Della exclaimed. "It's just like the middle of the forest."

"Let's see if Jacko is around," Hope said, placing an egg on a nearby stump. Some grass rustled nearby, and a twig snapped as a silver fox peeked out from behind a log. He approached warily, his head perfectly still, ears pricked, eyes focused on the tasty morsel on the stump. He didn't seem to be at all concerned about these smelly humans invading his home. He stalked his prey, circling around under some dense underbrush, and took the egg off the stump so cunningly that the humans hadn't even noticed it was gone. Suddenly Della felt a warm sensation running down the side of her leg.

"Jacko, bad boy!" Hope exclaimed, annoyed. "You must have an animal living with you at home, huh?"

"Yeah, a six-month-old terrier I got from a rescue shelter. How did you know?"

"Well, that's one thing that dogs and foxes have in common," Hope said, pointing to the big yellow stain on Della's light-washed jeans. "If they smell another animal's scent in their territory, they'll do their best to cover it."

"Well, I'm honored that he likes me well enough to claim me as his own!" Della laughed it off, not wanting her hostess to feel badly for what one of her animals had done.

"Wow, Brad," Hope said in a low voice out of Della's earshot. "She's the real deal. Better hang on to that one!" To Della, she said, "Come on over to the main house. I'll fix you up with something clean to wear, and we can clean those pants up for you."

"No need to go to all that trouble," Della said dismissively. "I practically grew up on a farm."

"Funny nobody taught you how to fish!" Brad grinned at her as she swatted at him.

Back at the main house, Hope showed Della to a dorm room, where two comfy beds sat side by side under the peaked ceiling of the old farmhouse. Sheer curtains billowed at the open window, letting in the fresh afternoon air, lightly scented with the smell of the animal pens outside. Hope handed her a pair of overalls and said, "Just bring your jeans down to the kitchen, and I'll throw them in the washer for you."

"I hate to put you to all that trouble," Della said.

"I was hoping to convince you and Brad to stay over," Hope confided. "I have to take an old friend in to the vet's clinic to have some tests done, and I'm shorthanded today because two of my student assistants are taking exams."

"I'd be glad to help any way I can," Della said graciously. "It'll help me get a closer perspective on what it takes to care for these animals on a daily basis."

"You can help with the feeding," Hope said appreciatively. "That's if Brad says you guys are staying."

By the time Della had changed into the overalls and found her way downstairs, Brad was settled into a chair in the big country kitchen with a hot cup of coffee in front of him. Hope was nowhere in sight, but a student was there doing kitchen duty and took her soiled jeans with a grin. "Hi, I'm June. Looks like Jacko ambushed you, huh?"

"Yeah, he got me with both barrels." Della grinned back.

"Sneaky rascal, that," June commented. "Would you like some coffee?"

"I don't know," Della said, looking at Brad. "What do you think about staying over?"

"I wanted to check with you before I agreed," Brad said,

considering. "Do you have too much work to do tomorrow to stay?"

"I think I can swing it," Della said, punching Madeline's number into her cell phone. "Just let me see if I can get someone to help me out."

Hope came through the door with an armful of fresh picked vegetables. "Fresh veggie stir-fry for supper," she announced. "Hope you're hungry!"

CHAPTER 24

After supper had been enthusiastically enjoyed and the clearing away done, Hope asked Brad and Della if they would come out to the barn to help her capture her old friend, Oscar, to take him to the vet. The three of them entered the flight cage, which was a long building adjoined to the barn by a connecting window. The large bald eagle was perched on a tree limb, looking rather nervous. He was holding his wings low, as if trying to decide whether or not to take off. His yellow eyes blinked at Della suspiciously, and he let out a high-pitched cry, his beak open threateningly as he shifted his talons to get a better grip on the perch. A net was strung under the perches high enough off the ground so that the birds would not injure themselves if they couldn't get airborne or fell while flying.

"Easy there, Oscar." Hope spoke to the bird calmly. "We have to go on a little road trip to see Dr. Christofer." She tried dropping a towel over the bird's head, but he was too quick for her. He spread those massive wings and swept up to a higher perch, blinking down at them from the wire-enclosed rafters.

"You're not going to make this easy for us, are you?" Hope said.

It took the best part of an hour to finesse the great bird

into a large cardboard carton. Once his head was covered, Brad had a firm grip on his talons, and Hope had a tape on his beak, Della stepped closer for a closer look at the magnificent creature.

"Careful, now," Brad told Della. "We have to make sure his feet are secured."

"Yeah," Hope said. "Even though he's an old and cranky bird, he can still take off a hand with those things."

"Why can't the vet come to see him here?" Della wondered out loud.

"He has to have X-rays done of his wings," Hope explained. "Did you notice how low he holds his shoulders? The vet thinks he has a deformity caused by arthritis, and it's causing him chronic pain. We have to find out if that's what is bothering him. He's lived here for five years, and he's always been cranky."

"Can they operate?" Della asked, scribbling notes and taking pictures.

"Very unlikely he'd survive," Hope said, her eyes downcast and a worried look on her face. "Well, anyway, I'm glad you guys could be here," Hope said. "Thank you very much. Some of these guys are like my children."

They loaded the large cardboard box with an indignant Oscar into the back of an ancient station wagon and headed out toward the dirt road, waving to June as they passed the farmhouse.

The station wagon bumped along over the rutted, dirt country road. In no time, they pulled up at the vet's clinic, where they were met by a middle-aged, no-nonsense veterinary assistant. Dr. Christofer came out of an exam room, and Hope introduced him to her friends.

"It's a hard day for Hope. Glad you could be here for her," Roxanne, the assistant, said out of Hope's earshot to Della.

"We're pretty sure the X-rays are not going to give positive news."

"Oh no," Della said fearfully, knowing the answer to her next question before she even voiced it. "So if the X-rays are positive for degenerative arthritis, what's his prognosis?"

"We're pretty sure the decision will be to euthanize. Oscar is by no means a social creature. The chronic pain will be affecting his behavior, making him too big a risk to live among people."

"I can see how that would be a cruelty to him," Della said.

"Trouble is, he's become a kind of mascot for the center," Hope said sadly, walking up to Della. "Thousands of schoolkids call us up on Skype to check in on him. They're all looking forward to the day when he'll be released. They're going to take it very hard if he has to be put down."

It could certainly impact the outcome of the amount of support they may garner in the funding competition, too, Della realized. This story will take some special handling, she thought, looking for a sympathetic angle.

The mood was somber as Brad, Della, and Hope bumped along the dirt track back to the shelter. A flock of wild geese flew in a V formation across the rainbow-hued evening sky as they headed back to the wetland to roost.

"I guess there goes my dream of securing funding for the waterfowl enclosure," Hope said somberly. "Oscar will be sadly missed if the worst happens tonight. The timing couldn't be worse with the competition closing next month. A lot of kids will probably stop voting if we have to put Oscar down."

"Don't worry, Hope," Della said, putting her arm around the woman's slender shoulder. "It's a great thing you're doing here. There are other ways to make it happen. You have to live up to your name and don't give up hope."

"You're right," her new friend said, wiping her nose with a tissue and smiling through her tears.

"When will Dr. Christofer know the results?" Brad asked gently.

"He's going to call me later tonight."

***

Later, as the staff joined Hope and her guests around the big kitchen table to hold a sort of vigil for Oscar, Della discreetly shot some pictures of the individuals who comprised this incredible group. Their caring support of their leader and mentor was clear as they told stories of Oscar's exploits during the time he'd been with them. If their hope and prayers could improve Oscar's chances for survival, they were here to do what they could.

Suddenly, the phone jangled on the wall. With trembling hands, Hope picked up the receiver.

"Hope for Life Animal Refuge," she answered. "Hi, Dr. Christofer. What's up?"

"Oh ... That's not the news we were hoping for," she said, rubbing a hand across her temple.

"Yes, of course. It will be kinder to do it while he's still under anesthesia. But I'd like to be there. I'll be out in ten minutes. Thank-you."

"Not good news, guys," Hope said sadly as she hung up the receiver. She shook her head as tears filled her eyes. "Arthritis is clearly showing in the X-rays. There's also a small tumor in his right wrist joint. Could even be cancerous. Kindest thing is to let him go," she said, wiping her eyes and nose.

Brad went to Hope and held her in a friendly embrace. All of the staff wanted to go with Hope to the vet's to bring Oscar's remains home, but Hope said no; she would go herself.

"We'll have a memorial service for him and put a tribute for him on the website," Della suggested.

Hope nodded, and Brad moved with her to the door. "I'll drive you."

The group broke up, then. Everyone moved out to where the animals waited for their keepers to give them their final feedings and make them comfortable for the night.

CHAPTER 25

After her chores were done, Della went out on the veranda to sit on the porch swing and wait for Brad and Hope to come back. As she made herself comfortable, her phone dinged with the tone that indicated a Skype call.

"Hi, Nana." She smiled as the screen popped open and her eighty-seven-year-old grandmother's kind face filled the screen.

"Hello, my beauty," the old woman chirped. "Where are you? I missed you tonight for our radio bingo date."

"Oh, I'm so sorry," Della said, remembering too late that she was supposed to have picked up the game cards and been at her grandmother's senior's residence at 6:00 p.m. sharp. "Something came up, and I had to go out of town."

"That's okay, my dear. I was young once. I remember how things used to come up back then, too." She cackled. "Your mother was here anyway. Not as much fun as you, but we did okay. Need young people like you around to keep me from getting old." She cackled again, wheezing.

Della could picture her Nana struggling to hold up the phone with her arthritic wrist.

"Damn rheumatism," she complained, wincing. "What I wouldn't do for a fifth of scotch."

"Nana!" Della scolded. "You know you can't drink alcohol with the drugs you're taking!"

"Oh, I know, girl." The old woman sighed. "Can't do any of the fun stuff anymore. Sucks to get old."

Della smiled at her. "You can't keep a good woman down," she said.

"So what were you up to?" Nana asked with an impish grin. "Was he taller than six two?"

"More like three feet," Della said, trying to put Nana off the scent of what she thought might be a big secret romance. "I'm at a wilderness refuge. My friend had to put her bald eagle down. She's been working with him for five years, but he developed really bad arthritis, and he can't fly properly now. He seemed upset that someone had to get his food for him because he can't hunt anymore."

"I know exactly how he must feel," Nana said, holding her arthritic wrist and painfully flexing her clawlike, old fingers. "Useless! If people were half as kind to their seniors as they are to their pets, they would put us out of our suffering when we get old and sick and depressed. Half of the existing old age homes are full of the walking dead—people just hanging around waiting to die. Who wants to be old and broken and dependent on someone else to wipe the drool off your face? It's so much kinder to let one die with dignity, like your friend did for her eagle. Keeping people or animals alive because their bodies are too stubborn to quit—that seems to be more for the family than the senior, don't you think? The native cultures got it right, you know. When the elderly got old and sick, they would let them walk away from the tribe, alone, to die. Animals do that, too. And then we have the dumb people who take men like old Dr. Kevorkian, who believed in assisted suicides for people who have excruciatingly painful, degenerative diseases, and throw them in jail. I tell you, girl, the world is a screwed up place."

"You know, Nana, you just gave me a fabulous idea!" Della said excitedly. "I just figured out how to help the refuge get their money!"

"What money?" her grandmother asked.

"They're trying to raise some money to expand their facility so they can rehabilitate waterfowl."

"Well, if anyone can help to raise money, it would be you," Nana said. "Go knock yourself out, girl. I'll see you when you get home. Don't forget to bring me some scratch tickets!"

Della shook her head, laughing at her irrepressible grandmother. "Love you, Nana."

"Love you, too, darlin'. Toodle-oo."

Della took out her tablet, and within twenty minutes, she had her tribute to Oscar written. She then e-mailed her editor at the magazine and asked him if he could wrangle her a spot on a national news magazine TV show. She attached her text file to it, told him more would follow, and hit send. She knew it was going to be a winner.

Running into the farmhouse, Della bumped into June in the kitchen and asked her if she knew if anybody had a good digital camcorder.

"Yeah, there's one in the office."

"Can I borrow it?" Della asked.

"I'm sure it would be okay with Hope," June said. "Just don't forget to put it back when you're done."

"Of course," Della promised, following June into a compact but neat office to retrieve the camera.

***

Later, Della smiled as she plugged a USB cable into the

camera and transferred the data to her phone. She'd hit the jackpot with the camera because it contained footage of Hope working with Oscar in the flight cage, and some of her and Dr. Christofer examining his injured wing and encouraging him to fly. He looked depressed, refusing to take a thawed, dead field mouse from the keeper's outstretched palm. Della had found some interviews as well. She had called her Nana back and recorded her comments. She e-mailed her saved file to her editor, along with a page of instructions on how she wanted the spot to be edited together. By the time Brad and Hope got back, the day had gotten the best of her, and she was sound asleep in the porch swing.

"It's been a long day," Hope said, yawning. "Why don't you take your little city slicker up to bed?"

"Don't let her fool you; she's tough," Brad said, as his warm gaze roved appreciatively over Della's soft curves in the pink Hello Kitty T-shirt she wore under the cute denim overalls. He tucked a hand under her knees, and lifting her easily in his arms, said goodnight to Hope, and headed upstairs to the dormitory.

CHAPTER 26

Brad opened the heavy door and crossed to one of the narrow beds, pulling back the covers and gently laying the sleeping Della on the sweet-smelling sheets. He pulled off her shoes and scratched his head, wondering if he should undress her. The bulky overalls with the clumsy looking hardware didn't look particularly comfortable for sleeping in, so he undid the metal buttons and hooks and slid them down her legs. It was only when he had them down past her thighs that he realized that she wasn't wearing any panties.

"Oh Lord," he groaned, instantly growing hard beneath the fly of his jeans. *Should have left well enough alone, but no, I had to go there,* he chastised himself. Della moaned in her sleep and turned on her side into a more comfortable sleeping position. Covering her with the soft sheets, Brad moved to the other bed, stripped down to his boxers, and slid between the cool sheets, preparing for an uncomfortable night.

***

The long day in the fresh air must have knocked him out, as Brad woke suddenly from a sound sleep. It was pitch-black, but some small noise had awoken him, and he listened, trying to identify the sound. A small sob broke the silence, and the figure in the other bed started thrashing around, muttering to an unknown assailant to "get away."

Pulling back the covers, Brad knelt on the floor next to the bed and shook Della's shoulder, softly crooning to her to wake up. "Sweetheart, wake up. You're having a bad dream," he whispered, brushing her damp hair back from her face.

Suddenly, Della's eyes opened, and she shot bolt upright in bed. "Brad, what are you doing here?" she gasped, her heart beating out of her chest. "I thought Oscar was attacking Nana." She shivered, drawing the covers close around her shoulders.

"Everything's okay," Brad said softly. "Poor old Oscar can't hurt anyone anymore," he said, rubbing her back.

"Oh right. I forgot." And she started to cry anyway.

"Shush now," he comforted. "Everything's okay." He shifted to sit on the side of the bed and pulled her against his chest, stroking her hair, undone by her tears, and not knowing what else to do.

"I seem to have this effect on you," he said, "every time we're close together with not many clothes on, at least."

"Wait, how did that even happen?" she asked groggily.

"You fell asleep. Hope assumed we'd be sleeping together. I thought you might be more comfortable if ..."

"You took off my clothes?"

"Yeah, sort of," he muttered, muffling his response in her strawberry-scented hair, which was driving him wild. He wanted to devour her.

"Thank you," she mumbled.

"Anytime," he answered reflexively, trying to ignore how sweet and soft she felt cuddled into his chest. Then he mentally kicked himself, realizing how pervy that had sounded even to himself.

Della started to giggle, and he was so relieved that she

didn't seem to think he had wanted to take advantage of her that he started to laugh, too.

"Well, you might as well get in here and finish the job," she said suggestively, reaching up and catching his earlobe between her teeth.

Her warm breath near his ear sent a spark of desire right to his cock, and he raised the sheets and slid in next to her, taking her lips with his as he tugged the ridiculous pink T-shirt over her head and filled his palms with her soft, warm breasts. Her nipples rose instantly as he teased and stroked them, and his tongue dipped into her hot mouth, showing her exactly what he was thinking of doing to her hot, wet pussy.

"Oh God, Brad. I missed you," Della said, reaching between them and taking his fully erect cock into her velvet fist. He fought for control as she stroked him, mindful of the fire building in his balls.

"Oh baby, I need to bury myself in that hot cunt of yours," he growled, sliding two thick fingers between her folds and brushing his thumb over her swollen clit. He swirled his thumb around the tiny bundle of nerves, and at the same time took one of her aching nipples into his mouth. He sucked hard, sending waves of need to her wet and ready center.

"Brad, don't make me wait any longer," she demanded, opening her thighs and thrusting her dripping pussy hard against his ramrod hard cock.

He moaned into her mouth as he grasped his cock and guided it to the entrance of her slick heat. Shuddering with pleasure, he pushed his length into her, feeling her adjust to his considerable girth.

Della could feel her toes curl as her muscles contracted, gripping him in her tight internal fist. He started to move, rocking her world as they gave and took exquisite pleasure from each other. He couldn't hold back any longer. He drew her closer, gripping her hips tightly as he pounded into her, racing toward the finish. He threw his head back, his face a mask of pure bliss, as her inner walls squeezed him, and he spilled his seed into her trembling body.

He buried his face into her neck as the tension drained from his body. He was reluctant to break his connection with her but relaxed as she cuddled him to her, stroking her fingernails gently down the length of his back.

"So good," he murmured almost incoherently, his brain fuzzily depleted of blood.

It was nearly a half hour later when Brad finally found the strength to roll off her, and she made a sound like a contented kitten. He padded into the bathroom to clean up, returning with a warm washcloth and a hand towel. He washed her gently in that most special place, and spread the towel over the wet spot they had made on the sheet. When he eased in behind her, pulling her against his chest, she nestled her sweet ass against his cock, which was once again becoming interested, and she settled in, her hand closed around his as he cupped her breast, lazily playing with her nipple.

"Go to sleep," he told his stirring cock as it twitched against her, refusing to be ignored.

She giggled, turning in his arms and slipping one silky thigh over his hip, instantly bringing his cock to full attention.

"Are you talking to me or him?" she asked, stroking a saucy finger down his length and caressing his balls.

"Woman, have mercy," he said, knowing that the sky was starting to lighten outside, and they both needed to rest.

Fuck it, he thought as her warm lips traced a line down his cheek and pressed against that sensitive spot just below his ear. Her fingers traced his jaw, and her warm, moist mouth latched onto his, promising all kinds of decadent pleasures. He accepted her invitation and pulled her up onto his chest, settling her sweet pussy just above his rock hard cock. He raised her hips and positioned her over his silken spear, burying himself once more in her tight, hot sheath. Throwing her long, dark hair back over her shoulders, she arched her back, taking him deeper as she ground against him, causing him to bite his lip in ecstasy, fighting with himself not to come. She crouched over him and started to move up and down, almost letting him slip from her body before taking him deep again, squeezing him tightly with her contracting inner muscles. His thick head rubbed against her inner wall, making her shiver with white-hot sensation. She hastened her pace, wanting to scratch that particular itch over and over until she was almost mindless with delight. Growling, he flipped her onto her back and thrust hard into her molten heat, driving the two of them to the brink of release.

Suddenly he stilled, his voice hoarse as he whispered in her ear, "Isn't that the most intense feeling in the world? Tell me how bad you want it, Della," he panted, forcing himself not to move.

"Brad, if you don't finish this, I'm gonna lose my mind," she gasped as her hips thrust up against him, imploring him to give her what she needed. He slid two fingers into her clenching pussy while teasing her clit unmercifully. Her eyes were dark pools of want, and her fingers plucked distractedly at her nipples, her whole body vibrating with need.

With a mighty thrust, he dived into her body, his finger still circling her clit as she shattered around him. On and on he pumped as her body milked him dry until he finally collapsed on her chest, spent.

CHAPTER 27

"Della, there's a call for you on the kitchen phone," June, the housekeeper said, knocking on the bedroom door. "Some guy named Phil Brennan. Says he's from Today Magazine."

Della opened her eyes, pushed her hair out of her face, and looked around at the unfamiliar furnishings. "Oh yeah, we're at the wildlife refuge," she acknowledged, and then suddenly realized she was alone in the room. Brad's bed was neatly made up, and her freshly laundered jeans and panties were laid on the dresser.

"Della, are you awake?" June's voice called out a little louder.

"Oh yeah, yeah. Please tell him I'll call him back in a few minutes, June. I was just getting in the shower."

"Okay. You have his number, right?"

"What? Oh yeah. Make it ten minutes, okay?" She was already in the bathroom with the water running. She glanced at her wristwatch. Ten o'clock! Mortified, she hopped in under the warm spray and grabbed a bottle of cucumber-scented bodywash.

***

A little under eight minutes later, she arrived in the kitchen, fully dressed, with her damp hair curling in a riot down her back. She spotted her cell phone on the kitchen table and, nodding her thanks to June, who was making fresh scones, walked out onto the shady veranda, dialing Phil's number.

"Well, hello, sleeping beauty," a brash voice answered. "I thought one was supposed to get up with the birds when one was out on the farm."

"You're a funny guy, Phil," she replied. "I wasn't expecting to hear from you this soon."

"Well, you're in luck. It's a slow news day," Phil retorted. "Truth is, when I read your notes and watched the video, I really got into the story, and I bumped it in front of a bunch of other stuff. The finished spot is really great. I wanted to see what you thought."

"Phil, you're a treasure. Hold on. I'm opening the file."

Once she'd finished reviewing the ten-minute file, Della was ecstatic. The piece was produced just the way she had wanted it—informative, empathetic, and with a touch of heartbreak, but finishing up with hope and a call for support. She got back to Phil and spent another ten minutes singing his praises. Promising him a steak dinner when she got back to work, she went to find June to see if she knew where Hope was.

She caught up with Hope, who, with Brad's assistance, was mending fences up near the coyote enclosure.

"Hi there, city slicker," Hope teased. "I see the morning got away from you."

"Yeah, you shouldn't have let me sleep in," she admonished Brad, who was busily brandishing a hammer and trying to look handy. He was admiring the shiny curls cascading down her back and her tight butt in the sinfully skin-hugging denim.

"You looked too comfortable to disturb," he replied, a twinkle in his eye.

"I have something I want to show you," Della said, waving her cell phone.

"Oh no, not more 'Lol Cats' videos," Brad protested. "I can't handle that much cuteness this close to lunchtime."

"No, this is even better. It's a Hope for Life television promo."

"What?" Hope said disbelievingly. "When did you manage to shoot that? Did I miss something? I didn't see any camera crew around."

"Actually, you shot most of it yourself. I just strung it together with my magic thread."

"Huh?" both Brad and Hope looked at her like she had lost her mind.

"C'mon back to the farmhouse. I'll put it on the big TV for you."

***

By the time Della got the appropriate devices hooked up to Hope's smart TV and everything was ready to roll, she had attracted quite an audience. All of the field workers and animal keepers were in for lunch, and June had made platters of sandwiches and poured pitchers of lemonade, which they all enjoyed while Della was preparing the presentation.

"Okay, here we go," she said as she pressed play.

The screen opened with Della, who introduced herself and gave a brief overview of the Hope for Life Wildlife Refuge, their mission, and their objectives. Della had done a great job with the videography, even with the simple equipment she'd had to use. There was footage of the sign at the main building and wide shots of the buildings and structures. Della had recruited a couple of the student guides to show some of the animals and explain the educational programs they ran. Della had interwoven pieces of footage already shot on the camera to paint a cohesive, interesting picture of what the refuge was all about.

Her audience was spellbound, and Hope watched, her mouth agape, as Della, using some of Phil's editing magic, introduced Oscar and told his story. She had incorporated the footage of Hope working with him in the flight enclosure and that of both her and Dr. Christofer examining his wings, showing how he was depressed because he couldn't hunt. There was a file interview with a little ginger-haired boy who had been visiting the refuge on a school trip. After he'd met Oscar, the little boy told how his brothers had been shooting at birds on their family's farm, and his big blue eyes were filled with righteous anger as he related his story.

"I couldn't believe Tom and Jed could be so mean. I mean, the birds weren't doing nothin' wrong. They were just catchin' field mice out in the crop fields. It was like they were killing them for fun, for sport. Well, I went straight to my dad, and he took their guns away and made them work extra time in the fields and donate the money to Miss Hope's refuge. Poor birds like Oscar here have been injured so bad they can't even hunt any more. It's just wrong."

By this time, Hope was sitting there with tears streaming down her cheeks. The screen opened once again on Della, sitting on the porch swing.

"Today, we had to say good-bye to Oscar. He has been an inspiration to so many children and adults who have visited Hope for Life and to those who have been fortunate to take part in one of their many fine educational programs. The damage done to his wings from his injuries had caused arthritis to set in, and he was in chronic pain every day.

"I'd like you to meet my Nana," Della continued in the video. "She has the same problem in her wrists as Oscar had. Here is what she would like to say."

The screen opened on Nana, sitting in front of her computer screen at home. Her poor arthritic wrist and her gnarled old hands were folded in front of her as she spoke. "Nobody knows how helpless and useless you feel when you live every day in pain. For a proud bird like Oscar, ending his suffering is such a gift to give him, letting his spirit soar, free of his damaged body. He will live on in all of you because he has touched your hearts and helped you to understand how important it is to respect and protect all of our wild creatures. Whenever we see animals being mistreated, we should step in. We can call people like Hope to give them a second chance at life. And when we can end their suffering, we should. Thank you, Oscar, and Godspeed."

The screen returned to Della on the porch swing. The camera zoomed in to frame her beautiful face. She said, "There is a way you can help. Hope for Life is registered in the Azarro Community Funding Project. Just by going online and voting, you can assist Hope and her team in helping even more animals. It won't cost you a cent. Just go online and vote for the Hope for Life Wildlife Refuge."

The screen zoomed in on Della's cell phone, displaying the web address for the Azarro Community Fund. And then it went to a wide shot of a flying bald eagle and a caption at the bottom of the screen that read, "In memory of our friend and teacher, Oscar, October 9, 2012." Then the video faded to black.

You could have heard a pin drop in the room, except for the occasional sniffle.

"Well. What do you think?" Della asked anxiously, looking at Hope.

"Oh, Della!" Hope smiled radiantly through her tears. "What a beautiful job. How did you ever put that together in such a short time? It's absolutely perfect."

The other team members added their congratulations, and everybody thought it would do wonders to raise awareness about the refuge and help them raise the funds they needed.

Brad, ever the practical one, said, "When is it going to air?"

"My editor is working on getting me a spot on a national news magazine show to air tomorrow night."

With that, Della's phone rang. "Hello, Phil?" she said, after reading the call display.

"Yeah, Della. Got that spot confirmed for tomorrow night on The Daily Happening airing at 7:00 p.m. central."

"Phil, you're my hero." Looking to Hope, she asked, "Do we have your approval?"

Hope nodded, tearing up again and grinning like a Cheshire cat.

"Don't forget to get a release from that little kid's parents and also the vet, your Nana, and the animal handlers," Phil cautioned.

"Already taken care of." Della smiled, signing off.

***

It was midafternoon and time for Della and Brad to head back to New York. Hope walked them over to the meadow, where the helicopter sat waiting and turned to Della, taking her hands in hers.

"Della, I can't remember when I've met somebody who, after only one day, it feels like I've known my whole life. I can't thank you enough for what you've done for me ... for us ... for the shelter," she said, throwing her arms around her and giving her a giant hug.

"It's been my pleasure." Della smiled. "I can't think of a more deserving story. I wish we could stay to be part of the memorial service for Oscar. But here's the tribute I wrote for him," she said, handing Hope a sheet of paper. "Maybe you'd like to have someone read it."

"Thank you," Hope said once again, wiping her eyes. "I have your phone number and e-mail address. I'll let you know how things go after the show airs."

"Yes, absolutely," Della said. "And you haven't seen the last of me yet."

"I should hope not," Hope said, rounding on Brad and getting up in his grill. "You make sure you treasure this girl," she said seriously. "And bring her back to visit often. Our house is open to you both, anytime."

"Thanks, Hope," Brad said, kissing her on the cheek and taking Della's hand. "She's pretty special."

"Oh, please, you're making me blush," Della grinned, opening the cockpit door and tossing her satchel inside. "See ya later, chickie," she said, jumping into the passenger seat and waving.

CHAPTER 28

Della and Brad had an uneventful trip home. It was hard to talk inside the helicopter with the noise of the rotors overhead and the radio intruding with the voice exchanges of the control towers, so conversation was held to a minimum. Every so often, Brad would point out landmarks and points of interest, but for the most part, they traveled in companionable silence. Della felt herself almost dozing off at times, having not gotten much sleep the night before. She hoped that Brad was faring better at the controls.

It wasn't long before they crossed the border back into the States and were headed back toward New York City. Brad popped the top on an energy drink, and she was sure she saw a twinkle in his eye as he glanced over at her nodding in her seat.

"Lots more air traffic in this neck of the woods," he commented. "Need your wits about you to land on the roof."

Della hadn't considered the skill it required to fly in among the tall buildings, with the updrafts from the heat emanating from the asphalt jungle below plus the hazards of other aircraft and everything else that might zip across your path. You certainly had to have good concentration to do what he was doing, especially after only a couple of hours sleep.

Della was glad when they finally put down on the big

circle marked with an H on top of the Jamieson Building.
The same overall-clad guy opened the cockpit door when
the rotors stopped turning and offered Della a hand down.
"Welcome home, Mr. Jamieson, Miss Rawlins. Hope you had
a nice flight?"

"Thanks, Robert. The bird's working fine. You'll see to
putting her away for the night?"

"Yes, sir," the young man replied.

Brad took Della's hand, and they made their way over to
where the elevator waited to take them downstairs.

"I'm just going to check the office to see if there was any
mail before I see you to your car," Brad said, taking out a set
of keys.

They walked through the reception area to Brad's office,
and Della took a seat in a comfortable wingback chair. Brad
rifled through a stack of envelopes on his desk, setting aside a
couple of priority pieces, which he would deal with first thing
in the morning. He noticed a squarish box with air mail stickers
all over it, wrapped in brown paper and tied up securely in
packing tape. The postmark was from Algiers, and there was
no return address.

"Strange ... This is the second mystery package I've
received this week, the first one being your lovely picture of
the caribou."

"Well, what are you waiting for?" Della asked excitedly,
moving to stand near the desk.

"Well, the postmark is from Algiers. Ryan sent me a message
to let me know he was sending me a souvenir. I guess that's
what it is. Doesn't look like his handwriting, though."

Brad pulled the wrappings off the box and then opened
the top and reached inside, pulling out a battered, old Nikon
camera with a faded, yet colorful embroidered camera strap.
He turned it over in his hands, looked through the viewfinder,

and turned on the digital display before Della really got a good look at what he was holding.

"What are you doing with my old Nikon?" Della suddenly exclaimed, coming up behind Brad and making him jump.

"How can that be your Nikon?" Brad asked with raised eyebrows. "It just got here from Algiers."

Della turned the camera over. There, scratched into the paint on the bottom of the camera body, were the initials DR. "See, Della Rawlins," she said triumphantly.

"How the devil did it come in the mail from the Algiers?" Brad wondered aloud, turning the camera over and checking the compartment that held the digital video card, finding it empty. "Looks like there are no pictures on it to give us a clue." The camera's display showed blank.

"The last time I saw this camera was in May 2011 in Abbottabad. This is the camera I loaned to Aaron the night the Navy SEALs extracted Obama bin Laden from Pakistan. Aaron was on the street when the helicopters raided the compound. I was on top of a building across the street. I didn't see what happened to it when he was taken prisoner. If this is the souvenir that Ryan said he was sending you, how did he get his hands on it? -And why did he send it to you? How did it get from Pakistan to the Algiers? And who has the video card?"

"All excellent questions," Brad said. "Ryan must think it's of some importance if he sent it to me like this with no letter or explanation. I think we should keep it under protection until we can get some answers. What do you think? I certainly don't want to keep it from you, but if Ryan took all these precautions, there must be more to it than meets the eye. He knows only that we've met and are friends. But why didn't he send it to your magazine or to your editor?"

"Seems like he wanted to send it to someone he could trust, and someone with little connection to me," Della reasoned.

"Yeah, but close enough to be sure it got back to you if necessary. Yeah, it's shady as hell. I think we should probably put it in the office safe until I can get hold of him," Brad said thoughtfully. "You never know what danger this might bring to your door."

"Have you tried to call him lately?" Della asked.

"Yeah, his office says he is out of the country with no known date of return."

"Is he in touch with his office, though? Has anyone heard from him?" Della asked with concern.

"He always tries to get in touch with the folks on Sundays. I'll check to see if they've heard from him," Brad said, punching a number into his cell phone. "Hi, Mom, how are you doing? ... No, it's Brad. Oh, you were expecting Ryan, huh? ... No, I haven't heard from him, either. Not in a couple of weeks. I guess he's busy ... The stores are doing fine ... Yeah, I'm keeping busy. Tell Dad I need to run some stuff by him. Tell him to drive into the city one day this week, or I can send the car. And let me know when you're coming. Oh, and Mom? If Ryan calls, tell him to call me right away, okay? ... Yeah, love you, too. See you soon."

Brad disconnected the call and turned to Della. "Nope," he said, "They haven't heard from him. Usually he tells someone when he thinks he'll be away for awhile, unless it's an emergency."

"This is starting to worry me," Della said. "I don't suppose he would have left a message on my home voice mail. He knows it's my camera. He gave it to me when his office was decommissioning some equipment a few years back. Said it would make a great backup camera if I was working in 'hot' zones."

"Can you access your voice mail remotely?"

"Sure, give me a sec." Della dialed into her landline and

grabbed a pen and paper out of her satchel. A series of messages played, mostly work-related stuff.

Close to the end of the recording, Ryan's voice came on the line. "Hi, Del!" he said, sounding overly friendly, as if he were drunk or something. "How's my girl? I've been out of town for a few days. Just got back, actually. A friend of yours asked me to put you back in touch with him. Call me when you get home, and we'll do lunch, okay? My cell phone died, so leave a message on my landline voice mail so I'll know when you get this. Be careful out there, babe. Get the picture?"

"What a weird message. That's so unlike him," Della said, replaying the voice mail.

"Yeah, but I'm even more worried after hearing that. He doesn't want to talk to you on his cell phone, and he's warning you to be careful, like there may be some reason you might be in danger."

"And you know it has something to do with the camera from that last part, "get the picture."

"Yeah. That camera is definitely going in the safe until we get some answers," Brad said, grabbing the offending article, unlocking and sliding open a door in his credenza, and spinning the combination lock on a bolted-in safe. "Maybe you should stay with me until we find out what's going on," Brad suggested.

"That seems a little extreme," Della said, shrugging off the uneasy feeling that had been growing in her since she'd heard Ryan's message. "I'm a big girl. I can take care of myself."

"Yes, Miss Independent," Brad said, rolling his eyes. "Well, I'm following you home in my car, and I'm checking out your apartment before I'll be satisfied to let you stay there alone."

"Okay, fine," Della said, holding her hands up in a calming gesture. "I'm not hiring any bodyguard yet."

CHAPTER 29

Brad turned off the lights and locked the office, and then he and Della took the elevator to the parking garage.

"Where's your car parked?" Brad asked.

"On a side street just around the corner," Della replied, pointing in the direction she had come from yesterday, though it seemed much longer.

"On Van Neisse," Brad calculated. "Okay, we'll take my rig over and pick yours up. Then I'll follow you to your apartment."

"Do you really think that's necessary?" Della asked, feeling he was being overly cautious, even for him.

"I didn't like the tone of that message," Brad said. "Ryan wouldn't have warned you to be careful unless there was something to be careful about. I don't think we should take any chances until we understand what all this is about."

Brad used his remote to open the doors of the Jamieson's branded Hummer, parked in its designated slot. Della slid into the passenger seat, which seemed miles away from the driver's seat. She noticed Brad, down on his hands and knees, peering under the truck with a small, bright flashlight. He went around the back and did the same with the other side. And then he reached inside and popped the release for the hood. He spent some time inspecting the contents of the engine compartment before he was satisfied that everything was in order.

"Brad, you really think this is serious, don't you?" Della asked quietly.

"From what you and Ryan have been involved with recently, it could be," Brad said, trying not to alarm her too much.

"But I wasn't identified in Abbottabad."

"But you don't know who might have seen you, and your picture might be on the Internet, linked with Aaron. Somebody might have put two and two together."

"But I don't have any information that anyone could use. If they knew I was in Abbottabad when Osama bin Laden was killed, it was already too late to stop the mission. What could they possibly want from me?"

"Except revenge?" Brad asked, one eyebrow raised. "You realize we're not dealing with rational people, right?"

Della nodded, twisting the handle of her satchel in her hands. "Well, at least it's not common knowledge that we are acquainted. Hopefully no one will make that connection, so you won't be in danger, too."

"We're not going to assume too much until we get more information from Ryan. Until then, we'll behave as usual but take no chances, okay? That means don't get caught alone, don't open your doors to strangers, and watch out for unusual people. I'm going to use my contacts to get some security to watch your apartment for now. I think it's a good idea that we not make it obvious we're connected, especially if it involves the camera, which it seems likely it does. Be careful what you say on the phone or text message or even in general conversation in your apartment."

"You think there may be bugs?" Della asked, wide-eyed.

"Again, we can't be too careful. I know the kind of things

that Ryan can be involved in. It's better to be safe. Does your apartment have in-house parking?"

"Yeah, it's underground. There's a security guard."

"Great."

By this time, Brad had, with Della's direction, found her little Ford Focus parked where she had left it. He got out and scoured the underside and under the hood with his flashlight. When he was satisfied it was free of explosive devices, he let Della get in and start it up.

"You know, instead of following you with the Hummer, I think I'll ride with you and just stay out of sight," Brad said.

"My football hoodie is on the backseat."

"Don't think it will fit," Brad said, holding it up in front of his broad chest. "But I can use this," he said, putting on her Patriot's ball cap, which had a nice, long sunshade.

Della waited while Brad parked the Hummer in her vacated parking space, and then with him slouched under a blanket in the backseat, they headed toward her apartment building across town.

On the way through the city, Brad had Della check every so often to make sure that nobody was tailing her car. They both relaxed a little when it appeared they weren't being followed. They approached her building, and Brad tried to make himself as small as possible under the blanket on the backseat of the compact car. Della swiped her tenant ID, smiled a good night to the security guard, and drove to her designated parking slot.

"Is the coast clear?" Brad asked Della.

"Yeah, all clear," she said.

"Okay, you get out and go to the elevator. Hold the door open. I'll be right behind you. What floor are you on, in case we get separated?"

"Seventh floor, apartment 714."

"Okay. Don't open the door until I get there, okay?"

"Okay."

Della waited in the elevator, her hand on the "open door" button, hoping that nobody was going to want to get in the car before Brad got there. Just as she was starting to get nervous, he slunk into the elevator, keeping his back to the security camera mounted to the ceiling. He punched the button to the sixth floor and, without saying a word to Della, left as soon as the door slid open at the sixth floor.

When the car arrived at the seventh floor, Brad was already there, and he'd started down the hall ahead of her. He paused when he came to the door to apartment 714.

"Wait—don't open the door," Brad cautioned, grabbing her sleeve as she reached out with her keys to open the lock.

"No, I know it's okay. Calm down," Della said.

"What are you, psychic?" Brad asked, eyebrows raised.

"No, just a little trick Aaron showed me so that we knew if anyone had been in our room when we were on assignment," Della said, reaching up and showing him a wooden toothpick that had been jammed between the top of the door and the doorjamb. "Sometimes we would stick a piece of invisible tape across the seam of the door. We always thought it better to do both—that way, if they found one, they most likely wouldn't look for anything else." She squatted down and peeled a piece of tape from the bottom of the door, holding it up triumphantly in front of Brad's nose.

"Why would you do that here?" Brad asked, puzzled.

"Hey, this is New York City. Haven't you heard about break-ins at apartment buildings? Wouldn't want to walk in on one of those creeps!" she said, shuddering as she remembered the man who had grabbed her outside the apartment in Abbottabad.

Della unlocked her apartment door, picking up the

toothpick that had fallen out of the doorjamb, and was relieved to find everything just the way she had left it.

"Tomorrow, we get an alarm installed," Brad said firmly.

The security buzzer sounded, startling both of them. The night doorman was on the phone.

"Miss Rawlins, there's a Ken Milman here to see you. He says he's from Securashield. He showed me ID. Do you want me to send him up? Oh, and by the way, there's a package here for you."

Della covered the mouthpiece and mouthed the word Securashield to Brad, who nodded.

"It's okay, Mark. You can send him up. But I want to speak to him first."

"Looks like you're not the only one getting a mystery package," she said to Brad, holding her hand over the mouthpiece of the phone.

"What? Give me the phone!"

When the CIA security specialist came on the line, Brad asked him to examine the package and to tell him what the return address was.

"It's from Major Ryan Jamieson, Riverview, New York."

"Okay, it's probably okay. Just take it outside and check it over. Call your superior and tell them we need your explosives unit over here to open it."

Della looked at him wearily. "This is gonna be a very tedious few days."

"Yeah," Brad said, putting his arms around her and drawing her close. "Maybe Ryan has a message for you, and we can see if it's necessary to take all of these precautions."

An hour went by before a knock came on Della's door. A uniformed security guard stood outside, showing his ID and holding a package and briefcase. Brad answered the door, checked the agent's ID, and listened as he gave his report from the CIA's explosives unit about the status of the package. It had been declared safe.

"Okay, you brought your kit, right?" Brad asked the agent, who nodded, and began doing an electronic sweep of the apartment. "Just to be sure," Brad said to Della.

Brad picked up the box on the coffee table and opened the cover. He pulled out an inexpensive cell phone. The enclosed sales slip indicated it was a prepaid phone, paid for by Ryan Jamieson the day before.

"Smart." Brad nodded. "Impossible to intercept or trace. It's the ideal way to talk without anyone being able to tap into the call," he said as the agent gave the thumbs-up sign.

"Great, now all I have to do is wait for him to call," Della said, looking exhausted.

"Yeah," Brad said, leading her out to the kitchen where he could speak to her alone. "Ken is going to stay here in the apartment tonight. Tomorrow, Securashield will put in the alarm system. I'd love to stay here with you, but I don't want to take a chance on someone making the connection between us until we hear from Ryan. Can you work from home?"

Della nodded.

"Okay," Brad said, taking her hand. "Just stay in until we hear from Ryan. We know you're safe here." He took her in his arms and brushed a kiss over her hair. "I can't stand the thought of you being in danger."

Della lifted her face to his, and he took her lips gently, feeling the tension in her body as he wrapped his arms around her, enveloping her in his warmth. As he deepened the kiss, she wished that he could stay with her in her bed, tangled with her in the sheets like they had been last night back at the refuge. It seemed like that was a month ago. It seemed like every time they got close to each other, something happened to pull the rug out from under them.

When he left—a short time later—she felt that familiar feeling of abandonment, even though she knew he wanted to be with her. She could feel it in his hungry kiss and in the hard pressure of his cock, snug against her belly. She could still feel his lips on hers as she gathered her bathrobe and pajamas and headed to the bathroom to take a long, hot bath. At least it was some relief knowing that Ken was there protecting her, and she could let down her guard for a few hours and rest.

Brad left the apartment, pausing until he heard Ken slip the deadbolt he had ordered installed. Keeping the baseball cap low over his face, he rode the elevator to the ground floor and exited the building by way of a side door, jogging several blocks before calling a cab.

She was safe, for now.

CHAPTER 30

It was Monday afternoon. Ryan punched in the code for his voice mail and played back his messages. There were two from his mother and three from Brad, the latter becoming more adamant about calling him back as soon as possible. Not knowing what he would say on the phone, Ryan felt it was safer to wait until he and Brad could meet somewhere secure, face-to-face, before he filled him in on what was going on.

He was more concerned about Della, but he knew that he had laced his message with enough information that Brad would know to put precautions in place for her. He figured that it should be safe now to call her on the prepaid cell phone. He pulled an identical model out of his jeans pocket and dialed the number he had scribbled on a scrap of paper. The phone rang twice before Della picked up and breathlessly said, "Hello?"

"Hi, Del, it's me," Ryan said. "Are you alone?"

"No, Brad has a security guard hired to stay with me."

"Great, I knew I could count on him," Ryan said, blowing out a breath of relief and running his fingers through his hair. "Did they sweep your apartment for bugs?"

"Yeah. Ryan, what's this all about?"

"I don't want to discuss it over the phone. Can we meet

somewhere, just the three of us? Somewhere where it wouldn't be odd that we might run into each other."

"How about my dad's offices? We all have him in common."

"Great idea. He should have some secure space available. See if you can book it for about eleven o'clock tomorrow morning. Call me on my new cell if you can get it set up. I'll call Brad."

"Okay, better give me your new number," Della said, ready to jot it down.

After ending her call with Ryan, Della immediately dialed her father's number. She explained, without giving him too much information, that she, Ryan, and Brad needed a secure place to meet.

"What have you gotten yourself mixed up in now?" her father groaned, thinking that, ever since Della had been old enough to play with boys, he hadn't had a moment's peace.

"I won't even know myself until tomorrow," she retorted.

Thankfully, he acceded to her request and got his long-suffering secretary busy clearing his late-morning schedule.

***

The next day, at 11:00 a.m. exactly, Della arrived at her father's office. He greeted her with a giant bear hug, and anyone watching would assume they were meeting for lunch. He ushered her into a briefing office.

Brad had arrived a half hour earlier, and he and Senator Rawlins had spent some time discussing several conservation issues he had on the table. He had taken notes in his tablet and set up action reminders in his calendar while the senator went to greet his daughter. Might as well put the time to good use.

Della stepped into the office. She was stunning in a tailored navy suit, lace camisole, and pumps. Her hair was pulled back into a tidy bun at the nape of her neck, and her makeup was flawless. Fleetingly, Brad wondered what she was wearing under her conservative outfit. He remembered that, when they had taken shelter from the bear under the Hummer, he had found her braless. He thought to himself that he'd really like to muss her up. He rose to his feet, buttoning his suit jacket, formally acknowledging her and hoping that no one would notice the bulge in his pants.

"Hello, Della," Brad said, taking her hands. "How are you?"

"I'm really tired of all this cloak-and-dagger stuff," she said. "Dad said that Ryan's not here yet?"

"No, not yet." Brad glanced at his watch. It was now quarter past eleven. All of their time was valuable, especially the senator's, who was on a tight timetable. He hoped that Ryan would hurry up.

Just then, Senator Rawlins ushered into the office a man who, at first glance, seemed to be of Middle Eastern descent.

Looking more closely, Della said, "Oh my God. Ryan, is that you?"

Ryan had been preparing to go back into the field. He'd had hair extensions put in, his hair dyed almost black, and a henna spray tan had stained his skin a dark mahogany. He was wearing eyeliner and dark brown contacts and could easily have passed for an Algerian national. He looked, if possible, even more handsome than usual.

"Like my new look?" He grinned, his white teeth gleaming in contrast to his brown face.

"Yeah, you're gorgeous," Brad said, annoyed, having noted the look of admiration that had passed over Della's face. "Now would you mind telling us what this is all about?"

"Absolutely." he said. Turning to Della, he continued. "Remember the night that bin Laden was killed in Abbottabad? You were positioned on the roof of a building across the street from the compound with a camera, and Aaron was positioned down on the street, almost in front of the entrance of the compound, also with a camera."

"That's right," Della said. "Aaron had my backup camera, my old Nikon. It was the same camera you'd given me years ago. You said the department was decommissioning some old equipment, and I could have it. You said it would be great if we were working in 'hot spots.'"

"That's right," Ryan said. "Brad, did you bring the camera?"

Brad removed it from his briefcase and laid it on the table.

"Della, is this your camera?" Ryan asked.

"Yes, you can see I scratched my initials in the paint on the bottom. I also registered the serial number with customs before I left the States and when I entered Afghanistan," Della said. "I loaned it to Aaron the night bin Laden was killed. I haven't seen it since—until it ended up in Brad's mail."

"Right," Ryan said. "I'm sure you saw that the digital storage card was missing from the camera." He opened the compartment and showed that the card was missing. "Most likely, it was removed by Aaron's captors. And when they were finished with it, the camera was probably discarded or stolen by one the guards."

"But how did it get from Pakistan to the Algiers?" Brad asked, puzzled.

"After the raid on the compound in Abbottabad and the capture and killing of bin Laden, many of the al-Qaeda fled to the Algiers and were incorporated into terrorist cells operating there. We've seen many familiar faces showing up in our current surveillance operations there. The camera probably was taken there and fenced in one of the marketplaces, which is where I found it.

"The thing is, these cameras had been used by our CIA operatives and were retrofitted with large capacity internal memory cards, accessible only with a USB cable that connects through a hidden port on back of the lens. Every photo that was shot was duplicated onto the removable storage card."

"Really?" Della said. "I had no clue."

"We never made our operatives aware of it," Ryan said, "in case they would divulge the information under interrogation. There was always a chance we could recover the equipment."

"So can we find out what's on the memory card?" Brad asked.

"Yes," Ryan said, producing a USB cable and an electronic tablet from his inside pocket. Removing the lens from the camera, Ryan plugged the cable into the hidden port and into the tablet. He fiddled with the tablet, and suddenly a series of photo frames popped up on the screen. There were pictures of Della and of Della and Aaron's adventures from the time they entered Afghanistan. There were photos of them interacting with the soldiers on the US base. There was even one of Della standing on the skid of a Blackhawk helicopter, dressed in fatigues and holding an M4 assault rifle.

"Oh my God. There's no doubt that whoever has the memory card knows all about Della," Brad said, sickened by the thought.

"Oh wait, it gets better," Ryan said, forwarding through the photos. The last dozen photos were fairly dark. They showed the helicopters descending on the compound in Abbottabad. There was one of the first helicopter nose-diving into the courtyard and then others showing the troops rappelling down and scaling the wall into the compound. Several frames showed the soldiers breaching the doors. And then suddenly the venue changed to another rooftop, where a group of figures were gathered. One taller figure, bearded and turbaned, stood out from the rest, silhouetted against the sky. He looked very familiar. The next frame zoomed in on the face. It was the Sheik, Osama bin Laden!

"But how can that be?" Della exclaimed. "That was almost the same moment the SEALs shot him inside the compound. Look at the time print! How could he be in two places at the one time?"

"Easy," Ryan said. "He was using a body double. Many Saudi oil barons and their family members do that to avoid assassination."

"So the man they shot inside the compound ..." Della said.

"Wasn't bin Laden." Ryan sighed.

"But they must have cross-matched his DNA when they got him aboard the Navy ship?" Brad questioned.

"Why do you think he was buried at sea so fast? No one had any proof that it wasn't him, until now," Ryan countered.

"So the administration is going with the story that we killed bin Laden, even knowing it's not true? But why would bin Laden not come forward and refute the story? Why would he let his people think that the West had conquered him?"

"Just think about it. Here was the perfect opportunity to end the hunt for him. He could go back into hiding and spend his time figuring out how to pull off the next 9/11. Then when it happens, he'll be resurrected. His people will think he's God, and they'll declare jihad on the rest of the world."

"So how does all of this affect Della?"

"Well, they know she was there. They don't know what she saw or what she shot. They think they have all of the evidence because they have the digital card, but they can't be sure. I had the contents of the memory card encrypted and sent electronically to the home office before I knew what was on it, before I left the Algiers. I'm just praying that our security there has not been breached. If so, they're going to want to contain the threat."

"You mean they'd want to see Della dead?" Brad growled, rising to his feet, hands on his hips. "I hope you're going to tell me that there's still time to get her into some sort of witness protection program." His eyes were trained on his brother like a .44 magnum, locked and loaded.

"Well, that's where things get a little tetchy," Ryan said, scratching his head. "You see, the administration has just as much to lose by this getting out. They would also want to contain the threat," he said. "Don't forget that the president is looking down the barrel of an election, and getting bin Laden is probably seen as his greatest accomplishment to date."

"So what exactly did you mean by 'contain the threat'?" Brad asked, a vein visibly pulsing at his temple.

"They'd lock Della away, somewhere like Guantanamo Bay, maybe a little better facility."

"Over my dead body!" Senator Rawlins, who had been silent until now, jumped to his feet. "I have spent my life serving this country. No child of mine is going to be sacrificed so that this administration can pretend they got that Saudi bastard!" he blustered, seething.

"Okay, this is what's going to happen," Brad said, having heard enough. "I'm taking Della out of here. We're going back to the cabin in eastern Canada. Nobody has linked us, and I can protect her there until things settle down."

"Just a minute!" Della said, her arms folded across her chest. Her father took one look at her, closed his eyes with a sigh and thought, *Oh boy, here it comes.*

"Nobody has asked me what I want to do," Della said, eyes flashing. "This is quite possibly the story of the century, and you just want me to run away and hide? Why can't I just break the story? What use would I be to any of them if it was all out in the open?"

"Della, you know I can't condone that," Ryan said, raising his hands helplessly.

"As much as I love you, Della, I can't go against the oath of office I took to uphold the integrity of the office, whatever that is," Senator Rawlins admitted somewhat brokenly.

"I'll support you in whatever decision you make," said Brad. "But I think we should let the professionals take their best shot at correcting this situation. I imagine the hunt is back on for bin Laden and it's of the highest priority?" Brad asked, looking at Ryan.

"Every high-level resource we have is being concentrated on this effort," Ryan said. "A very elite, dedicated force is ready to strike the minute we have confirmation of where he's hiding. There's no doubt we'll find him, and when we take him this time, there will be no fanfare, no mention in the press. It will all go away, just like JFK."

Della reflected upon how long it had taken the CIA to discover where bin Laden was hiding the last time. She didn't know if she had the stamina to hold out that long as a fugitive. She knew that Brad wasn't going to be able to protect her indefinitely, and she didn't want to put him in danger. But for now, it seemed to be her only option. Until they could figure out some other solution, she would have to hope and pray that Ryan could deliver on his promises.

"Dad, will you take care of Jack?" Della asked, tears spilling down her face.

"Of course, darling," the senator said, holding his daughter close.

"Make it look like you're leaving on a buying trip," Ryan advised Brad. "Dad can look after the stores till you get back. Don't go back to your apartment, Della. Brad will pick you up something to wear from the store."

A plan was quickly put in place, and Della stayed with her father while Brad left to make preparations for their departure.

Ryan came back into the office and sat down next to her on the beautifully upholstered settee. He took her hand in his and looked her deeply in the eyes. "Della, I'm so sorry that you're caught in the middle of this."

"All I can see when I close my eyes is Aaron waving his hands in the air and shouting, 'Osama bin Laden.' I guess he was trying to get the SEALs' attention to tell them about the other bin Laden."

"Yeah. I keep thinking about the young SEAL who thought he'd had the honor of taking him out," Ryan said, rubbing a hand over his tired eyes. "He was so proud that it was him."

"It's like a nightmare you can't wake up from." Della shook her head. "Look at all of the people I've put in danger—you, Brad, Dad, Hope, even my editor at Today. Everyone who knows me might be a target."

"Hopefully they don't know we have the photos," Ryan said, squeezing her hand. "If they think there's no proof, they won't be so interested in finding you." He squeezed her fingers between his and said, "Della, on my life, I promise you we will get him. I give you my word I'll get him for you and for Aaron."

They clung together as tears rolled down their cheeks, mourning their friend and Della's loss of liberty. It was a sad day to be an American.

CHAPTER 31

Ryan shifted in his seat in the cramped cabin of the commercial jetliner flying into Kabul International Airport. His was an indistinguishable face among the rows of seated passengers, and that's just the way he wanted it. In his pocket, he carried a passport issued to Hamid Zaher by the government of Afghanistan. It would allow him admittance into Algeria as well, without his having to provide a work visa. Fluent in Arabic and Persian with a smattering of Pashto and French, Ryan could move easily among the people of Afghanistan and Algeria without attracting attention.

As the plane touched down on the landing strip and the reverse thrust of the engines slowed it to a sedate taxi, Ryan grabbed his battered duffel bag and stood to join the rest of the weary queue waiting to deplane. He had a two-hour wait before boarding a Turkish Airways flight to his final destination, the city of Algiers, where his team awaited his return.

***

While Ryan was flying into hostile territory, Della and Brad were making tracks out. Brad had wasted no time preparing for a quick departure. He had made a couple of stops to load up the Hummer with provisions, clothing, and equipment to see him and Della through a two-week hiatus. That would at least give them some space to see what fallout there might be from Della's debut on national TV and whether it would spark a reaction from any of the American terrorist cells that may be affiliated with the al-Qaeda in Abbottabad or Afghanistan.

Having called Ken to check on Della's apartment and finding everything there secure, Brad had had Ken collect items from a list of essentials Della had made, as well as Jack and his portable pet carrier, food, and supplies. He had Della call her assistant, Madeline, and arrange for her to bring Jack and his baggage to her place until Brad could arrange for the terrier's pickup by the senator. He could take no chances that her place wasn't being watched. It was about five o'clock before he was ready to pick Della up, and he called her on the disposable cell phone and asked her to meet him at a busy shopping area a few blocks from the building where her father's offices were located.

"Ask your father to put you in an unmarked car with his own driver. And stay as close to the entrance of the drugstore as you can until I get there. I'll be driving the Hummer," were the only instructions he gave her.

"Is Dad picking Jack up at Madeline's?" Della asked worriedly.

"Don't worry about Jack. He's been looked after," Brad said firmly, brooking no further arguments.

Half an hour later, Della waited in her father's car, right in front of the drugstore as she had been instructed. She kept a nervous lookout for the not-inconspicuous, camouflage-painted Hummer, while the senator's driver, on her instructions, had run into the drugstore to pick her up some kind of hat and shirt she could use to change her appearance. She quickly changed into the newly acquired apparel, hoping no one would pay attention to her in her pencil skirt and pumps, sporting a New York Giants hat and jacket. She didn't have time to dwell on the strangeness of her attire before the large rig pulled up adjacent to the car, and she was motioned to get in. She slid across to the driver's side, rear passenger door and hopped out, scooting quickly up and into the Hummer.

The first thing she noticed, besides the driver—who took one look at the Giants fan wear and said, "Traitor," with a smug look and a twinkle in his eye—was the pet carrier sitting between them on the front seat.

"He looked so sad when you didn't show up to pick him up at Madeline's. I didn't have the heart to send him to stay with your father for two whole weeks. He looked like he wanted to come with us."

"Jack!" Della yelled, opening the kennel door and scooping the delighted puppy up into her arms. He covered her face in sloppy puppy kisses, wagging his stubby tail furiously, and she turned gratefully to Brad, her protector and savior, and the man who was risking his own life to take her to safety. She couldn't get past the lump in her throat to express her thanks. Her teary eyes said it all.

***

Back in eastern Canada, the phone hadn't stopped ringing off the hook since the airing of the television spot Della had produced for the Hope for Life Wildlife Refuge. People were looking to book tickets for tours, and schools were calling about field trips and wanting brochures sent about the distance education program. Some offered donations, and Hope had to put in a separate phone line to accept credit cards by phone, as well as through the foundation's website. Hope was ecstatic, and June was so busy answering the phone that they were going to have to order pizza for supper for the third night in a row. The community funding website was abuzz with votes for the Hope for Life waterfowl enclosure project as well. The vote count had jumped from a couple of hundred votes a day to a couple of thousand.

To make Hope's day even more exciting, she had received a call from the CEO of Ducks Unlimited, who said the organization wanted to come out to visit the refuge to see if there was some way that they could help with funding for the waterfowl enclosure. The folks at Ducks Unlimited had lots of ideas about how to attract different species of ducks to the area and would be interested in helping Hope expand her educational curriculum to include segments on duck behavior and life cycle and possibly even building an egg incubator and nesting shelter.

Hope was so excited that she had tried to reach Della at the apartment number she had given her, but the phone was answered by Della's voice mail. When she recorded her name and that of the organization, the line was picked up by a male voice, identifying himself as Della's assistant, Ken Milman. He had called Hope back on a secure line and wanted to ensure that she knew not to divulge Della's home number and address to anybody, whether the person was inquiring in person or by phone or e-mail.

"What's up with that?" Hope asked, puzzled. "Is Della in any kind of trouble because of the telecast?"

"No, no, ma'am," Ken replied. "Just some security issues. You know how TV stalkers can be."

"Sure," Hope said, uncertainly. "I can give out her magazine name and the editor's number, can't I?"

"Yes, ma'am, that's right," Ken affirmed. "Thank you for your cooperation. I'll be sure to let Ms. Rawlins know that you called."

***

In a shabby apartment in Brooklyn, New York, a young Afghani student sat hunched in front of an array of computer monitors and TV screens. He received his orders by e-mail from the Algerian cell of the Al-Qaeda in the Islamic Maghreb (AQIM) operating in the city of Algiers. His job as an analyst was to monitor television and Internet broadcasts over American networks, looking for information on persons of interest and reports of terrorist activities by the American media. He simultaneously ran seven news stations and many more web news sites, using word recognition software to flag specific words, names, and phrases.

When the report on the Hope for Life Wildlife Refuge aired on Monday night, a flashing red notification popped up on his number three monitor. The name Della Rawlins was highlighted, and the analyst pressed record, attached the file to an e-mail, and dispatched the message to the designated e-mail addressee.

CHAPTER 32

Ryan reached for his third cup of strong, black coffee. He'd been back in the Algerian capital for over twelve hours now, and the watching and waiting was already making him feel like his brain was going to bleed out his ears. It was such tedious work, but he had some of the best analysts—recruited and trained in terrorism by the CIA—at his disposal to pick up even the minutest of clues as to whether or not bin Laden was behind the scenes giving orders and leads as to where he might be hiding. It was slow going, hour after hour, monitoring the conversation in the bin Sharikh household.

The surveillance in bin Sharikh's office had been the hardest to configure. The techs had had quite a job hacking into his e-mail, and the computer was configured in such a way that they couldn't monitor the on-screen display. They had to rely on a mini cam inserted through a vent in the ceiling to see what was being displayed on his computer screen. It was a very poor connection, and they had been waiting for an opportunity when everyone was out of the house to go back inside and rework the setup. Unfortunately, since bin Sharikh had returned to Algeria, his home had become the headquarters for cell activity, and members of the group, in addition to members of the Sharikh family, were always present.

Ryan's attention was suddenly drawn to the video cam display of the office. One of the regular guys was at the computer, and he was on his feet staring at the computer screen, gesticulating wildly and shouting out to other members sitting around the living area. Ibrahim bin Sharikh rushed to his side, and Ryan clicked on the program that unencrypted the e-mail feed.

The last entry received came up on the screen. The sender's screen name was Brooklyn 40510 and the message read, "Della Rawlins, subject 01112001 identified, file number 255815, file 44298 attached."

With a sick feeling in his stomach, Ryan opened the YouTube video, and his suspicions were confirmed. It was Della's Hope for Life promo. Following the conversation in the office, and simultaneously pulling up the webcam display, Ryan could see bin Sharikh comparing Della's on-screen video with an eight-by-ten headshot he recognized as an enlargement of one that had been on the digital memory on Della's camera.

It was obvious that the cell had made the connection between the reporter who had been in Abbottabad the night bin Laden was killed and this American TV personality. As he watched, bin Sharikh furiously texted while giving rapid-fire orders to the other men. The computer guy typed a mile a minute, and Ryan knew the tom-toms were beating. It wouldn't be long before the net tightened on Della.

He regretfully pulled out his cell phone and sent a text to his brother, updating him on the status of the surveillance as it related to Della. He called his superiors and got clearance to send agents out to the Hope for Wildlife Refuge and the Today Magazine offices to provide protection, taking into custody and interrogating anyone attempting to gain information as to Della's whereabouts. He also alerted the security detail guarding Della's home and checked to be sure that Senator

Rawlins's security was informed of the danger. Anyone known to be associated with Della could be in danger.

By now, all of the analysts had converged on the data streaming out of the bin Sharikh home. Every packet was being traced, tracked, and monitored. One of the paths leading out of that office had to end at bin Laden's door. Although it brought one of his best friends directly into the line of fire, it was an opportunity that may have otherwise taken years to arise. The bait had been struck, the hook was set, and now they had to wait and let the line play out.

CHAPTER 33

Hope opened the door to the farmhouse kitchen and made a beeline to the coffeemaker. Grabbing a couple of chocolate chip cookies from the jar on the counter, she trudged over to the kitchen table and plunked herself down in one of the comfortable kitchen chairs. She was beat, and it was only three thirty in the afternoon. With both of her grad students back to school for the fall semester and all of her summer work grant students finished with their work terms, she and her four paid employees, plus any volunteer hands she could call on, were responsible for the operation of the refuge. Fortunately, money was freeing up with the steady stream of donations that had been pouring in since Della's TV promo had aired. Hope was holding interviews next week for a couple of keeper positions, so things should calm down a little once those people were trained and on board. In the meantime, Hope and her skeleton staff were putting in sixteen-hour days.

June entered the kitchen with an eye on the clock and bustled over to the refrigerator, tying an apron around her waist. She didn't even notice Hope sitting at the kitchen table until she spoke, causing June to nearly jump out of her skin.

"What's for supper?" Hope asked, trying to sound enthusiastic.

"Oh God, Hope! I didn't see you there!" June said, her hand pressed to her chest. "I was in such a rush to get supper started, and I got stuck on a call. Things have gotten a lot better since you hired that call center to take some of the calls, though."

"Yeah, it was too much for just one person to handle, especially with your housekeeping duties as well," Hope agreed. "Thanks for putting up with it for the last week, June. I had no idea when Della suggested doing the promo that it would get such a great response."

"Yeah, Della can really reel 'em in," June replied. "My last caller was really interested in her. He wanted to know in what city she was based and the name of her magazine. He even asked if we had an address or phone number for her."

"Oh my God, June! You didn't give him any information, did you?"

"No, of course not. You told me about that. No info except what's available on her biography on the net, right?"

"Right," Hope said, breathing a sigh of relief.

"He even asked me what her boyfriend's name is. Can you imagine the nerve?"

"What did you tell him?" Hope said, dreading her answer.

"I told him that Brad Jamieson was with her, but it's none of my business if he's her boyfriend or not."

"Oh, June, you didn't." Hope gasped and ran to the office to make a call. She waited impatiently for Brad to pick up on his cell phone, but the call went immediately to voice mail. She left a message to call her immediately. She tried his office, and his secretary informed her that he was gone out of town on a buying trip and would be away for at least two weeks.

"Is there any way you can get a message to him to call me?" Hope asked frantically.

"I can try his sat phone if it's really an emergency," the girl said reluctantly, hoping she wasn't going to get in trouble.

"This could be life or death!" Hope cried, deadly serious, and gave the young woman her contact numbers. "Ask him to call right away."

Hope stayed home and literally sat with the office phone in her lap, waiting for Brad to call her back. Around nine thirty, the phone finally rang, and Hope pounced on it, praying it would be him.

"Hi, Hope. Is that you?" The phone crackled with static.

"Oh, Brad, I'm so glad to hear from you."

"Yeah, it sounded urgent. What's up?"

"Looks like one of the workers accidentally let slip some information over the phone this afternoon."

"What kind of information?"

Hope cringed, hearing the concern in his voice. "I'm really sorry, Brad, but she let it slip that you were here with Della when she was here shooting the TV spot."

"Okay, Hope." Hope could hear the damage control tone in his voice as he started formulating a response to the new circumstances. "There's no sense beating yourself up over a mistake. We'll figure out the best way to handle it."

"Okay. I'm really, really sorry. Be careful, okay? Tell Della to be careful, too. I love you both."

"You be careful, too, Hope. The guard Ryan sent is still there, right?"

"Oh yes. He's a regular watchdog. He tried to shoot the coyotes the other day for trying to raid the Canada goose's nest. Claims he was practicing for terrorists!"

"Ask anyone—it's hard to get good help," Brad quipped. "Thanks for the heads-up, Hope. Be careful. Pray this will be over soon."

The call disconnected, and Hope stood in the middle of her

office, staring at the receiver. She hoped with all her heart that her friends would be okay. She hated this top-secret shit. How could you instill the importance of not giving out personal information to people when you couldn't tell them what was going on. And the more information you gave them, the more questions they asked. She was just not cut out to be a secret agent. She was shit at telling lies, and besides, it was way too stressful.

Hope endured a restless night. And the next day, she and one of her full-time helpers, Nancy, had to wrangle the other bald eagle into the station wagon to go see Dr. Christofer. She had to recruit June to oversee the midday feeding, so the calls had to be routed to the call center.

"Guess it's pizza for supper again tonight," she said apologetically to her assistant.

***

The visit to Dr. Christofer had taken longer than Hope had planned. The X-rays the doctor had taken had revealed buckshot in the bird's wing, and the doctor had recommended emergency surgery to remove the shrapnel rather than risk infection. Since the bird was already under anesthesia, it had seemed the best thing to do.

Now, hours later, she and Nancy pulled into the yard at the refuge. The place looked deserted. Agent Weston was nowhere to be seen, which was odd, as he usually met people at the gate, asking to see IDs and a lot of other nosy questions.

"Everybody must be in for supper," Hope commented. "Can you manage to bring Howard back to his enclosure? I need to check on the staff."

"Sure, Miss Hope," the girl said, hefting the large cardboard carton onto a nearby cargo carrier. "C'mon, Howard, time to go hop on your own roost," she said cheerfully.

Hope headed for the farmhouse, a sense of foreboding dogging her footsteps. She pulled open the screen door, and what met her eyes had her gasping and clapping her hands to her mouth in horror. June was sitting on a kitchen chair. The only way Hope could tell it was her was from the frilly kitchen apron. A black hood was over her head, and duct-taped around her neck. Her hands and ankles had been bound to the chair with tape, and a rope was tied around her waist, binding her tightly to the old-fashioned iron radiator. Her head lolled to one side, and Hope ran to her immediately, fearing the worst. She quickly grabbed the kitchen shears and cut the hood away from June's face. A wad of a dishtowel had been stuffed into her mouth, and she was barely breathing.

"Oh, June," Hope cried frantically, patting the girl's cheeks and praying that she would regain consciousness.

June's eyelids fluttered, and she slowly opened her eyes. There was a large bruise on her forehead and the red handprint of a vicious blow to the face on her cheek. She weakly gasped, "Water." And Hope shakily held a tumbler to her cracked and bleeding lips.

"Who did this to you?" Hope asked, reaching for the cell phone in her pocket and dialing 911. "Where is Agent Weston? Are the bastards gone?"

"I don't know who they were," June croaked, grateful for the removal of the gag from her throat. "They're gone now. Two guys came through the kitchen door. Must've come on foot and slipped by the guard. They slipped in while I was running the mixer and grabbed me from behind."

"Did you see them? Can you describe them?" Hope asked the shaking girl as she freed her from her bonds. "What did they want?"

"I only caught a glimpse of their faces reflected in the glass in the door of the microwave oven before they pulled the hood over my head. They were Middle Eastern, maybe East Indian—the accent you hear on telemarketing calls sometimes. They wanted to know where you were. I told them you were out. They tied me up, and I could hear them in your office. I don't know what they did to the rest of the staff."

At that moment, Nancy burst through the kitchen door, a wild look in her eyes. "Miss Hope, come quick! The barn door is jammed, and everybody's yellin' to get out. Oh my God, what happened to June?" she asked.

"I think we've been robbed," Hope improvised, suspecting worse motives behind the invasion but keeping them to herself.

Having given the necessary information to the 911 operator, Hope left June in Nancy's care and quickly sprinted to the barn. She could hear the staff banging on the door and demanding to be let out. The animals were upset by the racket, and the combined shouting and frightened animal noises had everyone's nerves on edge. Hope grabbed the handle of the shovel that had been shoved through the door handles on the outside of the barn door and kicked aside the broom handles that had been propped under the door closure to hold the doors firmly shut.

"Some protection you turned out to be," Hope accused the sheepish CIA agent. "Why weren't you at your post?"

"There weren't any visitors on the site, and I was giving the guys a hand with the feeding," he admitted.

"Come on back to the office and help me see what they got away with," Hope said, deadly calm.

**

By the time Hope and Agent Weston got back to the farmhouse, an ambulance and police cruiser had arrived. The paramedics had June on a stretcher and were waiting for the police officer to finish his questioning before transporting her to the nearest hospital.

"Miss Hope, can we ask you a few questions?"

"Sure. How about you talk to Agent Weston of the CIA first so he can brief you on the situation," Hope said, not wanting to upset her staff further with talk of terrorists and political intrigue.

Heading into her office, she was dismayed to see files, papers, and records strewn all over the floor. Her computer was open but, luckily, had logged her off, making it impossible to access anything without her password. On her desk was her last holdout to modern technology, her Rolodex. Cards were pulled out and strewn over the desktop and across the floor. A cursory glance showed Hope that two cards in particular were missing, the one listing Della's home address, e-mail address, and contact numbers, as well as Brad Jamieson's card, which had listed both his home address and business information, along with his e-mail and contact numbers. Her heart sank as she relayed the information to Agent Weston, and although she didn't know the whole story, she was sure it wasn't good that these people now had Brad and Della's personal information. She hoped that her trusteeship would not put them in more danger than they were obviously in already. She was glad that, wherever they were right now, at least they knew that they had been exposed as being connected and could take whatever precautions they had to in order to protect themselves.

Hope shuddered, thinking about the extent to which these people would go to get what they wanted. She was very thankful that none of her staff had lost their lives trying to protect her and her friends and she grieved the trauma that June had suffered when innocently caught in the cross fire. She wished a thousand plagues on the intruders and the people they worked for. For the first time, Hope realized there were worse people out there than poachers, animal abusers, and uncaring politicians. They couldn't hold a candle to these assholes.

CHAPTER 34

Ken Milman was well used to sitting idle. His training in surveillance had taught him patience. He had spent many a long and lonely night hyped on caffeine, his eyes and ears wide open as he watched his subject and waited. This job was super boring, though, because nothing was happening. Apart from the daytime comings and goings of the other residents on Della's floor and the opening and closing of the elevator door, not much changed on the static, closed-circuit TV monitor. Apart from a few people leaving phone messages, there wasn't much phone activity, either. There had been two calls where someone had phoned, but when the answering machine had cut in, they had hung up. He had tried to get a trace on these, but for the first one, there hadn't been enough time to capture the data. And the other one had traced back to an unidentifiable cell number, which could be a blocked ID or maybe a disposable cell phone.

Suddenly the computer screen went black, and all of the appliances went quiet in the apartment. Ken automatically released his weapon from his side holster and took it off safety. The city was prone to the occasional brownout this time of the year, but in this game, you couldn't take any chances. Silently, he crossed to the door of the apartment. Taking a quick look through the peephole, he noticed two subjects—dressed in coveralls and carrying toolkits—walking toward the apartment. They stopped in front of Della's door.

There was a sharp knock, and a male voice called out, "Building maintenance. We need to check your breakers."

Ken remained silent behind the door and risked another look through the peephole. One guy had a device on the door, something like a stethoscope, and he had earbuds in, listening. The other guy took a lock picking set out of his pocket, selected a tool, and inserted it into the lock. Ken could hear the clicking of the tumblers. When the lock released, and the door still wouldn't open, Ken could hear the two men swearing in some foreign language. He pressed the buttons on the alarm system that disabled the beep tones and pressed the silent alarm code, which would summon the NYPD to the apartment. He waited to see what the intruders would do next.

It seemed that the burglars had come prepared for anything, as one guy took out portable oxygen-acetylene tanks and a cutting tool. It took no time for him to make short work of the deadbolt. Several people passed the men, and they brazenly nodded and laughed with them over their fellow tenant losing her keys. In no time, the door swung open.

Brad watched as the two men systematically worked their way through the apartment, checking behind framed pictures on the walls, looking in cupboards and under beds, tearing the contents out of storage bins. When they found a couple of Della's cameras, they started talking excitedly and placed the equipment in a black duffel bag. They tried to break into Della's computer without success, but they rifled through all of the files pertaining to her foundation for the release of American journalists being held in other countries.

Ken knew that the NYPD would soon be arriving on the scene, but he wanted to let these guys commit as many felonies as possible before taking them into custody. He would enjoy having a crack at them during interrogation. He would be filing a full report with Ryan Jamieson as soon as they finished processing these two.

With that, heavy footsteps sounded in the hallway, and an authoritative voice yelled, "NYPD! Freeze!"

The uniforms burst through the open apartment door with weapons drawn, and Ken stepped out, holding his badge up, identifying himself as CIA. The two burglars gave up without a struggle and were taken into custody. Ken reset Della's alarm and locked the apartment door behind him as well as he could, and he and the police officers who'd arrived on the scene marched the suspects to the elevator.

Ken's patience had paid off. Things were about to get interesting.

CHAPTER 35

Brad and Della reached the Maine to New Brunswick border by Friday afternoon. The fall scenery as they'd driven through New England had been breathtaking. The trees were dressed in their colorful robes, and the air was fresh and had just started to acquire that little fall nip. All along the drive, farmer's fruit and vegetable stands had offered all sorts of bounty from the harvest. They'd stopped and bought baskets of plums, pears, and juicy apples, as well as blackberries, blueberries, and peaches. It was a veritable fruit buffet on the backseat. It was nice to take a break from driving.

"I'm gonna get a tummy ache if I eat any more fruit," Della said. "But it's sooo good!" The juice from the sun-ripened peach she was rapturously enjoying was running down her chin.

"You look delicious," Brad said, eyeing the juicy drop. And reaching out, he caught it and sucked the sweet liquid off his finger. His eyes darkened, and she knew what he was thinking. The small taste left him wanting more, and he pulled her across the bench seat and ravished her mouth, his tongue sliding against hers, the slippery contact reminding her of what it felt like to have his hard cock driving into her.

Her pussy clenched as the kiss got hotter, and she was soon arching her back, rubbing her pelvis against his straining cock, increasing the friction between them. They were both oblivious to the hoots and hollers of a bunch of skateboard enthusiasts who flew past, kicking up dust in the wake of their passing. She was shamelessly straddling his lap at that point, and when she realized how carried away they had gotten, she swung her leg off him and slid back over into her seat. She smoothed her hair out of her eyes with shaking fingers and attempted to straighten up her clothing, trying to regain some degree of modesty.

Brad grinned at her discomfiture and said, "We'd better save some for later." And he pulled back onto the highway, singing along to the country station that was playing on the radio.

"I really love your peaches, want to shake your tree ... eee ... eee."

They still had a way to go before they hit the highway that connected them with the 110, when Brad's Bluetooth signaled an incoming call. He listened to the message through his earpiece and gave a short reply about calling back. A short time later, a gas station came into sight, and Brad said he was going to pull in to fill up.

"I'm gonna go find the restroom," Della said. "Want me to pick us up some drinks and snacks?"

"Sure," Brad said. "You go on into the store. I won't be long."

When Della disappeared into the convenience store, Brad pulled out his cell phone and dialed his assistant's phone number. She answered on the first ring and gave Brad the message to call Hope. Not wanting to alarm Della, who was coming out of the store swinging a sack containing soft drinks, chocolate, and potato chips, he decided he would wait a while until he was alone to call Hope back. In the meantime, he felt maybe a detour was in order, instead of hitting the road right to their family cabin. Maybe it would be better to hide in plain sight for a little while and stay where there were plenty of other people. At the next interchange, he took the exit marked "St. Andrews by the Sea," and Della asked if they were on the right road to the cabin.

"No, actually. I think we should take a little side trip. Have some fun," Brad said.

"Okay, I'm up for that," was all she said, helping herself to some salt and vinegar chips.

Driving in on the New Brunswick side of the Bay of Fundy, Brad and Della were treated to pastoral views of lush green valleys dotted with white farmhouses, open fields, and half-hidden covered bridges shading seldom-used dirt roads.

Soon the rural landscape gave way to the seaside community of St. Andrews by the Sea. Prettily situated around the edge of Passamaquoddy Bay, the settlement was steeped in history and charm. Stately homes sat back from the streets on landscaped properties with immaculate lawns and gardens, shaded by centuries-old trees. As they approached the center of town, they passed fine craft shops and outdoor terraces of quaint restaurants and pubs. The streets were narrow here, and the architecture of the well-preserved buildings was a stunning example of their colonial heritage. Della was charmed by the town's main street and couldn't wait to visit the artisan's studios where blown glass, pewter, pottery, and designer clothing were offered for sale in the fascinating little shops. The seaside homes and sunny cottages added to the feeling of historical charm and quiet contentment. As they followed the shoreline at the bottom of the hill, where the low tide exposed the bottom of the bay, gently sloping away from the land, Brad reached for Della's hand and pulled her closer to him on the bench seat, his arm encircling her shoulders. Jack was enjoying a puppy snooze, cuddled into Della's thigh, and she lifted him onto her lap so that she could rest her head on Brad's shoulder as they soaked in the warm, salty breezes and felt the relaxation of the sleepy town wash over them.

***

Soon, the land started to rise again, and they passed a pristine golf course and more stately homes. As they neared the hilltop overlooking the community, the red-tiled roof of a magnificent Tudor-style hotel came into view, majestically spread out over the hilltop, surrounded by multihued gardens whose colors competed with the gaily painted wooden lawn chairs gracing its shaded veranda. The Algonquian beckoned to the weary traveler like an oasis in the desert.

"Oh yes," Brad nodded. "I think we can make do with this little hideaway for a night or two. What do you say, Della?"

"Yeah, I guess we could suffer it for a night or two. What do you think, Jack?" She laughed as the puppy yawned and stretched, sticking his rump in the air and wagging his tail.

***

While Brad checked in, Della took Jack for a walk around the grounds on his leash. Carpets of late-blooming flowers lined the flagstone pathways, and there were many private alcoves where guests could sit and enjoy the view. Jack enjoyed sniffing all of the flowers and trees and worked hard to leave his scent on as many of the plants and fixtures as he could.

Pretty soon, they found their way back to the reception area. And by that time, Brad had collected their bags and Jack's kennel from the car. A porter was ready to escort them to their room, located on the fourth floor. Brad gave Della a key card marked with the number 432.

After he had tipped the porter, who unloaded their duffels from the baggage cart, along with Jack's kennel, they were left alone to explore their surroundings. The room was fabulous. The wide foyer was tiled in rose marble, and then there were two steps down to a sunken sitting room. Fresh flowers graced an antique side table. A pair of brocade, wingback chairs and a velvet settee were grouped invitingly near an ornately carved mantelpiece, where a fire burned brightly, taking the chill out of the late October, afternoon air. A high-arched window topped wide double doors that opened onto a balcony, overlooking the gardens and grounds. Off to the side, the bedroom door stood open, and a white, four-poster bed spread with snowy white linens beckoned invitingly, piled high with fluffy pillows embroidered with the regal signature brand of the crimson A.

"Brad, are you sure this room isn't reserved for royalty?" Della asked, awed by the opulent decor.

"Tonight, you are my princess," he replied, stepping close to her and pulling her into his embrace.

His lips took hers in a whisper of a kiss, and the warmth of his body radiated toward her, drawing her to him like a moth to a flame.

"Do you know how much I care for you, Della?" he whispered, his lips softly touching her closed eyelids before tracking down over her cheek to nestle in the soft hollow below her ear. Her arms felt like polished silk beneath his fingertips, and her breasts were tempting him to tease their tightening peaks and turn her center to liquid gold.

Della ran her hands up over the soft material of his chambray shirt and started to slowly undo the small buttons. She put her lips to the base of his neck, and the fine chest hairs sprinkled there tickled her nose as she tasted his essence on her tongue. She freed the last button and pulled the shirt free from his jeans, smoothing her hands over the warm skin of his well-defined pecs and rippling abs. His body was lean and powerful, while hers was soft and curved with delicious secret places that demanded his exploration.

Her scent drew him to her like a siren song, and he lifted her into his arms and carried her to the bed.

Gently, he laid her down and drew her suit jacket off over her head. The sexy black lace bra barely concealed her creamy breasts, and the deep cleavage invited his lips to kiss her there. Craving his lips on her, she reached around and flicked open the clasp, and he drew the black confection away from her body and let it drop to the floor. His fingertips found her pouting nipples, and he lightly pinched them, one after the other, sending arrows of pleasure directly to her core. Soon the light pressure wasn't enough, and she drew his head to her breast, wanting to feel the hot desire of his mouth and the teasing of his tongue.

Wanting him to feel as turned on as she was, she stroked his hard cock through his jeans and ground her pelvis against him. His hand slid up the inside of her pencil skirt to find her perfect round ass. He groaned and flipped her over on top of him, so she straddled his hips as he pushed the tight skirt up to her waist. He found the lacy black thong, no barrier to his questing fingers. He undid the skirt and pulled it off over her head, and the glory of her body sitting astride him in nothing but a wisp of lace, thigh-high stockings, and patent leather heels was the sexiest sight he had ever seen. Reaching up, he pulled the pins from her hair, and cascades of dark curls came tumbling down over her shoulders, brushing softly over his chest.

"Oh God, Della, you're so beautiful. You take my breath away," he said, his eyes dark pools of desire.

She worked the button of his jeans loose and freed his straining cock, pushing his jeans and his underwear down his body. Not wanting to waste any more time, Della took his fully engorged cock in her hand and guided it to her entrance. She lowered herself onto his throbbing cock until she felt the head bump against her cervix. He felt so good, filling her, stretching her to her limits. She rose up until he nearly lost connection with her hot cunt and then slowly, teasingly, took him in again, squeezing him, rubbing him against that special spot on her inner wall. She sucked in air through her teeth and arched her back, her head thrown back with rapture. She circled her hips, intensifying the friction, till he thought he was going to burst. He reached up and cupped her breast, teasing her nipple while his other hand slid between their bodies and sought that little nub nestled between the slick folds of her pussy.

She gasped as he found it and flicked it with his fingertip, circling it until she cried out his name. She could feel the pressure rising in her core, and her inner muscles clamped around him, milking him for all he was worth. He couldn't stand it one second longer. He flipped her under him and drew her legs up until they were resting over his shoulders. He thrust into her slick pussy with his fingers until she was writhing under him. Then he grasped his cock and positioned it at her entrance to drive into her in one fluid motion. He pumped his hips in a steady rhythm, his rock hard ass muscles flexing with exertion, drilling into her trembling flesh as deep as he could reach.

Della cried out his name, begging him not to stop as she gave him everything she had. Her body clenched around him as an ocean of pleasure burst within her, coating him in her creamy essence. Brad felt his balls tighten as he rushed toward release. His lips found hers in a fiery brand as his hot seed spurted into her. It was a communion of souls—two beings joining together until they became one. They basked in the aftermath of their union, wrapped in one another's arms—heart to heart, mind to mind, physically and spiritually mated.

***

It was much later when Brad stirred. He withdrew from her slowly and kissed her softly on the shoulder. "Time for us to get cleaned up and figure out what we're going to do for supper," he said.

"Mmmm-hmmm," Della said drowsily.

"I'm gonna hop in the shower, and then I'm gonna run you a bubble bath. You have a look at the room service menu and see what you'd like for supper."

"Oh, good idea," Della murmured. "I'm starved, and I'm too lazy to get dressed to go out. I hope they have burgers and nachos. We can have a picnic in front of the fire in our hotel bathrobes."

"Sounds delightful." Brad grinned, wondering how he could have gotten so lucky to find this woman, so in tune with him, not wanting to get all dressed up and go out for a stuffy, overpriced dinner in a formal restaurant where you had to be uncomfortable for hours, when instead, they could kick back, watch a movie, enjoy a simple meal, and possibly make out. She was definitely a keeper.

He realized that he had to call Hope back, too. He didn't want to spoil the relaxed mood that he and Della had fallen into after such an enjoyable day. He would use the excuse of needing to take Jack out for a walk while Della was bathing to see to that obligation. He hoped it wasn't bad news. Things had been going well up to this point.

CHAPTER 36

Ryan and his team had not stopped analyzing the data that had streamed out of the Sharikh household in the forty-eight hours following the discovery of Della's ID. Every e-mail header had been traced back to its original source, and a picture of the lines of communication within the network was materializing.

Although the conversation was difficult to follow because a lot of it was coded, patterns were forming, which allowed them to identify who was leader and who was subordinate. There was traffic back and forth between Algiers, Afghanistan, and Pakistan and then a lot of incoming traffic from many parts of the United States to Algiers, cc'd to specific centralized hubs. Occasionally one or two of these hubs would send highly encrypted messages to a server in Spain. None of the techs had been able to pinpoint the end recipient, but they were using every trick in their arsenal—some a little shady—to get past the security barriers and obtain more information.

Ryan himself was working on identifying the coded references to Della and Brad. He was anxious to see whether forces had been dispatched to either of their home addresses or if any attempts were being made to track them by cell phone or by monitoring of financial transactions. He wished he had told Della and Brad not to use their credit or debit cards while they were away. He hoped that Brad would clue in to that danger. He had tried to reach his brother on the disposable cell phone that Della had taken with her, but they must have been out of range of a repeater. He would try later when Brad had his sat phone in service.

The cell phone in his pocket began to vibrate. He pulled it out and glanced at the display. It was a text message from Ken Milman, the agent assigned to Della's apartment. It read, "Caught two burglars at home. Now in custody, Ninety-Fifth Precinct. Will file full report after interrogation."

Holy shit, two rats in the trap, Ryan thought as he texted back that he'd be sending an agent to the precinct to supervise the interrogation. He immediately contacted the office to alert the director as to who they had in custody at the Ninety-Fifth Precinct in New York City. He so wished that Guantanamo Bay were still taking guests. This interrogation would probably require "advanced interrogation techniques" in order to get the information they needed in the shortest possible time. They didn't need the interference of other agencies hampering them in doing so.

***

On the other side of the globe, Ken had turned over the prisoners to his superior officer, Joe Miller, who had been waiting for their arrival at the Ninety-Fifth Precinct. Ordinarily, a crime linked to terrorist activity would have to be reported by the director of the CIA to the secretary of Homeland Security. Because this case was so highly classified, the director himself was directly involved in monitoring the interrogation. He knew that they could take no chances on botching this opportunity to get a lead on bin Laden.

The prisoners, Kahlil Aznan and Asham Zarifh, were being

kept in holding cells. As both had valid American citizenships, they were entitled to legal counsel, and both had refused to say anything without a lawyer present. As neither could afford defense council, they were on a waiting list for a legal aid lawyer to be assigned to them.

Joe Miller had been recruited by the CIA right out of college. Rising through the ranks, he had been assigned to a task force on terrorism long before the 9/11 attack. He had spent some time in Afghanistan monitoring al-Qaeda, and his background in psychology had earned him a spot on the interrogation squad during the roundup of bin Laden's associates after the 9/11 attacks. In the furor to track down bin Laden, he had seen men brought to their knees within hours, using techniques like waterboarding, sleep deprivation, confinement, and sexual humiliation, all of which was now highly illegal. These extreme measures did not often yield good intel, as detainees would make false confessions just to get the torture to stop. Joe knew that you could often catch more flies with honey than with vinegar, and he was an expert in getting information without having to implement these harsh interrogation techniques. It was amazing what you could achieve when you tried a softer approach.

Before council arrived, Joe requested to speak to the prisoners. An interview room with video and audio recording was made available. They set up a live feed to the director's office. The first prisoner was escorted in, and Jim lit a cigarette and sat down across from the prisoner, who was handcuffed and sweating profusely. His file lay on the metal table between them, and Jim started by confirming his name, Kahlil Aznan, and some of the basic information the police officers had collected. Joe took a sip from a can of Coke and noticed Kahlil eyeing it, swallowing thirstily.

"Are you thirsty, Kahlil? Would you like a drink?" Jim asked, fishing another can out of his jacket pocket.

Kahlil nodded, and Jim put the drink on the table in front of him, took the handcuff keys out of his pocket, and undid the handcuffs. Kahlil's eyes, which had been downcast up to this point, flickered briefly, and his demeanor relaxed slightly.

"You've been arrested on a charge of breaking and entering," Jim read from the report. "The apartment you broke into is rented by Della Rawlins. Says here she's a political reporter. She did some work over in Afghanistan and Pakistan. Looks like you might have known her." He took a pack of cigarettes out of his pocket, lit one, inhaled, and blew out the fragrant smoke. Kahlil's eyes followed his every move, and he wet his lips, drawing the secondhand smoke into his lungs.

Jim leaned forward, offering the pack, "Smoke?"

Kahlil wet his lips and accepted a cigarette, leaning forward as Joe offered a light.

Joe took a crumpled photo of Della out of the file and pushed it across the table at Kahlil. "This was found in the pocket of your uniform." Della's apartment number was scrawled on the paper. "We know that you don't work for building maintenance, and the tools you had in your possession were solely for the purpose of gaining entrance to the apartment. The only things you took were Ms. Rawlins's cameras, even though there was cash in her bedroom dresser, jewelry, and a gun in her night table.

"So how come an opportunist like yourself wouldn't bother with those goodies when they were lying out in plain sight?"

Kahlil remained silent, exhaling smoke from his nose, his eyes narrowed, his face unexpressive.

"We think you had specific orders to pick up the cameras and maybe even pick up Ms. Rawlins if she was around," Jim said, watching for Kahlil's reaction. "Things could go a lot easier for you if you told me who ordered you to break into Ms. Rawlins's apartment. Right now, you're only looking at a couple of years for B and E, but we have proof that you received communication by cell phone from a known terrorist source shortly before you went to the apartment. That puts you under the radar of Homeland Security and the CIA."

Kahlil's hands flew to his face, and a flicker of fear showed in his eyes.

"You know that you can be sent back to Afghanistan under the authority of the CIA and be sent for interrogation at one of our black prisons, don't you?"

It was obvious that Kahlil knew what he was referring to. Beads of perspiration broke out on his top lip, and the hand pressing the butt of the cigarette to his lips was shaking. "I am an American citizen," he replied.

"But it can be proven that you're involved in terrorist activity in the United States. That makes you an unlawful combatant. And that means that you can be taken under the authority of the CIA out of the country and interrogated. You can be imprisoned indefinitely without hope of ever seeing your family again. My colleagues in Afghanistan are not as friendly as I am. They will get the information they want.

"But we can save a lot of time and trouble if you just tell me who ordered you and Asham to break into Ms. Rawlins's apartment and steal her cameras. If you do that, we'll forget about sending you back to Afghanistan, you can serve your twenty-four months with parole for the B and E, and nobody has to know there was anything else going on. Asham has already agreed to it—as long as you agree to cooperate."

"But I was never told the name of the person giving the orders. I was only contacted through e-mail or text message. I never met anyone in person." Kahlil was obviously in distress, knowing all too well what went on in the American "black prisons." And it looked like he would rather take his chances on this side of the ocean than face what awaited him should he be extradited back to his homeland.

Jim pressed his advantage. "Nobody has to know anything. You give me your emir's contact information, and the judge will give you a slap on the wrist—and life goes back to normal."

Kahlil closed his eyes and dropped his chin to his chest. His body language bespoke surrender. "Okay." He sighed in defeat. "What do you need to know?"

It didn't take long for Jim to get the information he needed to start tracing the network back to its source. Both Kahlil and Asham verified what Jim and his associates had already suspected. The order to burglarize Della's apartment had come from Sharikh and had been ratified by the mysterious source behind the server in Spain.

The ball was back in Ryan's court.

CHAPTER 37

Phil Brennan stared at his computer screen. The cigarette he had lit was burning in the ashtray, forgotten, as he followed the news feed coming out of Algeria:

The Movement for Oneness and Jihad in West Africa reports the execution of a kidnapped Algerian diplomat in northern Mali. Tahar Touati, vice-consul of the Algerian consulate in Gao, was one of seven hostages taken in March 2012 during the Tuareg rebellion. The MOJWA had asked for the release of their imprisoned members in Algeria in exchange for the consular staff. Three of the seven hostages were released in July 2011. But Algeria had captured three more Islamist leaders, and the MOJWA had threatened to execute the remaining hostages unless Algeria released Necib Tayeb, a senior member of al-Qaeda's North Africa branch, al-Qaeda in the Islamic Maghreb.

Vice-consul Tahar Touati was executed on September 1, according to Agence Nouakchott d'information. Walid Abu Sarhaoui, the president of MOJWA's governing council, said, "We have carried out our threat. The hostage has been killed. Algeria had the time to move negotiations along but did not want to. We executed the hostage on Saturday."

However, Algeria's Foreign Ministry released a statement that read, "The statement announcing the execution of the

Algerian vice-consular official can only fuel surprise and justify the steps taken to try to confirm the accuracy of the information sent out late Saturday."

At the same time, Algeria's policy of non-negotiation or releasing convicted terrorists from prisons was seen by Sarhaoui as a hindrance to the release of the other hostages.

Wow, thought Phil, *the natives are getting restless*. He wished he had a correspondent in the area. There were still three hostages being held. There was likely to be a bloodbath there if the Algerians didn't back down. Wondering if there were any freelancers he could reach, Phil pulled up a list of Middle East correspondents currently working in Algeria. The name Brent Marshall stood out. He remembered Brent from a documentary he'd done on Iraq under Saddam Hussein, for which his team had won the Edward R. Murrow Award for best TV interpretation/documentary on foreign affairs. Brent had also covered a succession of crises between Iraq and the United Nations over weapons inspections.

Phil consulted his directory and searched for a contact number for his old buddy Gerry Raferty, CNN's senior international correspondent. If anyone knew how to get in touch with Marshall, it would be him.

***

Brent Marshall sat at his computer in his hotel room in the capital city of Algiers. He was intrigued by the offer from Today Magazine's editor to cover the story of the execution of Tahar Touati and the plight of the remaining hostages. Rumor had it that the MOJWA had raised the ransom on the consulate members from $18 million to $30 million, along with their demand for the release of Necib Tayeb. He knew that the region was volatile, but he had dealt with despots like

Walid Abu Sarhaoui before. Hadn't he been the only Western journalist to obtain an exclusive interview with Udai Saddam Hussein, the notorious son of the Iraqi dictator? He was excited at the prospect of penetrating the inner circle of the MOJWA. Rumor had it that this group had been sanctioned by the United Nations Security Council as a means of splitting the power of al-Qaeda in Northern Africa. Interesting territory to be explored.

Brent had heard that Ibrahin bin Sharikh was Sarhaoui's special lieutenant in Algiers and might be able to open the door to his being able to meet with the captain. For triple his regular fee, plus expenses, he would deliver a story to Phil Brennan that would put Today Magazine on the map.

CHAPTER 38

Brad and Della were having a lovely holiday. Being away from the city did Della a world of good. She had put the situation with Ryan and the whole threat from the Middle East out of her mind and firmly on the back burner for the time being and had adjusted to the relaxed, comfortable pace of life in the sleepy Canadian town of St. Andrews by the Sea. Brad had been at his most charming—lavishing her with attention, bubble baths, foot rubs, and a picnic in front of the fire. He had even taken on the task of taking Jack out for his nighttime walk. The doings of terrorists and dead dictators on the other side of the world seemed so far away.

"What would you like to do today?" Brad asked after they had awakened under the billowy, white covers of the comfy bed. Sun sparkled through the leaded glass window of the turreted bedroom, casting rainbow patterns all over the wall.

Della reached for him, and his arms snaked around her, molding her to his already hard body.

"I want to eat," she said, taking a playful bite of his shoulder.

He grinned lasciviously and tickled her as she made a grab for his package. He pulled her on top of him, nestling safely between her thighs.

"And then what?" He prompted, running his hands over her ass and up along her back.

"And after a really long time ..." She smiled seductively.

"Yes?" he encouraged, nibbling her neck, his hands fisting in her silky hair as he brushed his lips lazily over hers.

Her breath hitched as heat bloomed between her thighs. "I'd like to go shopping!" She grinned.

He swatted her ass playfully and exclaimed, "Killjoy!" He finally conceded, however, after she had kissed her way down his body. "Well, okay, I know when I've been beaten."

"I can be very persuasive," she told him, slanting a sexy glance from under her lashes.

"Wow, I should have held out longer," he teased, rolling her onto her stomach and reaching with his cock between her legs and slipping into her ready slit.

He couldn't get enough. Every way he took her felt as good as the first time. She spread her legs wider, encouraging him to go deeper, and he picked up the pace as she rocked back against him, increasing the tempo. The sensation of his balls slapping against her made her crazy, and she cried out with that little sound that really turned him on. He grabbed her by the hips and pounded into her, unable to stop or slow down. He was afraid he was being too rough with her, but her ecstatic cries of "Don't stop, ooh God!" spurred him on and was all he needed to bring them the release they both needed. He came so hard and so fast that he thought his cock would never stop pumping his hot seed into her.

He grabbed a handful of tissue from the bedside table and slowly pulled out, grabbing another handful of tissue to gently wipe between her legs.

Jack just cocked his head at them and whined, lying in his kennel. And they both laughed.

"Didn't know we had an audience." Della grinned, wrapping the fluffy hotel bathrobe around her gloriously nude body, rosy from their loving.

"Yeah, we taught him a thing or two," Brad said, rolling off the bed and heading for the shower. "Next thing we know, he'll be humping every pillow in the hotel."

***

After a tasty breakfast of French toast, Canadian bacon, and fresh fruit, which they ate out on the balcony, Brad and Della dressed in casual clothes and went downstairs to the concierge's desk to ask about sightseeing. He suggested they take a couple of touring bikes and go for a ride into town. Della was all for it, especially when she saw there was a big wicker basket attached to the front of the girl's bike where she could clip Jack's harness, and he could ride along with them. It took a little persuading to get Brad to agree, but Della promised to make it up to him later, so he acquiesced to her wishes. Once they got underway, he found it was quite enjoyable to ride along with the wind blowing through their hair. Brad liked the view from behind as Della pedaled, leading the way toward the older part of town.

The ride down the hillside was exhilarating, and as they paused for a moment to take a drink, Della noticed the wrought iron entrance to the Kingsbrae Gardens.

"Selected Garden of the Year by the Canadian Garden Tourism Awards," Della read. "Oh, Brad, can we go in?"

"Sure," he said, swinging his leg over the bike's frame, grateful to stow the damn contraptions in a nearby bicycle rack. He grimaced as he rubbed his aching ass.

"A little saddle sore," he commented as Della chuckled.

The gardens were still beautiful, even though it was late in the season. A comfortable, gravel walking trail wound through the property, showcasing over fifty thousand perennials in many themed gardens, ponds, streams, and old-growth

Acadian forests. Jack was having the time of his life, trotting along, following his nose, and stopping to sniff the many tree trunks, rocks, and bushes along the way. Brad was impressed with the variety of animals that made their home in the park— from the ducks in the pond to the winged creatures that inhabited the bird and butterfly garden to the alpacas that entertained the visitors taking a break at the café.

"Oh look," Della said, pointing to a sign near the door to the garden café. "You can dine here in the evening." She read, "Savour in the Garden will provide you with the very best fine dining experience. Chef Alex Hann will delight your senses with an award-winning, six-course tasting menu, featuring local game such as wild boar and red deer, as well as New Brunswick oysters, French pastries, and homemade ice cream for dessert. Call early, as space is limited. Choose one of our garden tables for a more intimate dining experience."

"That sounds lovely." Della sighed.

"Mmmm, oysters, you say? And delicious wine pairings, too. Let's see if we can get a reservation," Brad suggested, wiggling his eyebrows suggestively.

"Can we?" Della's face lit up. "Let's see if we can book the rose garden."

While Brad was making inquiries for dinner, Della browsed in the gift shop, buying some saltwater taffy; a pretty scarf for Madeline; and a bottle of creamy, rose-scented body lotion. She bought a sea captain's hat for Brad, thinking how sexy it would look with his wavy hair curling around his ears and his insanely blue eyes.

Jack was pulling on the leash to go when Della collected her purchases at the cash register, and Brad told her to go ahead and take him outside as he stopped a moment to browse on his way out.

The afternoon passed quickly by. Brad and Della

wandered through the local museum and stopped for a bite to eat at a little restaurant that served tall glasses of frosty Long Island Iced Tea and finger sandwiches. The delicate flavors of cucumber, deviled ham, and crab salad satisfied their famished stomachs, while the fancy homemade shortbread they were served for dessert melted in their mouths.

They wandered in and out of the artist's studios, marveling over the quality of the blown glass and pewter sculptures. Brad bought a very masculine letter opener, shaped like a dagger, and he insisted on buying Della a bottle of sultry French perfume when they stopped by the perfumery.

They were on their way back to collect their bikes at the Kingsbrae Gardens when Della spotted a dress in the window of the Haute de Couture Salon. The proprietress saw her looking at the gorgeous dinner dress displayed on the mannequin and beckoned her to come in.

"Ah, mademoiselle, that dress was made for you," the well-dressed woman said, her perfectly manicured hands slipping the dark rose chiffon off the display mannequin. "You must try it on."

"Yes, Della, I didn't bring anything dressy when I packed for the trip," Brad urged her. "The closest I could come at the store on short notice was pink camouflage. Try it on."

"Okay," Della said doubtfully, following the vision of chic back to the fitting room and disappearing into the small cubicle.

When she reemerged, dress on, the saleswoman clapped her hands and exclaimed delightedly, "Oh, mademoiselle, it fits perfectly. All summer, beaucoup des femme 'ave put it on, but don't 'ave the body or the length of neck to show it off. I would not let it go. I save it for the right one." She brought over a pair of silver sandals, and Della gazed at her reflection in the mirror. The soft chiffon crisscrossed over the bust. The neckline dipped low in front, exposing the curve of her breasts, and the back draped in a long cowl, nipping in at the waist and flowing over her hips. A light ruffled layer trimmed the bust like the petals of a flower, and the material floated as she moved, hugging her curves like a dream.

"You wear this without the brassiere, oui?" the saleswoman instructed, pointing to the visible straps of her underwear peeking out from beneath the soft bodice.

She pulled Della's hair out of the confining ponytail holder and arranged her dark curls around her shoulders. "Beautiful, non?"

Brad appeared in the dressing room doorway, holding Jack in his arms. He took in the vision of pure loveliness standing before the mirror. His heart gave a slight lurch, and he forgot to breathe for a second or two. The two women looked at him expectantly, and he said, without missing a beat, "What? Are you crazy? She'll take it!"

Della glanced at the price tag and gulped, digging through her wallet for her credit card, as she had spent all of her cash at the Kingsbrae gift shop.

"No, allow me," Brad said, handing the dog to the startled saleswoman and pulling some traveler's checks out of his wallet.

"No, Brad, I'll pay for the dress myself," Della protested.

"Please, let me," Brad said softly. "It'll be a treat for me to get to look at you all night in it." He softly cupped her cheek and touched his lips to hers.

***

Making their way back to their bicycles, they were having a bit of a struggle juggling all of the boxes and bags of their purchases. Jack had gotten tired, too, and he sat on the sidewalk, looking up at them woefully and refusing to walk another step.

"Poor puppy," Della sympathized, bending to scoop him up. "You're beat, aren't you, poor little dude?"

Jack stuck his pink tongue out and licked her face gratefully.

"Yeah, my rump can't take the trip back up over that hill, either," Brad said. "Here, hand me your cell phone."

He took a small business card out of his pocket and called the hotel. "Can you send a taxi to the Kingsbrae Gardens for Brad Jamieson, room 432? On second thought, better make it a van."

"And that's why you're the CEO," Della teased, smiling up into his eyes and giving him a smacking kiss on the cheek.

CHAPTER 39

Brent Marshall sat in his hotel room, waiting for his phone to ring. He idly reviewed the background information he had gathered in preparation for his much-anticipated meeting with Walid abu Sarhaoui,

Islamist leader and president of the MOJWA governing council. He was hoping to engage the leader in conversation about his group's ideology—what the MOJWA hoped to achieve by implementing Sharia, or Islamic law, in Algeria, and what had led the MOJWA to take the members of the Gao consulate hostage.

Brent had spent some time in Gao, speaking to the locals about the battle fought between the jihadists and the Malian government. They had taken him to the dusty parade ground that passed for Gao's main square. He had viewed the mounds of gray-black ash where the Islamists had burned the townspeople's CDs, cell phones, televisions, and all of their cigarettes—symbols of the immoral and unhealthy Western influence on Muslim culture. He had been shown a concrete pillar gouged with machete blows and stained with blood where they had cut off the hands of children who had been caught thieving. Brent had asked the people how they felt about this, and they had shrugged, saying, "They were just thieves–bad boys." At least under the Tuareg rule, the raping of women and children and the looting of shops and houses had been stopped. You might get flogged for smoking a cigarette, but at least the jihadists could restore order, even if it was order without compromise.

A group of Gao patrollers, loyal to the Malian government, had taken him to a nursery school filled with munitions they'd found hidden in a safe house just around the corner. The patrollers had opened a crate filled with Russian missiles and told him that supplies like this were stockpiled in houses all around the city, waiting for the infiltrators to use against the occupiers while innocent children played in their schoolyards.

Brent wondered if peace would ever be possible between the people of this region. There was so much hatred between the religious and secular groups. There was little room for compromise and so much effort put into trying to bend the people to the Islamists' will through the use of violence and terror—which, ironically, Islam categorically forbid. The Prophet Muhammad had demonstrated a life of patience in the face of insults and persecution, even forgiving those who had previously attempted to assassinate him. How then could violence be seen as the means to bring about peace?

There was such hostility toward the West—with its propensity to support dictators when it was convenient for oil and economic gain and to overthrow them when not, all the while preaching the free speech, democracy, and freedom that they didn't practice. In Brent's view, Muslims in the East, like non-Muslim Americans in the West, both hated injustice. Peace might be possible despite their free speech differences—but only by the peace-loving populace of both worlds joining together against injustice. Brent hoped that today's interview with Walid abu Sarhaoui might help to open unconditional talks between the opposing forces and that, with the withdrawal of coalition troops in Afghanistan, equilibrium might eventually be restored, allowing the way to be paved for resolution of the conflict. He wasn't looking for the Nobel Peace Prize, but he was hoping to allow Walid a platform to let himself be seen as less of a monster and more of a leader.

Just then, the door to the hotel room was kicked open. Five or six al-Qaeda fighters surrounded him, automatic rifles cocked and pointed at his head.

The leader, none other than Ibrahin bin Sharikh, addressed him in English, "Mr. Marshall, so nice to make your acquaintance. Abu Sarhaoui sends his regrets that he will be unable to hold interviews today. He thinks it only fair that we allow you to experience the real Africa the way our forefathers did and see how they were treated by you men of the West. I'm sure you will make of it a good story."

One of the men shoved a rag in Brent's mouth and pulled a hood over his head, jamming the butt of his rifle into the reporter's ribs as he forced him to kneel while the others duct-taped his wrists behind his back and shackled his ankles. His belongings were looted—the computer and camera equipment and anything of value—and he was hauled to his feet and marched out into the hallway and down the stairs, while the other guests and patrons of the hotel stayed well out of the way of the armed men.

Outside, a van was waiting, and Brent was shoved inside and whisked away through the busy, crowded city, where things like abductions and people being held at gunpoint were everyday occurrences. Brent thought about his wife and children and how they would soon become the center of a media circus, with him being the main act. He was about to find out what his life was worth to his family, his country, and his profession. He prayed to his God that he would find the strength to survive.

CHAPTER 40

Phil Brennan had been in the office since five in the morning. It was a habit left over from his days working at the busy New York news station, WABC-TV. He was two cups of coffee in when what was coming in off the news feed from Algeria caught his attention:

American foreign correspondent, Brent Marshall, working in the city of Gao, northeast Mali, was abducted this morning by armed members of an extremist Islamic group associated with al-Qaeda in the Islamic Maghrebor, or the AQIM as the group is commonly known. Marshall had been reporting on the recent assassination of Gao Vice-Consul Tahar Touati for Today Magazine, and it is rumored that he was to interview Walid abu Sarhaoui, Islamist leader and president of the MOJWA governing council, the group responsible for Touati's assassination, today. So far, no group has claimed responsibility for Marshall's abduction, and we have not been able to reach anyone at Today Magazine to confirm whether or not a ransom demand has been received. Brent Marshall is married with two children.

Frantically, Phil pulled up his contact list and tried calling the hotel where Marshall had been staying. All the agent at the reception desk would tell him was that Mr. Marshall was not answering his phone and was not in his room and had not checked out. Phil asked to speak to the hotel manager and was kept on hold for twenty minutes. Finally the manager came on the line and told Phil that there was no sign of Marshall in the hotel. All that was left in his room was some clothing—no bags, no computer or camera equipment, no ID papers. It looked like he had made a hasty departure. He demanded that the hotel bill be paid by the magazine should Mr. Marshall's credit card be frozen due to any trouble.

Phil's desk phone rang and his boss, Editor in Chief Andrew Pearson, asked him to come to his office.

Phil hoofed it up the three floors to the executive offices. Pearson's door stood open. His secretary waved him on in, shutting the door behind him, and he took a seat across the desk from the grave-faced editor.

"Phil, it's just been released that Brent Marshall has been abducted. We haven't been able to get confirmation from a credible source as yet, so we held the announcement, expecting there would be a ransom demand. This just arrived through the mailroom." A package wrapped in brown paper, about eight inches long by five and a half inches wide, lay on his desk, covered in stamps and airmail stickers, addressed to the editor of Today Magazine—no specific name and no return address.

"I'm waiting for the CIA to arrive to examine it before I open it."

A knock sounded at the door, and Pearson's secretary ushered two officials into the office, introducing them as Agents Joe Miller and Trent Starks of the CIA.

The gentlemen showed their ID's, and agent Miller asked, "Is that the package you called about, Mr. Pearson?"

"Yes, I hate to have the thing anywhere inside the building until you guys check it out."

"Yes, sir. This is Commander Starks, our explosives expert. He'll examine the package."

Commander Starks placed a bulky case on a side table and plugged in various cables and components. Wearing special gloves, he gingerly transferred the package to the machine. Several processes took place—X-rays, ion-mobility spectrometry, and gamma radiation. When Commander Sparks was satisfied the package was safe, it was handed over to agent Miller, who asked Pearson's permission to open it.

"Be my guest," Pearson replied, his expression tense.

Unwrapping the package, Agent Miller revealed a DVD case with yesterday's date scrawled across the cover in black marker. Pearson indicated a nearby DVD player connected to a flat screen TV mounted to the wall, and Miller opened the plastic case and slipped the disc into the machine.

An image of a heavily turbaned man of Middle Eastern descent appeared on the screen. He was heavily bearded and dressed in desert fatigues. Beside him, Ibrahim bin Sharikh and two other henchmen, their faces swathed in turbaned headdresses, stood, holding automatic rifles trained on the kneeling figures of Brent Marshall and one of the remaining consular hostages, Mourad Ghassas.

The unidentified Islamist leader, suspected to be Walid abu Sarhaoui, read a statement demanding that a ransom of €18 million each be paid for the release of the consular hostage and the American journalist. In addition, they reiterated their demand that the al-Qaeda leader Necib Tayeb be released.

Ghassas read a statement saying that he and his colleague had been treated well by their captors. He then made an appeal, calling on the Algerian government to negotiate with the kidnappers for his release. The camera then turned to Brent Marshall, who also read a prepared statement, calling on his government to stop supporting the French forces who were trying to restore the traditional government in Mali.

Phil and Pearson were dumbstruck when Marshall went on to say, "I appeal to my colleagues at Today Magazine who have seen, through the death of people like Aaron Giles, how far my captors will go to stop Western reporters from interfering in the business of al-Qaeda and its affiliates in the Middle East." Looking directly into the camera, Brent begged for his life, "To Della Rawlins, you, of all people, know that there is not much time for negotiation here. Please do everything in your power to help me get home. My life is in your hands."

The camera turned back to the turbaned leader, who said, "You have until twelve o'clock Wednesday to respond to our demands, or we will kill the first hostage. We will be in touch with instructions for Della Rawlins to personally deliver the €18 million ransom.

"That is all."

"So how do we get in touch with Ms. Rawlins, Mr. Brennan? I understand that you're her supervising editor?"

"That is correct," Phil admitted. "She has gone into a protection program in the wake of her partner's death. But there is a way that I can access her," Phil said, digging out his cell phone and retrieving Ryan Jamieson's card out of his wallet.

"Better not lose any time—we only have forty-eight hours," agent Miller said.

Calling Ryan's office, Phil was told that Ryan was out of town for an undisclosed period of time. He asked to speak to Ryan's superior officer and explained the situation and time constraint they were under, and the director assured him that the CIA would contact Agent Jamieson immediately.

***

Halfway across the globe, the news monitors at the CIA surveillance house had picked up the report of the American journalist's abduction, and they were watching the effect the announcement was having on the e-mail traffic on the Sharikh network. When Ryan got the call from the director informing him that Della Rawlins's name had come up as the person who was to personally deliver the ransom, he dropped his head in his hand and said, "You can't be serious."

"Oh, I'm deadly serious," Director Thornton said. "You'd better get her back from wherever you have her in hiding. We know she's the best bait we have to pull our friend out from under his rock. I don't have to tell you that this has to be handled very carefully."

Ryan used a secure line and dialed the special number he had set up with Brad.

CHAPTER 41

Della dressed carefully for her dinner date with Brad. She had spent a long time soaking in the huge, old-fashioned, claw-foot tub, up to her neck in rose-scented bubbles. Brad had peeked in at her before he left to take Jack for a long walk to tire him out so that he wouldn't bark and disturb the other guests while they were at dinner.

"Not going to fall asleep in there and drown like a silly chicken, are you?" He grinned, sitting on the edge of the tub and scooping a soapy bubble beard and mustache around her mouth and chin. "Oh look, it's the ayatollah," he teased.

"No. I'm just going to float here and pretend I'm a noodle," she replied, lying back against an inflatable bath pillow and closing her eyes.

"Delicious." Brad grinned evilly, dipping a hand under the foamy water and running it all the way up her thigh until her legs parted, and he stroked her sweet spot until she purred like a kitten. He couldn't resist taking a bubble-tipped nipple into his mouth and flicking it with his tongue until he had her sloshing water over the edge of the tub as she pleasured her clit with her fingertips.

She opened her eyes a crack and saw how turned on he was, and she reached a soapy hand over the side of the tub and tugged on his belt. "Wanna join me?" she enticed, sliding her other hand up to reach for the zipper holding his fully erect cock prisoner.

"Later, noodle." He grinned, evading her questing hand. "I'm gonna devour you with Alfredo sauce."

"And you know how I love chocolate for dessert," she reminded him with a sexy lick of her lips, which nearly had him ignore Jack's whines to get going and just slide into the tub with her, fully clothed.

As he placed a lingering kiss on her pouting lips, Brad promised that he wouldn't be gone long, and Della settled back under the blanket of bubbles to soak.

***

Brad shook his head as he stepped out the front door of their suite. He had never met a girl as naturally sensual as Della. Just one look from her smoldering eyes had him instantly aroused. She had gotten under his skin, making him want to do erotic things with her that he had never even considered doing with other women. She was in his blood. He lived and breathed her. He wanted her to be a permanent part of his life. He wondered if it was too soon, if she was ready to commit to him. He knew that she felt the power of the attraction between them, but was she ready to give her heart again?

"Whad'ya think, Jack?" he asked, reaching down to scratch the ears of the puppy, who was looking at him with his head cocked to one side, a fluff of dandelion seeds stuck to his nose, having just dived into a patch of the fading flowers on the side of the road. "Think your mom can love the two of us at the same time?"

Jack let out a sharp bark, and Brad wasn't sure if it meant "yes" or "come on, ya sap, let's go!" But they set out for their walk on a path that would always lead both of them back to her.

***

When Brad let himself back into their suite, Della was sitting at a vanity table, putting the finishing touches on her makeup. Her hair was shiny from her shampoo, and it cascaded down over her shoulders in glossy abandon. The dress fit like a dream, and without the confining bra, the natural shape of her firm breasts, with their perky tips under the flimsy chiffon, was enough to make his mouth water. She had just rubbed some of her rose-scented lotion into her arms and legs, and her skin glowed like polished silk.

Brad stepped to the hall table and took a long, velvet box out of their pile of shopping bags. He walked over to her and sat beside her on the vanity bench seat, slipping his arms around her and watching their reflection in the glass. He closed his eyes as he drew in the soft scent of her new perfume on her skin, and he knew that he would no longer be able to smell a rose without thinking of her.

"You are so beautiful," he whispered in her ear as her lashes lowered over the passion building in her smoky eyes. "You are the sexiest woman alive. I want to devour you, but I don't want to mess you up." He gently nipped her earlobe, and she shivered as his mouth traced a path along her jawline. He removed the cover from the velvet box and drew out a slender gold chain, from which hung a perfect crystal rose. He fastened the clasp around her neck, and the pendant rested there, sparkling like fire between her breasts.

"Oh, Brad, it's beautiful," Della breathed, watching the crystal sparkle against her skin. She saw the emotion in his eyes and laid her lips on his, soft as a butterfly's touch, and whispered, "Thank you. I love it." He had been waiting so long to hear her say those three little words to him.

Della laid out food and water for Jack. And shortly after she'd finished, Brad emerged from the bedroom, his tall and powerful body tucked into black trousers, a soft black turtleneck, and a casual jacket. He wrapped a black cashmere pashmina around her, and they left a light on as they closed the door on a snoring Jack, safely tucked into his kennel.

A sleek, black limo waited at the hotel reception entrance for them. The chauffeur stepped out and said, "Good evening, sir, madam," and held the door open for them to board. They were whisked away to the wrought iron gates of the Kingsbrae Gardens, which had been transformed to nighttime elegance with the lighting of thousands of lights. The maître d' met them at the reception desk with menus and led them down the softly lit path to the privacy of the rose garden. They were seated in an arbor surrounded by climbing roses, and the maître d' plucked a long-stemmed fuchsia rose from a nearby vase and bowed formally, saying, "Please allow me to welcome you to Savour in the Garden. The rose blushes at your beauty, mademoiselle. Please accept it as a token of our appreciation for choosing to dine with us tonight."

The dapper Frenchman expertly placed linen napkins in their laps and offered menus and a wine list. He took their drink order and then made himself scarce, returning only to fill their water goblets and ask if they would like their patio heater turned on.

It was a very warm night for October, and the crescent moon hung low in the indigo sky. The soft glow of candles on the tables was all that lit the space besides the stars sprinkled across the heavens.

Brad took Della's hands in his. "Are you warm enough?"

With the soft pashmina around her shoulders, Della nodded and told him she was perfectly comfortable.

A waiter returned with their drinks, telling them he would be back in a little while to take their dinner order. They perused the selections, each of which sounded more delectable than the last. Della finally settled on a rocket pear salad made with fresh arugula and balsamic dressing, and Kingsbrae duck with an orange demi-glace, fingerling potatoes, and a medley of fresh harvest vegetables. Brad chose the New Brunswick oysters, fresh from Passamaquoddy Bay, followed by rosemary-basted lamb shank, and a savory potato croustade served with roasted root vegetables.

Brad asked Della's preference in wine, and they settled on a nice cabernet sauvignon to complement their main course.

For a while, they were content to sit back and enjoy the romantic ambiance. Soft music was piped into the garden through hidden speakers, and Brad asked Della if she'd like to dance. Aching to be held in his arms again, Della smiled and nodded, and they wandered over to a pretty, wooden gazebo, where another couple was enjoying a slow dance. Brad took Della in his arms and fitted her to his hard contours. Her arm slipped inside his jacket to encircle his waist, and he held her other hand close to his chest. His arm slipped under the soft pashmina, and she felt his long fingers stroke the curve of the bare small of her back as they swayed together, the melody soft and sultry on the night air. Too soon, the song ended, and Brad pulled her to him and kissed her with a restrained hunger, just enough to whet their appetites.

They saw their waiter approaching with their appetizers, and they sat down at their table as he expertly served the sumptuous fare. Brad's oysters were served on the half shell, and the look on his face as they slipped down his throat made her believe in the famed aphrodisiac quality of the delicate shellfish.

"How hungry did the first person to eat an oyster have to be to try that?" Della teased. "Be careful not to crack your tooth on a pearl," she laughingly warned.

"You mustn't confuse eating oysters with pearl oysters," Brad informed her. "Different altogether, although food oysters can occasionally produce pearls. This species is most likely the Eastern American oyster, very commonly found in Atlantic waters," he said sagely, causing Della to roll her eyes.

"You know way too much about animals," Della said. "I don't want to know anything about ducks or lambs. I'd prefer to just think about meat as delicious proteins found on styrofoam trays in my local supermarket."

"Ah, yes, we must get back to your lessons in duck hunting when we get back to the cabin. Ideal time for it right now with the ducks migrating south. Can't have you going back home to Michigan without bagging your first duck! What would all of my customers say? 'Brad, your girlfriend can't hit the broadside of a barn. What are you thinking?'"

"Am I your girlfriend?" Della asked, swallowing the last delicious forkful of salad and resting her fork on the delicate china plate.

Brad took a minute to consider his answer, not sure whether he should make light of the question or treat it seriously. Deciding to be bold, he took her hand in his and looked her deeply in the eyes. Placing a kiss on the back of her hand, he said softly, "I'd really like you to be."

A smile tugged at the corner of her mouth as she regarded the man who had stolen her heart, calmed her fears, and made her feel whole again. "I'd be proud to be your girlfriend," she said.

He closed his eyes, pressing a kiss into the palm of her hand. Opening them again, he saw in hers the promise of a love beyond all reason, without reservations, enough to last them a lifetime.

***

The shrill ringtone of the emergency contact cell phone that Brad had kept close at hand ever since leaving New York intruded upon the tender moment. As Brad pulled it from his jacket pocket, he was tempted to fling it as far into the middle of the duck pond as he could, but then he saw his brother's name on the call display.

"What?" he answered rudely into the phone. "We're having dinner. Can't it wait?" he said, pissed to have to think about anything except Della on this magical night.

"Brad, you have to bring Della back immediately. Something has developed. This is it, time to rock and roll. Where are you? I'm sending a chopper."

Brad filled Della in on what Ryan had told him, and with that, the bubble burst on the sweetest interlude that Della had ever experienced in her life. With that one call, she was plunged right back into that dark night of terror. All of a sudden, the scent of the garden was cloying, the shadows menacing, and behind every shrub and rock along the path, there lurked a monster. Della felt tears of frustration and fear well up beneath her eyelids. Why couldn't they just stay here where it was safe, away from the world of madmen and foreign governments?

Her heart felt empty, but she clung to Brad's hand as they rushed back to the hotel to gather their belongings. JFK's famous quote popped into her mind. "My fellow Americans, ask not what your country can do for you—ask what you can do for your country."

Yeah, Della thought, and just look where it got him.

CHAPTER 42

Della and Brad were on their way back to New York City. Della was trying her best not to think too much about the reasons for their hasty recall. She could feel the familiar sense of panic rising in her breast. She tried to put her mind back at the restaurant, in the rose arbor with Brad, drinking dry red wine in the warm candle glow, kissing, teasing, and seeing that look in his eyes. It had been too good to be true. The nightmare had returned. Brad couldn't wake her from it this time—he could only sit helplessly by as they waited to hear what was in store for them next.

The chopper landed on a helipad atop the building that housed Today Magazine. The paper's boardroom had been commandeered by the CIA because its clandestine station in New York City had been destroyed when the Twin Towers had collapsed in the September 11 attack on the World Trade Center, and it had not as yet established a new base of operations.

Ryan was there, along with Agent Miller and others from Homeland Security and the National Security Agency. All of them had been briefed by Director Thornton and Ryan, who was acting director of covert operations for the African region.

Della and Brad were drawn into a private office with Director Thornton and Ryan. The director was not crazy about the idea that people with absolutely no security clearance were involved in one of the most sensitive operations of his career. They were shown the ransom video, and Della was sick to her stomach by the blatant attempt to force her to expose herself, using her foundation for the return of captured journalists to lure her right into the lion's den. Had she not known what evil lurked behind their demand for her to personally deliver the ransom, she probably would have gone on a crusade to raise the money, walking right into their trap, never to be seen or heard from again. The challenge now, was to get bin Laden to expose himself.

* * *

The decision of the president to involve the National Security Department in what was being called Operation Lion's Den had given Ryan access to some of the most brilliant hackers in the world. He had immediately put them to work analyzing the data coming out of Algeria and, in no time, had confirmation that the IP address behind the firewall of the server in Spain was the alpha dog of the network. Everyone of importance reported to that address. Ibrahim bin Sharikh had a direct line of contact. And they had been able to sufficiently decode the identifier for Della's name to know that the person behind the firewall was aware of her.

Might be time to tighten the screws on our friend Sharikh, Ryan mused. I bet my old friend Major Thomlinson at the NATO base in Algeria would like to have a crack at squeezing some information out of him. He figured they could set it up as a retaliatory hostage taking and take Sharikh to the black site in Morocco, right next door to Algeria. The major was quite familiar with torture methods and would have no issues using them to break Sharikh. He got in touch with the major, and together, they devised a plan.

It wasn't long before Ryan got the call that Ibrahim bin Sharikh was in custody. Major Thomlinson left the city of Algiers and drove west. His passport and uniform identified him as a prison guard from Medea, and he had official papers indicating he was transporting a prisoner back to his hometown of Marrakesh, Morocco. He joked with the Spanish border guards near the Moroccan city of Oujda, tossing them a package of Turkish cigarettes as they let him through, and he drove onto the base of the Atlas Mountains. He could have traveled southwest along the coast, through the city of Casablanca, but time was of the essence. So he took the caravan route from Fes and wended his way past the old French foreign legion forts and palm oases that had once dominated the trans-Sahara desert trade to the bank of the Ziz River near the city of Rich.

There stood Tazmamart, a military prison run by the Royal Moroccan Gendarmerie, the military men who had incarcerated those who had plotted against King Hassan II in the 1970s. For a long time, the authorities had denied the existence of the Tazmamart prison, but stories of the atrocities that had taken place there were legendary, and it had become a symbol of military oppression.

Rumor had it that conditions had been terrible under Moroccan control. The prisoners were put in cramped, single-person, underground cells for twenty-four hours a day without enough headroom to stand upright. They were allowed no human contact, no light, and very little in the way of food or protection from the summer's heat or winter's cold. There was no medical treatment for injuries caused by torture or diseases like tuberculosis. There were also allegations of executions. All in all, thirty-five prisoners—more than half of the people incarcerated at Tazmamart during the eighteen years it was open under Moroccan control—died before the prison was finally closed in 1991.

Nowadays, with the permission of the Moroccan government and with the financial assistance and direction of the CIA, the facility was being used as a secret detention and interrogation center by the US government to detain alleged unlawful enemy combatants. An important aspect of the black site operation was that the legal status of the detainees was not clearly defined. In practice, inmates in black sites had no rights other than those given by the captors. What better place to bring a scumbag like Ibrahin bin Sharikh?

As Major Thom, as he was known, drove up to the guardhouse of the intimidating structure, surrounded by crumbling stone walls topped by bales of razor wire, with guards armed with automatic rifles staring down at him from the watch towers, cold sweat ran down his spine. Time was short. And he had a job to do.

CHAPTER 43

Back at the Sharikh household, anarchy reigned. With the leader of the cell snatched right out from under their noses, ambushed by a group of supposed French and Malian soldiers while he was running a shipment of guns between safe houses, nobody knew who the new leader was. And therefore, nobody was following orders given by any one lieutenant because no one had been identified as the alpha leader. Several of the higher-ups had been vying for that honor before Sharikh had arrived back on the scene, and they all had opposing views on the way hostage taking should be handled. Most of the contenders for cell leader would gladly let the opposing forces kill Sharikh in a heartbeat rather than lose their prized bargaining chip, the American journalist, or pay out any of their illegally procured funds to secure Sharikh's release.

Mahamadou Kabare was Sharikh's tech guy, in charge of communications. He could see the whole organization unraveling before his very eyes. He had often seen Sharikh texting and e-mailing a particular e-mail address when important events were being planned or discussed. Kabare knew that, unless somebody in power took over their operations, they would eventually fall prey to the occupying forces. He logged on to the computer and composed an e-mail to user Amir al-Mu'minin, which, loosely translated, meant "Commander of the Believers."

Addressing the recipient in the same manner he had seen Sharikh use, he typed:

Amir al-Mu'minin,

Forgive me for contacting you without authority, but it is with a heavy heart that I must report to you that our esteemed leader, Ibrahin bin Sharikh, has today been taken hostage by what appears to be French-Malian forces in retaliation for our capture of the American journalist, Marshall, in the city of Gao, Mali. We have not as yet received a request for ransom or offer of exchange from his captors.

There is much dissention among the members of the cell at present, and it is my fear that, without the emergence of a strong and powerful leader, this organization will fall prey to the occupying forces of the city of Gao. As loyal lieutenant to bin Sharikh, I beg your intervention to restore direction to our group and strengthen our resolve to bring jihad to the realm of these oppressors.

Almost immediately, a return message appeared in Kabare's inbox. It read:

Brother Mahamadou Kabare,

Praise be to Allah, in whose name we carry out the holy struggle jihad - to raise the word of Allah above the words of the unbelievers. Although our brother Ibrahin bin Sharikh has been taken prisoner, it is our common goal to liberate Muslim lands from its oppressors and restore Sharia to our people. That must be our common focus.

A request popped up on screen for the user to switch to digital telephony. When Kabare accepted the link, there was a collective gasp through the team of CIA agents engaged in monitoring the conversation between Kabare and the mysterious Amir, as well as from Kabare himself.

The picture on the screen was of none other than Osama bin Laden, looking a little older and a bit worse for the wear, but definitely the Sheik himself.

"Mahdi," Kabare breathed, meaning "rightly guided one." He was recognizing Osama bin Laden as the Muslim equivalent of the Messiah in the Christian faith—the chosen one, raised from the dead, divinely chosen to direct the revival of religion.

"Yes, my brother, the time is right for me to reveal myself to you as the Imam Mahdi, destined to expel the new crusaders—the Americans and Israelis—from the Abode of Islam in the name of Allah.

It has been made clear to me that, with the capture of our esteemed brother Ibrahin bin Sharikh, a new Wialyat must emerge, one of the most faithful, to become the hearing ear of Allah. There is a special mission that you all must engage in to prove who has attained the closest nearness to Allah.

Do you remember the story of the great saint, Shayk Ahmad Jaam, who used to travel on a lion wherever he went? In every city, it was his habit to ask the people of the city to send him one cow for his lion's meal. One day, he traveled to Baghdad and sent one of his disciples to Shayk Abdul Qadir al-Jilani, commanding that a cow be sent to him as a meal for his lion. The great Shayk Abdul was aware of the saint's coming and had arranged for a cow to be kept for the lion. As the disciple took the cow with him, an old stray dog that used to sit outside the home of Shayk Abdul followed him. As the cow was presented to Shayk Ahmad Jaam, who signaled the lion to commence feeding, the lion ran toward the cow. But the old, weak stray dog pounced on the lion's back, caught it by the throat, and killed it by ripping out its stomach."

"There is such a stray dog soon to be coming from America. Sharikh has already baited a trap for her, although he was not careful enough and got caught in it himself. This qybah, this bitch, must meet its end, if I have to catch her by the throat and rip out her stomach myself."

"But Amir, what about the hostages?"

"We will use the American reporter as the cow—to lure the qybah into the lion's den. And then we will spring the trap, and that will be that. No more hungry lion. Let me tell you what you must do ..."

CHAPTER 44

Della and Brad had been waiting for hours in Phil's office at Today Magazine. There was no way of knowing how the kidnappers were going to get in touch with Della with instructions for delivering the ransom, so the best plan of action was to sit tight. Contact had been made with Washington, and the €18 million had been approved by the president under some sort of emergency budget through the Special Activities Department. The money had been delivered by armored car and was sitting on a desk in a locked office with an armed guard.

"I wonder how they're going to protect me if I have to bring the ransom to the terrorists by myself," Della worried, as she and Brad sat together sipping coffee and watching the hands of the clock tick off the minutes.

"I don't know. I guess it depends on what the captors demand. No doubt they've planned for several contingencies, but whoever responds to this with you will have to be able to fly by the seat of his pants."

"Yeah, too bad they can't use a body double for me like bin Laden did," Della said.

"Don't be too sure on that," Brad said as a female agent walked past the office door, looking remarkably like Della.

The door opened to the office next door, and agent

Miller strode purposefully toward them. "Della, it's the call we've been waiting on. Now, remember, like we discussed, stay calm, listen carefully, and agree to whatever they say. Everything is being recorded. Try to stall for time if you can. We have your back regardless what they ask for."

Della was a bag of nerves inwardly. But outwardly she squared her shoulders, remembering that a man's life lay in the balance. And she followed Agent Miller into the room where a battery of equipment was in place, ready to record and hopefully track the call. Agent Miller fitted a headset and mike over her ears, and the recording agent nodded to her as he clicked open the line.

"This is Della Rawlins," she said, nervously twisting the coiled headphone wire around her fingers.

A heavily accented voice answered. "Listen carefully," the voice said. "Go to LaGuardia airport. There is a reservation in your name for American Airlines flight number 603 departing at gate number 35 at 9:00 a.m. When you land, you will go to the taxi kiosk and dial 20071825; ask for Raoul. You will receive further instructions at that time. You will come unarmed, unaccompanied, and without any communication devices, either portable or concealed. You will be watched at all times while you are in transit, so do not attempt to make contact with anyone until we make contact with you. Do you understand?"

"Yes," Della replied.

"No slipups, no tricks, Ms. Rawlins. You come alone. Keep in mind the deadline is tomorrow at 12:00, or Mr. Marshall will be executed."

"Yes, I understand." Della nodded.

"Oh, and Ms. Rawlins?" the voice said. "Don't forget to bring the money."

"How am I supposed to get that through customs?" Della asked warily.

"Oh, I'm sure your friends at the CIA will help you with that," the voice sneered, and then the line went dead.

The communications tech shook his head. The trace had only led back to the Sharikh household. No news there. The only thing noteworthy was that the former tech/communications guy was now the one giving orders.

***

On Ryan's end, there were no new leads, either. The team had watched Kabare deliver the ransom information to Della. And following that, the usual missive had been sent to the Spanish server. But despite their best efforts, no one had been able to get past the security firewalls to the end user. Ryan pounded the desk in frustration. What was he supposed to do, let Della walk right into bin Laden's lair without any protection, without any wire, and without any tracking device? He'd be damned if he'd let it happen. He had told her he'd have her back, and neither hell nor high water would stop him from keeping his word.

On the other side of the world, Brad was coming very close to losing his cool. He had cornered Agent Miller and was up in his grill, his every body hair raised and his posture threatening. He was a force to be reckoned with. Agent Miller was tempted to call the military police and have him forcibly removed and put in a holding cell until this was all over, but he feared that would not bode well for Ms. Rawlins's co-operation in the mission.

"How the hell are you planning to protect her?" Brad's voice vibrated through the thin walls of the news editor's office. "She sure as hell is not going out of my sight until you give me a detailed plan of how you are going to track where she's going and how you're going to get a team in there to take that bastard and all of his little cronies out, not to mention keep her alive."

Della was glad she wasn't on the receiving end of the tirade that followed, but she heard Brad loud and clear when he insisted that he be included in the highly classified conference call that was due to take place any minute with the directors, chief of security, and secretary of defense to decide on a plan of action. The alternative was to forget about Della's participation in the mission.

When Brad stormed back into the office where she was waiting, she was ready to give it to him with both barrels. She stood facing him down, all five foot seven inches of her.

"Where do you get off making ultimatums on my behalf to the chief of security? I think I have some say in what I will or will not do. Do you really think that Ryan is going to just let me walk in blind without a plan? This is way beyond your area of expertise, Brad. Stay out of it!"

"Look, Della, there's too much at stake here for me to just sit on my hands and do nothing. I've read The Art of War, and I know more about the skill of manipulation than most of these guys have ever learned. How else could I have gotten where I am? I'm not about to let you put yourself in harm's way without knowing what they're planning in case things go sideways. Please, please trust me," he said, taking her hands in his. "I will not let you become collateral damage in their frenzy to put a cap on this particular well."

Della was upset by his actions and the implication that he didn't consider her intelligent enough to look after herself, thinking that she would just fall in line with these war hounds' plans without considering the danger to herself. She was smart enough, though, to recognize Brad's experience in dealing with high-level executives and politicians and grudgingly admitted that he probably knew the game of hardball better than she.

"Okay, look," she conceded, "I know that you're the one looking out for my best interests here. But I'm a big girl. I'm not afraid to see this through. I will follow the CIA's orders to the letter—whatever you and they think is prudent to achieve our objectives. I trust your judgment. Just don't think you can speak for me. I want to know what you're thinking before I decide what I'm going to do. Deal?"

"Okay, deal," Brad agreed. "Della, don't think I doubt your intelligence or your bravery. I don't know another living soul who has more of both than you. I just can't bear the thought of anything bad happening to you." He brought her hands to his lips, closing his eyes. His breath hitched, and she could sense how hard it was for him not to give into his emotions and cling to her. She was having some difficulty with that herself.

"Brad," she whispered, touching his cheeks, dark with stubble, "I love you. We're gonna finish this, and then we're coming home, and I'm washing my hands of the whole damn lot of it. The politicians can duke it out between themselves. I'm finished with politics."

"I hear ya, little girl," said a booming voice from across the room.

"Daddy!" Della cried, running across the room and flying into her father's outstretched arms.

CHAPTER 45

Della sat in coach seat 3B of the American Airlines Boeing 747, flying out of LaGuardia, New York, to Gibraltar, Spain. The flight had a stopover and a plane change in London's Heathrow as well, so she didn't know what to expect. The CIA had investigated the reservation and was planning for every contingency. Della's arm still hurt where the GPS homing device had been implanted under her skin. Ryan had sourced a chip that was undetectable by normal electronic scanners. The CIA was using them in all field agents engaged in covert operations. To anyone examining Della, it would appear to be a birth control implant, and it had worked perfectly so far. The techs could clearly see her blip on their GPS map, which was "requirement one" on Brad's list of requirements for Della's participation in Operation Lion's Den.

"Requirement two" had been eyes on Della both in flight and on the ground. As it would have looked suspicious to add a passenger to the manifest at this point, the CIA's answer was to replace one of the flight attendants with an undercover agent who would report her every movement.

"Requirement three" was to get Brad on a separate flight arriving about the same time as Della so that he could keep his eye on her himself. He wasn't above going in disguise so as not to attract attention. Surprisingly, the management team was not against this requirement. They needed as many backups as possible in case of something unexpected happening.

It had been a long, anxious night, and Della grabbed a nap while they flew over the Atlantic. She didn't stir until the captain's voice came over the cabin speaker announcing their descent into Heathrow International Airport in London.

The stopover in Heathrow was tight, and Della would have just enough time to meet her connecting flight. She joined the queue waiting to deplane, holding tightly to the red leather tote bag containing the ransom money. She felt rumpled in her sand-colored, linen pants and matching trench coat, and she was dying for a coffee. No one approached her as she sat by herself in the British Airways lounge near gate twelve, waiting for her flight to be called. Across the seating area for gate eleven, a tall, gray-haired gentleman sat holding a walking cane and reading a newspaper while he surreptitiously watched the young, dark-haired lady in the light trench coat nervously twisting the handle of the oversized red tote bag she held on her lap. British Airways announced the boarding call for flight 803 to Gibraltar, Spain, and the gray-haired gentleman watched until the woman showed her boarding pass and entered through the gate to board the aircraft. When he received confirmation from the flight attendant that she was safely seated, he relaxed and waited for his own flight to be called.

***

The sun was rising as the British Airways flight approached the airport on the Gibraltar Peninsula. Della couldn't believe her eyes. The airport was small, with one of the main runways extending right out into the ocean. As they circled over the densely populated city, she was shocked to notice that the main runway ran right across a major highway, and it looked like traffic had to be stopped in order for planes to land or take off. The plane descended, and she closed her eyes as they swooped lower next to the gigantic Rock of Gibraltar, saying a little prayer that they wouldn't end up in the ocean. Finally, with a reassuring bump and lurch, the airliner touched down, and the engines roared into reverse thrust, swiftly slowing the giant bird into a gentle roll. Della, glad to be alive so far, gathered her scattered wits together and mentally went through the checklist of things she had to do once she got off the plane. The piece of paper in her pocket had the name and phone number of her contact, and she touched the edge of the lined paper for the hundredth time since leaving New York to reassure herself that it was still there.

As the plane rolled to a stop in front of the terminal building, she joined the throng of passengers waiting to disembark. Following the line of passengers into the arrivals area, Della bypassed the escalator leading to the baggage claim area and followed the signs to the taxi kiosk. She fished the crumpled note from her jacket pocket and picked up the receiver at the booth, dialing the number.

A voice answered, "Quieres un taxi?"

Reading from the paper, Della answered in her best high school Spanish, "Puedo hablar con Raoul, por favor."

"Un momento."

There was a slight pause, and then another voice answered. "Raoul," it said.

"Yo soy Della Rawlins," Della identified herself.

The speaker answered in accented English. Della had to listen carefully to understand what he was saying.

"Hola, Ms. Rawlins. Please go to the taxi area outside the main terminal building to your right. There you will see a line of cabs marked Gibraltar Cabs. Find the car with number 28285 on the trunk. Show the driver your passport, and he will take you to your destination."

"Thank you. Gracias," Della said, jotting down the number.

She gathered the handles of the heavy, red tote in her hand and headed toward the exit. She could see the taxi queue and left the air-conditioned building, stepping into the seventy-six-degree heat. Walking down the line of taxicabs, Della's eyes frantically scanned the numbers painted on the trunks. There it was—28285. She opened the rear passenger door and slid inside, showing the driver her passport. A pair of dark brown eyes regarded her from underneath a turbaned headdress.

Suddenly, the door locks engaged, and the driver took off, driving quickly onto the roadway that crossed the airport runway just before the warning lights came on and the gate started to close, indicating an incoming flight. Della looked out her window and saw the approaching jetliner bearing down on them. The cabbie gunned the engine, and the car made it to the other side just as the wheels on the jetliner touched down with a screech, and Della started to breathe again.

***

Behind them, Brad beat on the headrest of the seat ahead of him as the cab driver berated him in Spanish. All he could see were the taillights of the ramshackle cab ahead of them as it sped toward the opposite gate while the jetliner came in for a landing. It was a good ten minutes before the gate slid open again, and he yelled at the cab driver to catch up with the other cab as he frantically texted Ryan to feed him Della's coordinates.

***

Luckily for Brad, Della's driver felt confident that he had shaken any pursuers and had headed around to Gibraltar's Westside, outside the northern end of Gibraltar Harbour. Della read the signage indicating they were entering the Ocean Village Marina next to the airport runway. She fervently hoped that the GPS implanted in her arm was working, and she slipped off her jacket, thinking that the device would have an easier time registering to the satellite.

The cab pulled up to a berth where a sleek and expensive yacht was moored. The name painted on the back read A A Advocate. Two burly men, obviously holding automatic rifles inside their jackets, stepped toward the car, and the cab driver released the door locks. One of the men reached inside and grabbed Della by the arm, pulling her roughly out of the car. She was forced up the gangplank and onto the vessel, clutching the red tote bag and trench coat to her breast. She was forced down a flight of stairs into a large lounge area, where the gunmen scanned her with an electronic wand and patted her down to be sure she wasn't armed or wearing a wire. They confiscated her cell phone and then cuffed both of her ankles and wrists to a chair and pulled a hood over her head, tying it tightly around her neck. Satisfied that their prisoner was secured, they left to go up on deck to prepare for departure. Their instructions were to get away as quickly as possible.

Della tugged on the handcuffs, but the chair she was tethered to was bolted to the floor, so there was no way she was getting loose. Luckily, she was sitting with her back to a window, so she tried to angle her arm so that the GPS unit would still register to the satellite. It was the only way that Ryan and Brad could track her movements.

The hum of the yacht's motors indicated that they were pulling away from the dock. Della sent up a little prayer that, wherever she was being taken, someone would be able to follow her.

CHAPTER 46

Major Thom drove around to the prisoner intake gate at Tazmamart prison. He showed his ID and prisoner intake forms, and the guards slid the gate open. He drove the van up to the door, got out and went around to the back of the vehicle, and opened the armored door. His prisoner sat stoically, handcuffed and shackled, eyes downcast. The major released him from the van and nudged him with an automatic rifle, signaling him to get out.

The door to the prison swung open, and the prisoner was led past the courtyard area to one of the detention buildings. He was directed down a set of stone steps, and as they descended into the depths, the light got progressively dimmer. When they finally reached the cell block, the air was musty, damp, and cold, and it was practically dark. The major stopped outside a cell door and unlocked the prisoner's shackles. He instructed him in Arabic to undress, and once he'd complied, he pushed him inside the cell and locked the door behind him.

Sharikh looked around in the dim light. The cell was less than ten feet long and four feet wide. But the devious part of it was the ceiling, which was too low for a person to stand upright. You could only sit on the filthy cot or stand and bend over. There was no toilet, only a six-by-six-inch hole in the floor. The smell was terrible. Sharikh chose to sit on the cot, and he could hear from a distance the sound of a dog barking and screams of inmates. His thoughts took him back to his imprisonment in Guantanamo Bay, where he had been beaten; intimidated; humiliated; and, until it had become illegal, waterboarded. He still had nightmares of drowning because of that. If the person administering the torture didn't know what they were doing, you could very well end up with brain damage from oxygen deprivation. Although he had been waterboarded up to thirty times a day, he had not broken. He knew that, if they'd found out what he had been up to in Afghanistan, he would never have seen the light of day again, so his lips had remained tightly sealed. Luckily, the prisoner transfer had come up, and he had been released.

Now he wasn't sure who his captors were. If it was the French-Malian occupation, he was only being held as a retaliatory hostage for the American journalist, Marshall. And he would probably be released when the American's magazine raised his ransom. If, on the other hand, the Americans somehow knew about his other activities …

He heard another prisoner screaming out in agony, and shivers went up his spine.

***

Sometime later, Sharikh heard the clank of a door and the sound of approaching footsteps. The major was back, but this time he was accompanied by two soldiers. They were all dressed in American fatigues.

"On your feet, inmate," he ordered.

Sharikh obeyed, his heart sinking as he realized his predicament. The major threw him a pair of shorts, and one of the guards handcuffed and shackled him. He was taken from his cell and marched past row upon row of cells until they came to a heavy, metal door. They were entering the interrogation center. As the door clanged open, Sharikh's eyes were blinded by the garish light.

They had passed by a cell where an officer was shouting at a prisoner who was on his knees, shackled to the floor, while another officer stood by with a snarling Rottweiler—in attack mode. It was all the dog handler could do to hold it back. The beastly animal's jaws snapped, and its guttural growls and snarls left no doubt as to what the prisoner's fate would be should the interrogator decide to let the dog loose. Separated by a thin wall, the next cell had held a prisoner stripped to his underwear and shackled to a board. The interrogator was shouting questions at him, and whenever he was displeased with the answers, he shocked him in the side or legs with a cattle prod. The man was swearing innocence to whatever the interrogator was accusing him of, and his body was slick with sweat, his face a mask of terror, his eyes wild and full of pain. Tears ran down his cheeks, and spit drizzled out of the corner of his mouth. His cry was a keening wail of agony. They had also passed an empty cell, where the tools of torture resided. Several reclined boards were set up with leather restraints for the head, wrists, and ankles. Sharikh's captors had led him past several closed doors, where he could hear the muffled cries of prisoners and the shouts and threats of interrogators.

Soon he had been brought into a stuffy interrogation room. A Taser sat on a side table, plugged into a charging unit. He was seated at a metal table, and the two armed guards stood behind him, their automatic rifles at the ready.

Major Thom closed the door and turned toward the prisoner. "Ibrahin bin Sharikh, you have been a very busy boy since you were last a guest of the US government. To say that the accommodations here at Tazmamart are not quite so well appointed as those at Guantanamo is an understatement. But if you are co-operative, you might find your stay with us to be a short one. If you decide to be unco-operative, you will find your stay will be even shorter." The major smiled as if he had made a clever joke, and the two guards smirked. "Now, I am not going to waste our time asking you stupid questions about your cell or your activities. Your headquarters has been under surveillance from the minute you set foot back in Algeria. Months before then, actually. We've traced your network all over the globe, and many of your contacts are being investigated as we speak—people like Brooklyn 40510, Alibamobad_911, and al-Mu'minin." He took particular notice of the prisoner's facial expressions and demeanor as he mentioned the last username. Sharikh was visibly shaken. His eyes darted to Major Thom, and his Adam's apple bobbed as he swallowed nervously.

"We know also about the kidnapping of the Gao consul members and your very nasty treatment of your French and Malian prisoners of war." He shook his head and tut-tutted. "You people don't have much experience in how to get information out of prisoners, do you?" He barked out a laugh. "Your compatriot Hakimh had never experienced the sting of the Taser before," he said, taking the instrument out of the charger and stroking the head over the prisoner's jugular vein. "Now, let's play a little question and answer. If you answer right, you go through to the next round. If you lie, you get the buzzer, okay? First question. "Why did you ask Della Rawlins to deliver the ransom for Brent Marshall in person?"

The ready light on the Taser gun shone red in Sharikh's eyes as he answered, "It was ordered by my commanding officer."

"And what is his name?" Thom asked. "Remember, we've had you under surveillance for months now."

Sharikh's mind raced to find an answer to satisfy his tormentor but not give too much information away. "He goes by the name Amir al-Mu'minin. I have never met him. I only communicate with him through e-mail."

"Arrrrrr ... Wrong answer," Thom said, letting the Taser fly.

The prisoner reeled from the electric shock, his body seizing and bucking on the ground.

"Now, come on. That was only a little tickle." Thom chuckled teasingly.

"Hey, Major Thom, you can use that gun in drive stun mode, too. That way, we won't have to drag his ass back to his cell, and you can stun him up to five times unless he has some sort of heart illness."

"Is that so?" Major Thom said. "Why thank you, Lieutenant. That's some very useful information. Amazing technology, isn't it?" he asked sarcastically, holding the instrument up to the prisoner's face and reloading the clips. "Just in case," he said.

"Now then, let me remind you of a conversation you had with the amir over video telephony, where you called him 'the Mahdi.' Why did you call him that?"

The major was bluffing, knowing that bin Laden had revealed himself to Kabare but betting he had also confided in Sharikh in order to get him to do his bidding. Everybody wanted to be Wialyat, the ear of Allah.

Sharikh could not move his body. The electrical currents were tearing through his nervous system like fire through his veins. He tried to focus his concentration on reaching toward the ear of Allah to help him block out the pain. He prayed for all he was worth to raise himself above it as he answered, "He told me he was the chosen one."

"Not the chosen one. The Messiah, the one raised from the dead. You saw his face. You know his name."

The Taser was inches from Sharikh's neck. The major prompted him by making an "O" sound.

The Taser came closer to the prisoner's neck. He closed his eyes, but his resolve wavered, and his voice burst forth a betrayal. "The Lion Sheik." Sharikh lay panting, his eyes closed, cursing his weak mortal body.

Major Thom persisted relentlessly. "But that's not his real name, Sharikh. What's his real name?"

Sharikh started to weep, his breath coming in great gasps. He realized that his tormentors already knew his commander's name. "Osama bin Laden," he cried.

"That's right. Good man," Thoms said, relaxing his posture and patting him on the shoulder. "Now that wasn't so hard, was it? Take a minute to compose yourself. I hate to see a grown man cry." He poured a glass of water and pushed it toward the prisoner, who gulped it down greedily.

Thom gave him a minute or so to recover, and then, sitting on the edge of the desk, tapping the Taser against his leg, he said, "So Osama bin Laden wants Della Rawlins to come here to deliver the ransom money in person. To him. Is that correct?"

"I was already taken into custody when the arrangements were made. I don't know anything more."

"That's true," the other lieutenant said. "Kabare delivered the instructions for Ms. Rawlins's ransom delivery. He"—the man indicated Sharikh—"was already in custody."

"Where is the Sheik hiding?" Thom brought his face close to the prisoner's. "Tell me now, or things will get much worse for you."

Sharikh gathered his strength to resist the major's will. He knew that he would be dead either way—whether he died right here in this place or gave them what they wanted. The amir would see to that. Shaytan was whispering in his ear to give in to the American warlords, while his loyalty to the Mahdi urged him to stay silent.

Major Thom saw the warring emotions cross the prisoner's face. He knew that the information was very close to the surface. It would take just a little more persuasion to force it out. "Sharikh, I am not a cruel person. But sometimes doing my job means that I have to do things I don't want to do in order to get information that we need. I don't like to make people suffer. And really, if you don't give up the information, we still have people tracking your boss down. It's just a race to the finish as to whether I get the information or some tech whiz kid breaks through a motherfucking firewall. It's only a matter of time. You're a mere termite in the scope of this operation. You might as well give me the information. You're very, very dispensable." He said the last word menacingly, right into the prisoner's face, the spit from the word dispensable spraying over him.

"By the way, that's a pretty little wife and daughters you have there back in Algiers. Our men just might pay them a visit, have a little fun. They've been cooped up over here for months now with no female companionship, if you know what I mean. Too bad your cell has been rounded up. Nobody's home to protect them now." He shook his head sadly.

Sharikh reared up and roared, "American pigs! Yankee bastards! Sons of dogs. May Allah bring his wrath down upon you and your children. May he smite you with the mighty sword of jihad!"

"Take him out to Interrogation Two," Major Thom said, unimpressed by the prisoner's outburst.

They were getting closer to Sharikh's complete capitulation.

The armed guards unshackled the prisoner and took his battered body up the hall to another interrogation room. There in the middle stood the same dreaded tool of torture that Sharikh had faced at Guantanamo Bay. The guards restrained his hands and feet and forced his head into the leather fastenings. The major stood nearby and gave the order for the water buckets to be filled. A cloth was placed over Sharikh's face, and the water bucket was raised and poised to pour.

The major gave Sharikh one last chance to concede defeat, but his faith in Islam and his desire to be found a worthy believer would not let him give in. He shook his head, and immediately the water flowed over the densely woven cloth, filling his nose and mouth, and the familiar feeling of drowning made the panic rise in his breast. The major gestured for the water to stop, and he pulled the cloth off Sharikh's face.

"This is not fun for any of us, Sharikh. Have you had enough?"

"Fascist pig!" Sharikh spat.

"Well now, boys, I guess he wants some more." Thom gave the signal to resume.

Every five minutes or so, he stopped the procedure until he noticed the prisoner was weakening.

"You know, Sharikh," Major Thom said, "bin Laden's no Mahdi. Do you know he hired someone who looked like him to take his place the night the Navy SEALs shot him in Pakistan? What a coward. He let his family be collateral damage while he watched from a rooftop a couple streets away. Now he's shacked up in some Spanish hacienda, probably in the lap of luxury, while poor saps like you risk your lives to defend him. Are you that stupid? Is he going to protect your family when he did nothing to protect his own? He's a fake, a fraud. It's not worth your life or your family's safety. Give him up, Sharikh. It's just not worth it."

Sharikh was gasping for breath. He made no motion to indicate whether he was ready to comply. Tears streamed down his face as he processed what the major had said. Had he been duped all this time, looking for guidance from a God with feet of clay? What of his family? He thought of his loyal wife, who would follow him unquestioningly into the heart of darkness. He thought of his beautiful daughters, who wanted to go to school in America—to get an education, they said, and to learn about the world and try to understand why their world was in such turmoil. How could they be protected with no father to watch over them? He prayed to Allah to forgive him, to show him the path to be a worthy believer. He had lost faith in those who professed to know the way. Jihad was over for him. With his surrender, he earned his twenty pieces of silver. "He's at his lawyer's home in Majorca—Giovanni Di Stefano, in Son Vida," he gasped, exhausted.

Major Thom gave the signal to stop interrogation. Sharikh was released from the waterboard. The armed guards were left to clean him up, get him some dry clothes, and take him to a regular cell, while the major hurried off to make contact with Ryan and the rest of the team.

CHAPTER 47

The AA Advocate had been cruising along for hours, and nobody had come to check on Della. She really needed to pee. She tried clanking the handcuffs against the chrome of the chair base, but she couldn't make enough noise to attract anyone's attention. She was thirsty, too, and the hood was making her feel very claustrophobic and overheated. She felt around for something, anything that could help her. Her fingers came into contact with a device on the wall. It felt like a radio with a row of buttons. She pressed the first one. Nothing. The second one. Static. The third one. Now she could hear people talking loudly over a hissing sound, and she realized it must be an intercom to the upper deck.

"How much longer till we get there?" a voice said in Spanish.

"Perhaps another half hour," another man answered. "You can see the island just coming into sight."

"Are we taking her right to the house?" the first man asked.

"Yeah, but we take her in by the back entrance. The boss doesn't want anyone to see her there."

"She must have only got a one way ticket, sí?" another voice asked, causing the other two to laugh.

"All I was told was to get her there, lose any tail, and not let her be seen. Maybe the boss is getting a little on the side this weekend with the wife gone to the mainland shopping."

"Maybe we get to watch on the security cameras, sí?"

The other men laughed.

"Maybe with the hood and handcuffs, she's into the kink," the first man joked.

"Better go check on her," the second man ordered. "Don't want to damage the goods."

Della pushed the button again, and the intercom went silent.

Soon she heard footsteps coming down the stairs from the upper deck. She heard the man come into the lounge.

"Por favor, señor, necesito usar bano," she said, begging to be allowed to use the bathroom.

"Un momento," the man grunted.

And Della could hear the clink of keys as he grabbed her wrist and turned the key in the lock. He took her by the upper arm, pulled the hood off, and led her over to a door and turned the handle, pushing her inside.

Della somehow managed to wiggle her pants down with her wrists shackled and relieved her bladder, which had been on overload. She straightened her clothes and looked around to see if there was anything she could use to send a message to Ryan or Brad, if they had even been able to follow her. She grabbed the bar soap on the vanity and pushed open the blind covering the bathroom window. Quickly she scrawled "Della" backward on the window with the soap so if they were searching for her, at least they would know which boat she had gotten off.

She replaced the blind and then grabbed a Solo cup out of a dispenser and gulped down a couple of glasses of water as the guard pounded on the door for her to hurry up.

The guard grabbed her ass as he marched her back over

to secure her to the chair again, and he ran his hand up her leg as he fastened her ankle shackle. As he squeezed her breast, he said close to her ear in Spanish, "Hey, belleza, maybe you'll have some time left for me after Di Stefano is finished with you, sí?" And he pressed his erection aggressively against her thigh.

Revolted, Della shrunk away from him and hunched her shoulders, and he laughed, patting her cheek before he slid the hood back over her face, tying it tightly around her neck.

"I look forward to it, putita," he growled, calling her "little whore."

The man left the room, and Della was visibly shaking. What had she let herself in for? And where were Brad and Ryan? Suddenly the name Di Stefano registered with her. Wasn't that the name of Saddam Hussein's lawyer? The one who had represented hundreds of high-profile villains, including the likes of Charles Manson and Harold Shipman, without a valid law degree? She remembered that the man had been tangled up in Ponzi schemes in Europe and that his name had been linked with some other lawyer named Fiol or Fioli in Majorca, who had tried to bring charges against President Obama over 9/11, saying, that instead of being killed, bin Laden should have been "pursued, arrested, tried, and convicted on behalf of the victims of some terrible and appalling atrocities." He'd said, "The killing of bin Laden was even worse as it took place in foreign territory, Pakistan, without the permission of that government."

Well now, Della thought. It seems like our friend bin Laden has crawled into a cushy cave in Majorca with a fine nest of nasty vipers, and it appears that I'm about to make their acquaintance.

CHAPTER 48

Giovanni Di Stefano and his guest were relaxing on the shaded terrace of his €20 million home, located on one of the very best and most extensive plots on Son Vida. The property enjoyed a sensational 360-degree view from the Bay of Palma to the mountains. The main house boasted a galleried, vaulted reception hall with marble floors and walls, a dining room, five bedrooms and five bathrooms, and a library and office, along with a gourmet kitchen with a breakfast area, a bordega with tasting facilities, a self-contained music and recording studio, plus a two-bedroom staff apartment with its own living area, kitchen, and utility and laundry rooms. The separate indoor pool/guesthouse boasted a lavish spa, sauna, wet bar, and two complete guest apartments.

From the covered, south-facing outdoor terrace, the two men could enjoy total privacy while enjoying the sea view, in combination with beautifully landscaped gardens and the sparkling mosaic-tiled outdoor pool. Giovanni made sure to keep the staff well away so that even the guards and servants who worked in the villa were unaware of the identity of the villa's guest.

Giovanni's life of crime and ill-gotten gains had funded it all. One judge had described him as "one of life's great swindlers." He had been referred to as "the Devil's Advocate" for his work for some of the world's most notorious criminals. His client list included such figures as Saddam Hussein, Slobodan Milošević, Charles Manson, and Serbian paramilitary leader and indicted war criminal Arkan. He was one of the most convincing, conniving, conscienceless, colorful, and creative thieves around. Recently he had been accused of twenty-seven charges of deception, fraud, and money laundering between 2001 and 2011, which included "tricking people into thinking he was a bona fide legal professional."

The truth was, Giovanni had never gone to law school. He knew a lot about the law, but his knowledge was all self-taught. Once the authorities caught on that he might be a fraud, the British police and the Law Society had started an investigation. As a result, he had been arrested in 2011.

The Law Society had declared that Di Stefano was "not a solicitor or a registered foreign lawyer or a registered European lawyer." Further, the organization was unable to verify either his legal qualifications or his status as a foreign lawyer, despite going to considerable lengths to do so and despite having asked Di Stefano himself for the information. The Law Society of Scotland and the Ordine Degli Avvocati of Rome had also said that Di Stefano was not a registered solicitor.

Di Stefano did not see any of this as an impediment to his career. All he needed was a bona fide law firm through which he could act as agent, and he was back in business. His greatest claim to fame was the size of his balls. He once commented that he would "defend Adolf Hitler or Satan." His mantra was "defending the indefensible," and he believed it so much that his autobiography bore that same title. When asked about his motivation, he replied, "No one's ever asked, 'Does Satan have a case? Does he have a good case?'" Of course, the judges who had heard the many trials of fraud, money laundering, and embezzlement against him found him to be a swindler without scruple or conscience.

Giovanni had always admired Osama bin Laden. In an interview, he had recounted meeting Osama in 1998. When asked what he was like, he had replied, "I found he had a handshake like a priest. Warm. And secondly, he had a wonderful manner of speaking. Very … soft. A calming effect. Almost like a psychiatrist, in a way."

Osama had had Giovanni handle some shady deals with Majorcan developers, and he had found the Italian a very useful and skilled "advocate." When the American forces had supposedly killed him, Di Stefano had proved a most helpful and trustworthy friend, in not allowing his estate to be carved up among his family. He had found ways to protect much of Osama's wealth by tying funds up in trusts and timed investments, such that Osama still had a good bit of power behind his name, even though he was technically "dead." When he staged his triumphant resurrection and return to power, he would still have the wealth behind him to assert his leadership. Giovanni would be well placed as his trusted financial and legal adviser. It was a very useful and symbiotic (not to mention profitable) relationship.

Naturally, the plucking of this last thorn in Osama's side, this Della Rawlins, was a task that had Giovanni's name stamped all over it. With his fortress located in the opulent and politically benign playground of Majorca, conveniently located outside of the hot zone of Afghanistan and Pakistan and close to the new territory of North Africa, it was an ideal place for Osama to deal with the loose ends of his former life and prepare for his triumphant return. The last thing he needed was the infidels, the American interlopers, breathing down his neck, trying to hunt him down. He was the Lion Sheik. It was time to bare his teeth and unsheathe his claws. He would rid himself of this annoying putita, this brazen qybah. Did she really think that she, a mere woman, could stop the Imam Mahdi, the "rightly guided one" chosen by Allah himself? She was soon to feel the mighty power of jihad as her blood was spilled in the name of Allah. She would be a worthy sacrifice.

The holy celebration of Eid al-Adha (the Festival of Sacrifice) fell on the tenth day of Dhu al-Hijjah, the last month of the Islamic lunar calendar. It was the day when Muslims celebrated the willingness of Ibrahim (Abraham) to follow Allah's command to sacrifice his own son Ishmael. To honor this selflessness, the faithful would bring animals to the holy place to sacrifice. Human slaves had been offered up in the past, but no human sacrifice had been made publicly in years. One day soon, they would drive the infidel Christians and Jews out of the holy city of Makkah, and the faithful would once again be able to complete the Hajj, the pilgrimage into the holy city. Yes, Miss Della's sacrifice would perfectly complete the final ritual of the Hajj, thus completing his own spiritual cleansing and confirming his rightful place among the faithful as "the chosen one." Allah, all praise to his holy and exalted name, would be pleased.

In the meantime, he had every right under Islamic law to claim her as his slave, as she had been captured as a spoil of war with the Americans. And though he had no desire to use her himself, he would give her to his men and let them enjoy the pleasure of her body until such time as it would be of use to him. Perhaps he would have her tongue cut out as well, to show the Americans what his people thought of Western journalists publishing their lies and ill-informed versions of what was really happening in their country. Yes, the Americans needed another lesson to learn with their eyes, as they refused to open their ears. Maybe he would have her ears cut off as well and send them to the president as a reminder of his refusal to listen. Miss Rawlins would pay well for the effrontery of thinking she could face the Lion Sheik in his own den.

CHAPTER 49

Brad was beside himself. "Can't you squeeze a few more knots out of this old tin can?" he asked the commander of the SSK 760 antisubmarine sub in which he and Ryan and a team of Navy SEALs special forces were presently hitching a ride to Majorca.

Ryan kicked him and mouthed, "Shut up!" as the commander replied, "We're running at top speed, son. We could have come out here in a 340-foot attack sub, doing thirty knots, but you can't maneuver that in shallow water. You do want to sneak up on the bastards, don't you?"

"Yes, of course, Commander. Please excuse my brother. It's his lady friend who's been taken hostage. He's a little on edge."

"Understandable." The commander nodded. "Just let us do our jobs, and we'll get you there shortly." Turning to his first mate, he gave the order, "Rise to periscope depth."

All Brad knew was that they had tracked Della's GPS tracking device signal, and it had come to a stop at this location.

***

When Brad had lost visual on Della at Gibraltar Airport, his frantic call to Ryan, who was monitoring the operation from the nearby Spanish Naval Port of Rota, had his brother reaching for the phone to request the US Navy's fastest submarine out of Gibraltar Harbour to follow Della's GPS signal.

Luckily, Brad had arrived at the quay just in time to see the AA Advocate leaving port. He had frantically asked a nearby boater if a girl carrying a large, red purse had been seen getting on the yacht, pleading with the boater and explaining that he thought his girlfriend had been kidnapped. When the man confirmed Della's description, he fed the information back to Ryan, who by this time had received the call from Major Thom, confirming bin Laden's likely location to be Di Stefano's address in Son Vida Estates, just outside of Palma, Majorca.

When the port authority had confirmed that the AA Advocate was registered to Giovanni Di Stefano, Ryan knew the lion was in his den. They were going to need a smaller, stealthier craft that could maneuver in the shallower coastal waters off Majorca. They didn't want their quarry to know they were tracking him down, and they couldn't waste any time with Della already in his clutches. Ryan had picked up the phone and dialed a direct number to the commander of the US forces in Gibraltar; he'd requested the use of the commander's fastest submarine tender to transport a small antisubmarine SSK-class submarine to Majorca to support his special ops team in a highly classified, covert mission.

***

"Your young lady's name wouldn't happen to be Della, would it?" the commander asked Brad, indicating for him to take a look through the periscope. Brad peered through the eyepiece and realized that he was looking at the side of the yacht, the AA Advocate, which was anchored in a private cove near Porto Pi. There, scrawled across a porthole window on the starboard side was the name "Della."

"She's still alive," breathed Brad.

"Always knew she was a smart girl," Ryan commented when he had had a look through the scope. "Her tracking device is signaling not far from here," he commented, watching a light flash on a handheld GPS receiver. "Just let me zoom in on the map of the Son Vida area. There!

"Bring up a satellite map on those coordinates."

In minutes, they not only had a satellite picture of the estate; they had real-time video of the entrance, which had an electric gate and two armed guards. Two other armed guards were patrolling the grounds with dogs, and several more were posted around the house itself.

The team took a few moments to examine the scenario as if it were a training exercise. Together, they came up with their plan of attack. Two intel officers would be onboard to provide support. The sub was armed and ready with computer-guided missiles and direct communication with the agents in the field. They were ready, to a man, to get this job done, to get the rats exterminated, and to get the hostage and the team out safely.

Ryan had been in close contact with the war room in Washington, where a tense roomful of brass reviewed and evaluated each piece of intelligence as it was relayed to them. The situation boiled down to this: The United States had no beef with Spain. Despite the body of evidence that had been exposed to support the theory that bin Laden was present at the Di Stefano estate, they still did not have concrete confirmation. They were putting several hundred million dollars worth of assets and personnel, not to mention the lives of a couple of innocent civilians, on the line to go in and make that assertion.

High-powered lawyers discussed the contravention of international law, and members of the Security Council talked about the threats to national security being brought both to Spain's door and to homeland security. But if bin Laden was there, they couldn't let him escape again.

After much discussion, the president finally spoke. "Gentlemen, I think we have to rely on the strength and intelligence of our men and women in the field to get this done. Let's give them a chance to do their jobs."

Finally a consensus was reached, and Ryan got the go-ahead from the chairman of the Joint Chiefs of Staff to deploy.

"Okay, suit up, boys. We're going in," Ryan ordered.

Ryan saw Brad move forward with the divers who were already donning wet suits, preparing for the onshore landing.

"Brad, I need you here to monitor Della's tracker," Ryan said, knowing that the request sounded weak at best, with two other agents staying on board.

"Not a chance in hell," Brad replied, pulling on the tightly fitting suit. "I'm going in with you."

Knowing it was senseless to argue when his brother dug in his heels, Ryan said, "Look, we don't have time to argue about this. If you're coming, stay out of the way and do what I tell you."

"Okay, fine," Brad agreed, just to get his brother off his back. "But just so you know, we're not coming back without her."

"Roger that," Ryan agreed.

One of the intel agents approached Ryan with hard copy of the satellite shots he had received from their base, showing pictures of the Di Stefano estate, which extended from the private cove where the yacht was moored uphill to a sprawling Moroccan-style villa surrounded by a ten-foot stone wall. A large golf course flanked the left side of the property, providing lots of cover, and no other homes were in close proximity. It was unknown as of yet if the wire on top of the wall was electrified. The other agent was working on getting blueprints and schematics of the building, which would be sent to each of agent's tablets. For the five-man special ops team, it was a fairly easy breach. The trick was to get in silently. There was no margin of error with Della's life at stake.

The divers proceeded to the airlock. They did a last-minute check of their communications earpieces and mikes. They were ready. Two agents stepped into the airlock and gave the thumbs-up, and the airlock filled with seawater. They repeated the process until all SEALs were deployed. The last man out disconnected a pressurized rescue module from the side of the vessel, in case it was needed to bring Della to the sub.

Outside of the vessel, the light gray hull of the submarine was almost invisible against the light sand of the ocean floor. The divers swam the short distance to the deserted beach and swapped their swim fins for boots. They concealed their air tanks, fins, and the rescue module behind some bushes and geared up for combat. Ryan went over instructions for their plan of attack, going over diagrams of the grounds and floor plans of the house.

"Boys, we shoot to kill. Dead men tell no tales," he needlessly reminded them. "The code word for a successful kill on the target will be same as last time, Geronimo."

With that, he gave the signal to advance, and the team started up the hill, invisible under cover of the rough of the golf course. Not even a bird was disturbed from its roost as they passed unnoticed up the hill.

CHAPTER 50

Della had been escorted off the AA Advocate in handcuffs and shackles, with the hood in place over her head. She had been allowed to carry the red, leather tote with the ransom money with her, and the weight of it was heavy on her shoulder. She had been led down a shaky ladder, put aboard a small boat, and tendered to a beach, where she had gotten aboard a van and was taken to a gated villa. Suddenly the van stopped, and the men conversed in Spanish. They were directed to go around to the back of the house to the service entrance. The air here was scented with flowers and freshly mown grass, and the sun shone warmly on Della's bare arms. A guard in a dark suit holding an automatic weapon waved the group through and locked the wrought iron gates behind them. The van stopped in front of a door in a long stone wall that led to an underground entrance. The air was cooler here, and Della shivered as they descended the stone stairs.

She heard the men open a lock, and she was pushed inside the opened door to a spacious apartment. Once they were inside with the doors locked, the hood was removed, and Della looked around at her surroundings. She was standing in the utility area of the servants' quarters. Through the open door to her left, she could see commercial washers and driers and other laundry equipment. To her right were storage cupboards with cleaning supplies, mops, brooms, and several vacuum cleaners. She was met by a woman dressed in a maid's uniform, and one of the guards told her to help the prisoner freshen up and have her ready in a half hour to be taken to the villa. The guard locked the red tote in a nearby storage locker and pocketed the key, and the men left, locking the door behind them.

"Hola. Mi nombre es Carmelita," the woman said. And she led Della through a hall to a windowless bedroom with an adjoining bathroom. She locked the door and crossed to a closet, where she took out an intricately embroidered, traditional Afghani women's tunic and pantaloon set and laid them on the bed. She placed some clean towels on the vanity in the bathroom and indicated that Della was to freshen up and dress in the clothes provided. She would be back in "quince minutos" to make sure she was ready for the guards who would be taking her to meet "tu maestro," her "master," as Della translated. She didn't like the sound of that. If this Di Stefano thought she was his slave, then he had another thing coming.

Della was relieved of the handcuffs and shackles and was left in the stuffy bedroom. The first thing she did was look for a mode of escape. It was pretty much useless, however. There were no windows or unlocked exits. The ceilings and walls were heavily stuccoed, making escape unlikely without power tools. Knowing that flight was futile and with the task still before her of delivering the ransom and securing Brent Marshall's release, she got on with the business of making herself presentable. She hoped to God that Ryan would deliver on his promise of "having her back."

***

By the time Carmelita unlocked the door again, Della was

showered and dressed in the clothing that had been provided to her. Carmelita took her to the kitchen and gave her a tray with a glass of fruited tea and a sandwich, and Della gratefully accepted the food. It had been sometime yesterday when she had last eaten.

Soon, a knock came at the door, and the sound of a key turning in the lock announced the return of the guards. They once again handcuffed Della's wrists but left her ankles unshackled. Carmelita fixed a matching veil over Della's hair. One guard thrust the red, leather tote bag at her and led her through the apartment to a door that opened into a corridor leading to the spa area. They passed the indoor pool, which led to the exercise area and a lounge with a bar. They marched her through the sitting area, which opened onto a rotunda. They stopped outside a polished wooden door, and the guard knocked softly.

"Pasa," a voice commanded.

The guard opened the door and said, "Esta es la señorita. Della Rawlins, señor."

"Ah, Ms. Rawlins, do come in." A tall, balding man rose from behind a large, polished desk. His piercing eyes peered at her from behind shaded, wire-rimmed glasses. His hook nose was distinctly Italian and curved down toward a thin mouth. He looked to be in his mid to late forties and exuded an air of confidence and competence.

"Welcome to my home. Let me introduce myself. I am Giovanni Di Stefano," he said, "attorney to the famous and infamous. Some people call me the Devil's Advocate because I defend the indefensible." He extended his hand and took both of Della's shackled hands in his. "I am delighted to make your acquaintance. I understand that you have enjoyed quite a distinctive career as a photojournalist and have covered many political conflicts in your short but colorful career. I wasn't fortunate enough to meet your partner, Mr. Giles. He had returned to the States before I became aware of his presence in Pakistan. Had I known of his plight, perhaps I may have been of some assistance in securing his exchange back to the United States. I'm sure that my friend"—he paused as a tall, turbaned figure, dressed in a tunic and the traditional dress of the Afghani Muslims, silently entered the room—"would have found that amusing."

So intent were they in their appraisal of each other—predators and prey—that they took no notice of the operation taking place outside.

***

The advance team had reached the rock wall surrounding the Di Stefano estate without incident. Ryan gave the hand signal for the men to spread out, with the two to his left to take care of the guards at the gate while the two to his right were to hunt down and take out the perimeter guard and dog. Ryan knew the floor plan to the mansion by heart now, and his focus was on the office window to the left of the grand front entrance, where he could see the back of Di Stefano's balding pate seated at his desk in a chair upholstered in a magnificent tiger skin. The sheer curtains at the windows obscured his view of the other people in the room, but the thermal imaging sensor in his hand told him three people were present.

Suddenly the crackle of static that preceded a voice message came through the earpiece in Ryan's helmet. "Atlantis to Alpha Leader, can you read? Over."

A few minutes passed while Ryan repositioned himself to talk and not be heard. He spoke softly into the mike. "This is Alpha Leader. Over."

"Home Base, Agent Swift, sir. There's been a change of plan."

"What the fuck are you talking about, Swift?" Ryan whispered as loudly as he dared.

"Sir, we just got new orders from brass. You have twenty minutes to Geronimo, or else we send in the heat."

"You serious?" Ryan asked incredulously as his eyes assessed the scene, noting the guards down at the gate with neat bullet holes through their foreheads, their bodies dragged to the side and out of sight. One of the SEALs stood guard while the other entered the servants' quarters at the back of the house.

"Yes, sir. You have five more minutes to confirm visual on target, and then countdown begins. You have twenty minutes to Geronimo, repeat that, twenty minutes to Geronimo before we launch."

"Fucking Christ," Ryan swore once more at the perfidious bastards in Washington. "Roger that. Stand by, Home Base."

Ryan switched to com mode on his mike. "Attention all units, we have five minutes to confirm target and twenty minutes to Geronimo, or else the brass is going to light this place up. All units copy?"

"A Dog Five, we copy. Front gate is secure."

"B Dog Five, copy. Sons of bitches. Perimeter is secure."

"Alpha Leader, reconnoiter left wing for confirmation of target. Be ready to deploy TG."

"Roger, Alpha Leader. Servants are confined to their quarters. All clear."

Ryan checked his wristwatch. Three minutes to cross the courtyard and ... Go!

Taking the lead, Ryan crossed the open space, keeping to the shrubbery to screen himself from view. He crept stealthily to a position directly under the open office window and slowly raised a mirrored scope to allow him to see inside.

It took him several seconds to adjust the scope's light exposure and focus. Two minutes ticked by until, finally, he nodded to his backup and gave them the thumbs-up.

Confirming his partner's signals in his field glasses, the SEAL spoke into his mike, "A Dog Five for Alpha Leader, target is confirmed. Repeat, target is confirmed."

CHAPTER 51

"May Allah greet you, Ms. Rawlins." Osama bin Laden spoke in his soft tone. "Praise be to Allah, the Lord of the Worlds."

Della was momentarily tongue-tied as she turned to meet the man the world thought of as the "face of terror." Although the man was still a tall and imposing figure, bin Laden's face showed the lines of someone who lived with chronic pain. His beard had grayed, and he walked stiffly. Nevertheless, a shiver ran down Della's spine as she beheld the man who had ordered the deaths of almost three thousand of her innocent countrymen on her home turf and had killed thousands more in embassy bombings, roadside bombings, and suicide bombings. Where did the evil reside in this seemingly peaceful, priestly looking man?

"Mr. Bin Laden," Della acknowledged, "I came at the request of your people to deliver the ransom money for my colleague, Brent Marshall. But it seems your staff," she said, including Di Stefano in her assessment, "is determined to treat me as a prisoner." She indicated her handcuffs.

"May the peace of Allah be with you, Ms. Rawlins," bin Laden said. "It seems that we were destined to meet again since that fateful night in Abbottabad when we became acquainted through the lens of your camera."

"My partner and I were in Pakistan on a diplomatic

exchange. It was quite by accident that we learned of the raid on the compound in Abbottabad."

"Then you and your partner are not only liars and intruders, but like the rest of your countrymen, you are also opportunists," Bin Laden accused. "Much like your colleague, Mr. Marshall, you are all interested in 'getting the story,' but you refuse to hear what our people want you to hear. You are so interested in portraying us as monsters and terrorists that you refuse to acknowledge the years of struggle and the battles our people have fought—to uphold the laws of Islam and to keep tribe after tribe of infidels from invading our lands, laying siege to our most holy places, raping and killing our women and children, and stealing our resources."

Bin Laden moved to a nearby credenza, picked up a crystal water jug, and poured a cool drink into a tumbler. He took a seat in a leather chair across from where Di Stefano sat observing them, his fingers steepled.

Bin Laden spoke again, quietly. "I am just a man—one whose heart aches and whose blood boils at the atrocities you crusaders have committed against my country under the guise of 'freedom' and 'democracy.' You get into bed with the Israelis and the Jews to destroy our culture and keep from us what we hold most dear. Have you no conscience? No will to learn and to understand the will of our people? Because of your tyrannical interference, you have forced us to take the fight to your door, to attack the pillars of your culture that you see as your strength, to let you feel the outrage and see the perfidy of an attack against the very fundamentals of your existence. How many of your people and our people will your government sacrifice to your gods of money and power?"

"It seems to me, Mr. bin Laden, that the greatest hindrance to peace is the inability of people to be able to separate religion and politics. One group wants to control the land

and use its resources, while another group wishes to dominate and hoard the wealth to itself, manipulating its people to do its will through the use of their religious beliefs. It's a game as old as time."

"Our people do not go to America and tell you that you cannot go to your holy places. We do not put sanctions on your exports to starve your farmers and cripple your people with poverty. How can we expect to live as equals when your so called 'superpower' government bullies us by sending in attack forces, bombing our cities, going on witch hunts with drones, and killing our people without arrest or trial? Where is the justice you believe in? How can there be real negotiation or meaningful discussion between nations when you give no credence to our culture and take sides in wars you don't understand? We are forced to drive you out and cripple you like we did in Afghanistan with the Russians. Where is that 'superpower' today? Lying in ruin. Dismembered. All praise to Allah, with whose help and guidance, we will do the same to the United States, rather than yield our birthright to the crusaders and the Jews."

"Mr. bin Laden, isn't it better to take a diplomatic approach to resolving these old grievances through meaningful discussion and upholding the resolutions agreed upon by representatives of all governments in the United Nations?"

Bin Laden's face contorted in fury. "Do not speak to me about United Nations when your government will train and supply arms to opposing forces in conflicts they know nothing about or else to serve their own objectives. Your country's corruption and manipulative powers know no bounds."

"Mr. bin Laden," Della tried again, feeling powerless to make any inroads with him, as his grief and contempt for the years of invasion and betrayal had hardened his heart into a coal of hatred, cynicism, and distrust, "perhaps it is through the journalists, the watchdogs, and the analysts that the real truth about what needs to be done to achieve lasting peace and accord in the Middle East can be revealed. The political and economic issues have to be identified and dealt with without cloaking the issues in religious guises. I agree the powerful countries need to back off and allow the opposing nations to address their differences, mediate agreements, and put aside old grievances. But it will only work as long as everyone benefits. Look at the waste of resources—in money, munitions, and the blood of the youth of our countries. Someone has to stop the madness. Someone has to throw down the arms. When does the cost of being the occupier, the victor, become too high?"

"I have dedicated my life, my family, and my fortune to Allah's use. I continue to trust that he will lead us to victory as he has in the past. It is the duty of every Muslim, as is spelled out in our holy scriptures, to defend the faith, to put their lives and the lives of their children and their families and everything they have to the use of Allah, from whom all blessings and glory be given. Blessed be the faithful and the children of Islam."

Della could have hit her head repeatedly against the marble of the wall. There was just no possibility that this man could be persuaded that there was any way to achieve the goals of his ideology other than through war and terror. If Allah himself descended from the clouds, bin Laden would think it a trick to thwart him from reaching his objectives. For one who purported the arrogance of the United States in holding to its objectives, Della wondered how bin Laden thought he was any less so in allowing his country and his people to be decimated by this holy war. "Mr. Bin Laden, I have come here of my own free will to pay for the release of a man who I feel has been fair in his reporting of events and conflicts and objective in his commentary on the ideologies of groups and individuals of all ethnicities and religious sects. I am willing to give up my freedom to take his place if you will release him to go back to his family. He has committed no crime or insult to deserve to be held hostage, especially when the condition of his release has been met."

"Ms. Rawlins, it is not acceptable in our culture for a woman to make demands of the men in control of her fate. However, in light of our discussion today, I feel that you are a forward thinker, and although it is impossible to justify the actions of the government of your country, and though you have been misguided in your previous actions, you do have a commendable, if naive and idealistic, view of how the world of politics should be run. As I am sure you have discerned, it is impossible for me to release you to go back to America with the knowledge that bin Laden is alive and well—all praise and gratitude be to Allah from whom all blessings flow to the faithful. The time is not yet right for me to reveal that truth to the world.

"I will, however, order Mr. Marshall to be released and will send word to his paper that they can arrange for his transport back to the United States immediately." He indicated to Di Stefano to accept the ransom money from Della and to make the call to affect his order.

"As for you, you will remain here as Mr. Di Stefano's guest until such time as I need your cooperation in future operations. You will have no contact with your countrymen or allies, and you will accede to any requests I make of you without question or rebuttal. Is that clear?"

"You mean, effectively, that I am your slave?" Della asked carefully, fully understanding the interpretation of the term under Islamic law.

"If you wish to think of it in those terms," bin Laden agreed.

"Don't think for one moment that I have forgotten your complicity in supporting your Navy SEALs in the execution of the order for my death. Nor have I forgotten about your partner's intention of bringing word of my escape back to your commander in chief so that he could once again set his dogs on me. I do not forgive my enemies so easily, especially one with such a silken tongue, uttering words of peace and understanding. Was it not your Eve who tempted your Adam to eat from the poisoned apple? I will not so easily be tempted by you, guyyah."

He turned to Di Stefano. "Instruct your guards to take her away and lock her up. Spare no method of securing her. She has proved deceptive in the past."

With that, bin Laden stood and made a move to slip back behind the draperies, intending to pass through a concealed doorway to his inner apartment.

Unbeknownst to him, a small mirror caught his reflection, and a message was relayed. Out in the harbor, a timer flashed to life on a harpoon missile housed in a steel tube mounted atop the submerged sub.

"Mr. Bin Laden, your holding me here will not prevent my government from knowing that you are still alive. Look at the picture files on my phone. Those photos were retrieved from a secret drive on the camera in Aaron Giles' possession, which turned up in a market in Algeria. They are now in the possession of the CIA, who have many of your men in custody. It will only be a matter of time before your location is known to them, and that's if my GPS tracker hasn't already given them your location."

Twenty … nineteen … eighteen …

"Giovanni, did you not scan this charrira for electronic devices?" bin Laden asked, visibly shaken by Della's revelation.

"O-Of course, Amir," Di Stefano said, stuttering in his haste to reassure bin Laden of his security team's thoroughness in protecting the secrecy of their location. "Here is her phone."

With that, a small, metal cylinder came flying through the open window of the study and rolled across the floor, emitting tear gas. Bin Laden made a grab for Della's shackled wrist and pulled her in front of him as he quickly moved the tapestry aside and exited the room. Several other cylinders crashed through the glassed-in ceiling of the rotunda as bin Laden dragged Della's struggling form behind him, making his way to the main staircase and descending to the spa area below.

Di Stefano quickly tapped out a message on the computer keyboard on the desk in front of him until he could no longer see, as the tear gas blinded his eyes. He grabbed his chest, the crushing pain squeezing his lungs as saliva dripped from his mouth and threatened to choke him.

Seventeen ... sixteen ... fifteen

Behind the closed door they had just come through, Della could hear the sound of explosions and gunfire as the Navy SEALs breached the guarded entrance of the villa. Precious minutes were lost while the advance team identified that their prime target was escaping with the hostage. Ryan ordered the team split up and block all exit points while they located the target with thermal imaging.

Fourteen ... thirteen ... twelve ...

Bin Laden struggled to hold on to the girl, who was putting up an impressive fight. They entered the pool area, and Della used her legs to try and trip him while she twisted her body and sank her teeth into the hand gripping her arm.

"Wald il qahbah!" bin Laden screamed as blood ran down his arm. He drew back and landed a stinging slap across Della's face that made her ears ring.

She retaliated by snaking her shackled wrists over bin Laden's bent head and around his throat. His hand went to the chain at his neck while Della jumped on his back, pulling her wrists as tight as she could. Bin Laden stumbled and fell to his knees. With seemingly superhuman strength, he forced the chain apart, and Della's arm muscles were no match for the Sheik's superior strength. He reached up and grabbed her by the hair, pulling her off his back. Dragging her to the edge of the pool, he pushed her head underwater and held her there while she thrashed and fought for release.

Eleven ... ten ... nine ...

Suddenly, with the sound of shattering glass, two Navy SEALs shot their way into the pool house through the plateglass wall directly in front of bin Laden. One SEAL grabbed him by the robes and pulled him away from the edge of the water. He lost his grip on Della, and the other SEAL jumped into the waist deep water and immediately started to administer mouth-to-mouth resuscitation.

"What do you want me to do with this, Ryan? Can I finish him off?" the young SEAL asked eagerly.

Della had started to cough and come around at this point, and Ryan was able to place her gently on the pool deck. At that moment, Brad and another SEAL came running into the pool house, weapons drawn. When Brad saw Della lying on the pool deck, vomiting water and gasping for air, he immediately ran to her side. The medic with him was beside her in seconds, taking her vitals and listening to her heartbeat, which was a good thing because, with the shock of finding Della, Brad had forgotten every shred of poolside first aid he had ever learned.

Eight ... seven ... six ...

Meanwhile, Ryan strode over to where bin Laden was being restrained facedown on the pool deck, the young corporal's boot planted firmly in the small of his back.

"Turn the bastard over," Ryan ordered.

The young corporal obligingly removed his foot from bin Laden's back and pulled him into a kneeling position facing Brad.

"You're not so scary now, are you, old man?" Ryan taunted the stoic rebel leader.

Bin Laden raised his head and spat at Ryan and the American flag he wore proudly on his uniform. "May Allah curse you and all your countrymen to the fires of hell for all eternity," he growled, teeth bared and the fire of jihad burning brightly in his eyes.

"Not today, old man. It's your turn to say your prayers for good this time," Ryan replied. He took out his handgun and pulled a special bullet out of the chest pocket of his uniform. It had been made from metal recovered from ground zero, where the 9/11 disaster had taken place at the Twin Towers in New York City. "This is from the families of the two thousand nine hundred and ninety-six people you're responsible for killing in the 9/11 attack."

He gave the bullet to his partner, who had his weapon trained on the middle of bin Laden's forehead. He took out another bullet, which he carefully loaded into his own handgun. And this one is from my best friend, who your men tortured and killed just for taking your picture. He would have been proud to look you in the eye and tell you what a scumbag you really are." Ryan chuckled.

Bin Laden closed his eyes and chanted in Arabic, praising Allah and seeking his blessing in the afterlife.

Five ... four ... three ...

Ryan nodded to the other SEAL, who loosened his grip and let the Sheik sink to the floor. "On my count, head and heart, for God and Country ... One ... two ... three ..."

"For Islaaammm!"

Two shots rang out simultaneously, just as bin Laden's eyes

came open and he screamed his faith to the heavens. The light of his earthly existence faded to black, and his body slumped backward onto the floor. A halo of red pooled around his head, where a small hole had appeared in the place where his third eye was rumored to be, and a river of blood flowed from the hole in his chest, tinting the pool water with a reddish stain.

A crackle came over Ryan's radio from the last SEAL, who was standing guard outside the compound. "A Dog Five, Geronimo, Geronimo, Geronimo EKIA," Ryan said into his shoulder mike, indicating that the enemy had been killed in action.

The field op's voice came back over the radio, "Roger that, Alpha leader."

The voice of Agent Swift responded. "Atlantis standing down. Operation Lion's Den is complete. Congratulations, sir."

***

The medic who had been tending to Della found her to be stable, so he turned his attention to bin Laden's corpse, drawing two sets of blood and bone marrow samples, as well as DNA swabs, and placing them in sample tubes to go back to the lab to be tested. He withdrew a body bag from his field kit, and the corpse was prepared for extraction.

Outside, a Chinook helicopter approached the villa and landed on the back lawn, whipping the sparkling water in the outdoor pool to whitecaps. A cleanup team disembarked to remove all traces of the operation from the property. The advance team boarded the aircraft, along with the body bag containing bin Laden's remains and the handcuffed figure of Giovanni Di Stefano, who knew better than to threaten the Navy SEALs with legal action for his "unlawful arrest and detainment." He knew he was lucky to be alive, and any threat to divulge the identity of the man he had been aiding and abetting could easily earn him a bullet hole through the head. He knew also that the Spanish government had been about to seize his property on Majorca due to his evasion of paying taxes, and he would be facing many years at the hands of the Majorcan Gendarmerie had he remained there without the protection of the Lion Sheik to save his slippery skin.

Brad cradled Della in his arms. Her neck was bandaged, and she wore a cervical collar to protect her against further injury. The medic had given her some medication for pain, and her stomach felt empty and queasy after inhaling the chlorinated pool water. She was rather pale and worse for wear, but she had never looked more beautiful in Brad's eyes. He kissed the top of her head softly and tried to make her as comfortable as possible in the cramped seating area of the Chinook helicopter. The SEALs were in high spirits, slapping each other on the backs and letting off some steam after the intense operation they had just completed.

"Thank God we don't have him to worry about any more," the guy who had pulled the trigger along with Ryan said, slipping into the seat behind Della and Brad. "That woman of yours is amazing," he said to Brad. "When Ryan and I were advancing toward the pool house, we could see her inside, jumping on the old lion's back and trying to rip his throat out with her bare hands." He shook his head in amazement. "Craziest thing I ever saw in battle."

"Yeah, she really is something special." Brad smiled fondly, holding the woman he loved as the sedative took effect. The woman he loved. His heart was so full of what he felt for this woman that he had all he could do to keep the tears of pride and relief from rolling down his cheeks.

Ryan slipped into the seat in front of them and saw the raw

emotion in his brother's eyes. "I guess this marks the end of a great career for Della in foreign espionage and diplomatic service, huh, bro?"

"You got that right," Brad growled back. "From now on, she'll be reporting on fuzzy ducklings and baby pandas being raised in captivity."

"Pity," Ryan replied, picking dirt out of his fingernails with a wicked-looking, military-issue field knife. "She has real potential."

"Yeah, and she's going to realize it by becoming my wife as soon as I can arrange it."

Ryan laughed and grabbed his brother in a playful headlock. "Maybe I can persuade her to take a walk on the wild side and come work for me."

"Fuck off and go find your own woman," Brad replied, a mite less jokingly than his brother expected, and he couldn't resist teasing him further.

"Well, don't forget—I saw her first," he said, grinning as he saw the light of competition darken his brother's eyes.

"What are you two griping about?" Della's eyes fluttered open momentarily as the deep male voices roused her from her drug-induced slumber.

"It's okay, sweetheart," Brad soothed her. "Ryan is only being his usual annoying self."

"That's okay then," Della replied, out of it. "He always was a cocky son of a bitch."

And all of the Navy SEALs roared with laughter as Della wondered what was so funny.

Brad and Della were cuddled up together, spooning on her couch in front of her big-screen TV. Jack was splayed on the floor, sound asleep, his legs stretched out behind him like a sleepy frog. Brad reached over and picked up the half-empty bottle of red wine to refill their glasses, and then he settled Della comfortably back in his arms as she flicked through the stations for something interesting to watch. He nuzzled her neck, and his hand ran up her back and over her shoulder, which was encased in soft cashmere.

"How's your neck doing?" he asked, lightly running his lips up the delicate column to the hollow behind her ear.

"It's fine since I took the muscle relaxant the doctor ordered," Della answered, shivering in pleasure as he ran his lips along her jawline and finally claimed her lips in a lazy kiss. His hand strayed under the soft sweater to her bare breast, and he could feel her nipple rise as he traced circles around the pink areola with his thumb.

"Mmmmm," she purred like a contented cat, arching her back and letting the familiar heat build deep within her core. She nestled her butt more tightly against his pelvis and she could feel his cock growing hard against her.

Since they had returned home, Brad had not let her out of his sight. He had been so attentive to her injuries, placing hot compresses on her neck and applying antibiotic cream every four hours to make the bruising fade. He made her fruit smoothies and chicken soup and had taken excellent care of her. She told him she was getting spoiled and that, if he continued to lavish such attention on her, she would become a horrible narcissist.

"Want a nice, warm bubble bath or a shower before we go to bed?" Brad suggested.

"I'll wash your back." He smiled sexily into her eyes. "Your front, too," he added, lavishing tender attention on her other soft mound.

Della turned in his arms and wrapped her arms around his neck, pulling his lips down to hers and taking his questing tongue into her mouth. He left her no doubt as to where his thoughts were as his agile tongue danced with hers, slipping and sliding in an erotic ballet.

Suddenly, something on the television caught her attention, and Della turned her head toward the newscaster, who had interrupted the scheduled program with a breaking news report.

"President Obama was bombarded with questions today as he held a press conference at the White House in response to the illegally hijacked airing of what appears to be a recently recorded video from Osama bin Laden, who had been reported to have been killed in a May 2011 covert mission by the CIA Special Forces in collaboration with the US Department of Defense and the Navy SEALs. Bin Laden claims that the president has lied to the citizens of the United States and that the Navy SEALs' so-called 'successful' operation to hunt him down and kill him was only a ploy to garner him votes to win the November 2012 presidential election."

In the video, bin Laden warned the people of the United States that the jihad against the United States would continue until all of the infidels had vacated the holy cities and the children of Islam had taken back control of their lands. There was a close-up on bin Laden's face as he directly addressed the president and once again accused him of lying to his own people. Now that his duplicity had been revealed, no nation could trust his word on any treaty or accord. And if he wanted to have any credibility with the people of the Middle East, he must take immediate action to recall American troops out of Afghanistan as he had promised and break his alliances with the Israelis and Jews. If he did not comply, many more American citizens, including women and children, would die on their own turf, just as his own were being killed now in their own homes through air strikes and drone attacks.

Following the airing of the video, the newscaster went on to report on the recapture and second killing of bin Laden by the joint CIA/Navy SEALs forces at the Di Stefano villa in Majorca. And he gave a brief biography of the Italian "lawyer" who had harbored bin Laden after he had fled Pakistan.

Della couldn't believe her ears. Why had she put her life at risk, going over to Majorca to face the Lion Sheik in his own den if the whole story was going to be released upon his death anyway? Brad knew from her incredulous expression exactly what she was thinking.

"I bet that little news bomb had the president's advisory team scrambling for cover this morning," Brad commented.

The president's rebuttal speech had him throwing himself on the mercy of the citizens of the United States to forgive him for taking action to "draw bin Laden out of hiding by letting the public think he was dead."

The Republicans were having a field day, condemning the president for his duplicity in misinforming the public and claiming that the country could no longer trust him. The president countered by allowing photos of the mission in

Majorca; a very dead bin Laden; and his minion, Di Stefano—who, no doubt, was responsible for releasing the story upon his capture at the hands of the Americans—to be made public.

Much praise was given to reporter and humanitarian Della Rawlins for her role in bringing about bin Laden's capture and ultimate assassination, as well as the release of foreign correspondent Brent Marshall. The report once again brought up the death of Aaron Giles as Della's former partner and his role in trying to lead the SEALs to get the right man in the original mission. He was recognized once more for his extraordinary patriotism and bravery, and file footage was shown of his casket being carried off the military helicopter, while newer video of Della showed her climbing out of the military helicopter at Edwards Air Force Base.

Della sighed as the reporter went on to comment on the state of current hostilities between the terrorists, extremists, Israelis, Palestinians, and the American forces near Gaza. She shook her head as the age-old battle raged on with the same old players, just operating under a different name. "I don't think there's much hope of things ever changing over there," she lamented, "not while there's money and oil at stake."

"Not very likely," Brad agreed. "The best thing we can do is tell people about what you experienced firsthand and let them tell the politicians what role they want their country to play in bringing about lasting change. Look at the results you got when you told the story of Hope for Life. Hope has been swamped with offers of help and support. You have a natural gift for letting people see the truth. I hope we can partner together in the future to let more stories be told. You have an amazing gift to give the world."

Brad thought that this was the perfect moment he had been waiting for to ask Della a very special question. He reached into his pants pocket and was about to draw out the small, platinum band that sparkled with several carats worth of brilliant diamonds. But at that moment, the phone rang. Brad sighed and reluctantly reached across to the portable phone sitting on the coffee table.

"Hello, Ryan," he said, noting the name that had come up on the call display.

"Hey, Brad," his younger brother greeted him. "Did you see the news report that just aired on CNN?"

"Yeah, Della's upset. She took all that stress and responsibility on her own shoulders, trying to protect the president, when they already had a contingency plan ready if the truth came out."

"I can understand her being pissed off. I'm sure the administration would have preferred the outcome where the public was none the wiser. The old bastard, bin Laden, would have been taken out once and for all, and that would have been the end of it. But I guess now it's up to the court of public opinion whether the president did the right thing or not."

"Yup, I guess what he does from this point on will tell what kind of leader of the free world he really is."

"How's Della feeling? Other than pissed off, I mean?" Ryan inquired.

"Here, ask her yourself," Brad replied, poking a sleepy Della, who was presently lying with her head on his chest, enjoying having her back massaged by her willing sex slave.

"Mmmmph," was all that she could manage when Brad held the receiver to her ear.

"Hi, Del. How are you feeling now?" Ryan asked. "Ready to get recruited for CIA boot camp?"

"Go away, Ryan," Della groaned. And then to Brad she said, "A little more to the right, sweetheart. Ooooh, that's the spot. Can you do it a little harder? Mmmmm, yeah. That's perfect ... mmmm."

"Just wanted you to know that we have a security detail assigned to you guys until further notice."

"Uh-huh ... Thanks ..." There was the sound of heavy breathing and then kissing.

"Well, I can see that you two are busy, so I'll say good night. I'll drop by and see you sometime tomorrow."

"Okay, night, Ryan," Della replied, hitting "end call" and dropping the phone to the floor.

Suddenly, the phone rang again. Della grabbed it off the floor and growled into the receiver, "Look, Ryan, I really can't talk right now. Your brother and I are about to have some really steamy sex, so I'll talk to you tomorrow, okay?"

"Excuse me. Is this Ms. Della Rawlins, formerly of Today Magazine?"

"Yes, yes, this is me—I mean she," said Della, stumbling over her words, trying to gather her scattered wits as she crawled off Brad and sat up on the sofa with her sweater half-off and Brad still working on the button of her jeans.

"This is White House secretary Jean Shea calling for President Barack Obama. Are you able to take his call? Or shall I have him call back at a more convenient time?"

"Oh, no, no, Ms. Shea. It's fine. Please put him through." Della grabbed Brad's questing hands and mouthed the words "It's the president."

"Mr. President, Ms. Rawlins is on the line," Della heard the secretary say.

"That's fine. Thank you, Jean," President Obama replied. "Hello, Ms. Rawlins—or should I call you Della? I've heard so much about you over the past couple of days I feel that we're already well acquainted."

"Hello, Mr. President. Please call me Della. It has been quite an eventful couple of weeks. Quite nerve-racking by most standards. I'm starting to have a new appreciation for the Bond girls, I must say," Della blabbered on nervously.

President Obama laughed and replied, "Indeed, you handled yourself very well under pressure from all reports I've heard, and I wanted to tell you personally how grateful I am for the job you did. I can only imagine how much courage it took for you to knowingly enter the lair of this fundamentalist madman, risking your life to protect your country and to save the life of a colleague. You are to be commended. I stand in awe of the true patriotism you have shown."

"Thank you, Mr. President. After this morning's news release, I felt that what we did was sort of in vain, in light of the story all coming out anyway. I'm sorry that we hadn't anticipated them blowing the lid off of it."

"Well, I've learned that, in politics, you can't always be prepared for every contingency. It's like the man said: 'You've got to roll with the punches.' As president, even after listening to all of my advisers, I still have to go with my gut. And my gut said we needed to take care of this guy now. Without your participation, this could have dragged on for God knows how many more years, and thousands more lives could have been lost."

"That's true," Della said. "He did say that he thought you weren't hearing what he was telling you, and he was planning another attack to eradicate the Americans and Jews out of the holy cities."

"There you go. What you have done, Della, although it may seem so violent an act, is actually an act of peace. This man was such a barrier to peace and such a catalyst for hatred. Although there are many who share his ideologies, I'm hoping that there are leaders among them who truly want to put the war behind them and will work to find the common ground to peace in the Middle East. I hope that you will continue to report on things as they develop and evolve in this region. It's important that the people are able to see through unbiased eyes the history and struggles that these people have endured and know that we will take responsibility to right the wrongs and will try and forge a new relationship, learning from the mistakes of the past."

"Thank you for your vote of confidence, Mr. President. I wouldn't have been able to take on this challenge without the backing of the Navy SEALs and the advice of my partner, Brad Jamieson. They are the true heroes coming out of this mission."

"We as a nation are very grateful to you all. Michelle and I are planning to host a dinner and reception in your honor here at the White House. We look forward to meeting you in person and hearing about your experiences."

"Thank you, Mr. President. I am truly honored by your invitation."

"That's fine, then. I will have my secretary call and arrange a date. Della, there's one more matter I wanted to mention to you."

"Yes, sir," Della replied, racking her brain to think of what else she might have to discuss with the president.

"With regard to the ransom money we released to allow you to lead the mission into Majorca ..."

"Yes, sir. I understand that the SEALs recovered the money from Di Stefano's office just after they took him prisoner and killed bin Laden. I trust that it was returned in full to the treasury?"

"Oh yes, of course it was. In light of the great service you have done and the cost savings realized in not having to expend further funds to continue the mission, we have decided that a portion of the €18 million ransom money recovered will be turned over to your foundation for the recovery of journalists being held hostage in foreign countries. As I'm sure you are aware, it is not our policy to negotiate with terrorists. But in light of the positive results you were able to achieve, we feel that this money will be wisely used to bring our people home without the direct involvement of government. I'm sure you realize the importance of confidentiality in keeping the source of the funding just between us?"

"Yes, of course, Mr. President. You can rest assured that my foundation will use the utmost discretion in disbursing these funds."

"That's fine then, Della. I will have a check sent over to your office tomorrow. Once again, thank you so much for everything you've done. The country is in your debt. Good night, Della."

"Good night, Mr. President," Della replied, hanging up the phone and letting out her breath, which she had been unconsciously holding.

"That was President Obama," Della said, her mind reeling, trying to process the call.

"Yeah, I gathered," Brad replied, waiting patiently for Della to elaborate.

"He and Mrs. Obama want to host a dinner and reception in my honor at the White House."

"Awesome! That new rose dress won't go to waste after all," Brad teased.

"And that's not all. They're going to grant some of the ransom money that was recovered back to my foundation for the return of journalists held hostage in other countries. Isn't that fantastic?" Della grabbed him in an excited hug. "There's nothing else that can top this day! I am just so happy!"

"Oh, I think I can top that," Brad said, pulling the two-carat sparkler out of his pocket and holding it out for her inspection. "Della Rawlins, will you do me the honor of marrying me?"

Della's eyes filled with tears, and she could hardly get a

word out around the lump that had formed in the back of her throat. She threw herself against the solid wall of Brad's chest and kissed him with all the passion and love that filled her heart and soul.

When Brad finally raised his head, ever the practical one, he said, "So, can I take that for a yes?"

"Yes, you idiot," Della said, swatting him with a pillow.

***

Stay tuned for more adventures with the Jamieson family as Brad's brother, Ryan, meets his match in Behind the Firewall, the next book in the Jamieson Brothers series.

Printed in the United States
By Bookmasters